Craving Absolution

by Nicole Jacquelyn

Craving Absolution
Copyright © 2014 Nicole Jacquelyn
All rights reserved.
Editor: Pam Berehulke
Bulletproof Editing
Formatted by: Danielle Benson
Cover Artist: Sommer Stein
Perfect Pear Creative Covers

ISBN-10: 1500529745
ISBN-13: 978-1500529741

No part of this book may be reproduced or transmitted in any form or by any means, electronic or mechanical, including photocopying, recording, or by any information storage and retrieval system without the written permission of the author, except for the use of brief quotations in a book review.

This is a work of fiction. Names, characters, businesses, places, events, and incidents are either the products of the author's imagination or used in a fictitious manner. Any resemblance to actual persons, living or dead, or actual events is purely coincidental. The author acknowledges the trademarked status and trademark owners of various products referenced in this work of fiction, which have been used without permission. The publication/use of these trademarks is not authorized, associated with, or sponsored by the trademark owners.

Also by Nicole Jacquelyn

THE ACES MC SERIES

Craving Constellations
Craving Redemption
Craving Absolution

Dedication

To the girls who don't feel comfortable in their own skin.
Someday, you will.
And it will be spectacular.

Contents

Prologue	1
Before . . .	5
Chapter 1	6
Chapter 2	13
Chapter 3	29
Chapter 4	39
Chapter 5	47
Chapter 6	55
Chapter 7	62
Chapter 8	71
Chapter 9	78
Chapter 10	83
Chapter 11	93
Chapter 12	102
Chapter 13	108
Chapter 14	115
Chapter 15	123
Chapter 16	129
Chapter 17	136
Chapter 18	141
Chapter 19	148
Chapter 20	154
Chapter 21	161
Chapter 22	165
Chapter 23	171
Chapter 24	178
Chapter 25	182

Chapter 26	188
Chapter 27	194
Chapter 28	201
Chapter 29	207
Chapter 30	209
Chapter 31	216
Chapter 32	223
After . . .	232
Chapter 33	233
Chapter 34	238
Chapter 35	246
Chapter 36	249
Chapter 37	258
Chapter 38	265
Chapter 39	273
Chapter 40	281
Chapter 41	285
Chapter 42	288
Chapter 43	296
Chapter 44	301
Chapter 45	308
Chapter 46	314
Chapter 47	318
Chapter 48	322
Chapter 49	327
Epilogue	333
Acknowledgments	345
About the Author	347

Prologue

Farrah

My feet were asleep. I'd been kneeling for so long with my ass resting on them that they'd gone past the tingling stage and had moved straight into the can't-feel-them-at-all stage. It was a bit of a relief, the only relief I was feeling at the moment. I'd been vomiting or dry heaving for what felt like forever, in between moments of falling asleep with my head on the toilet, so any part of my body that I didn't actually have to feel was a blessing. Even my fucking fingernails were tired.

I was in my underwear with my arms wrapped around the seat of the toilet, shivering on the bathroom floor when he found me.

I'd fallen asleep early the night before, not even taking the time to wipe off my makeup or brush the hair spray from my hair. Remnants of black eyeliner had turned to streaks of black all over my face, and my bouffant hairstyle had morphed into bed head that would take an entire bottle of conditioner to salvage. Needless to say, it wasn't my finest moment.

Any other time, I might have been embarrassed that he'd seen me that way. I'd come so far in the past few years, and I never wanted him to have to save me again. I wanted to be a person he knew he could count on. Solid. Dependable. But at that moment, I couldn't feel anything but relief.

Thank God he was there.

I raised my head wearily, opening my mouth to call his name, but before I could utter a word I started heaving painfully again, dry heaves that made my body jerk and my stomach muscles scream in pain. He stood there watching me silently until I was spent, and at first I didn't realize anything was wrong. I was too busy resting my forehead against the cool porcelain, completely unconcerned with anything beyond swallowing over and over, trying to keep the retching at bay.

By the time I noticed how odd it was that he just stood there, he'd begun to speak in a low hiss.

"I can't believe this shit."

I turned my head to the side in surprise, so exhausted that lifting it was out of the question.

"You told me you were done with this shit. Gram's been calling you for fucking hours, Farrah. What the fuck?"

"Sick," I mumbled, closing my eyes. God, I was so tired. Why wasn't he helping me? Couldn't he see that I needed his arms around me?

"Yeah, looks like it," he said with a sneer.

I blinked back at him, my eyesight blurring as sweat broke out on the back of my neck. Something was wrong. What the hell was happening?

"Gram called and said she couldn't get a hold of you. So I thought, thank God I'm in town, right? Because I was afraid you were hurt, dead on the side of the road somewhere—"

His voice started going in and out. I tried to focus on what he was saying, but his words seemed to just fade to nothing and then became inordinately loud.

Was he yelling? It sounded as if we were in a tunnel.

"Same old shit . . . fucking druggie . . . done with this . . ."

"Cody—" I groaned, trying to cut him off. It wasn't what he was thinking. Couldn't he see that this was different? He must not have heard my voice or maybe he just chose to ignore me, because within seconds he was turning away from the door as the first sharp pain burst through my belly, stealing my breath.

Oh fuck. Where was he going?

He couldn't just be leaving me. There was no way he would leave me. He wouldn't do that.

Oh God.

Oh God.

But I was wrong.

I wasn't sure how long I lay on the floor after he was gone. It could have been minutes or hours before I had the strength to drag myself out of the bathroom and across the hall to where my purse lay on the floor in my bedroom. The pain was nearly overwhelming, and tears ran down my cheeks as I fumbled around for my phone. I knew it was in there somewhere, and I keened in frustration as I fumbled past my wallet, makeup, and hair supplies.

I'd never been more scared in my entire life.

Somehow, I eventually tipped the purse completely over and my phone came tumbling out. My hands shook so hard it took me two tries before I could find the contact I needed, and by that time I was weeping in agony.

"Hello?"

"Gram." I moaned pitifully, pulling my knees to my chest until I was curled into a ball. "I think something's wrong with the baby."

"Oh God, Farrah! I'll be right there, darlin'. Hold on," she ordered as my best friend's toddler tried to talk over her in the background.

I dropped the phone in relief, wrapping my arm around my waist and rubbing softly as I gingerly lay down on my side. A few seconds later Gram's shadow passed by my window, and sobbed in relief as I heard her slam open my front door.

Knowing that I would soon be safe had my mind racing back to the look of absolute disgust in Cody's eyes, and I bit the inside of my cheek to keep myself from screaming.

He'd assumed I'd betrayed him, and he was going to lose his fucking mind when he learned his mistake. I knew him; over the past couple of years his thoughts and feelings had become more familiar to me than my own, and I knew he wasn't going to recover from this.

Cody had become yet another person who let me down, something he'd promised over and over again would never happen.

He was the betrayer, I thought, before mercifully passing the fuck out.

Before . . .

Chapter 1

Casper

When my parents were killed in a home invasion and my sister, Callie, hooked up with her boyfriend, Grease, I couldn't understand what the hell was in his head. I mean, I knew that my sister was beautiful. She got the best traits of both our parents, and I knew guys dug her. But their relationship was just *different* from the very beginning. It was like Grease couldn't stay away from her. He was determined to protect this scared sixteen-year-old kid—to claim her as his—even though he barely knew her.

    I didn't get it, and it freaked me the fuck out. All I could see was that he found this vulnerable chick, and he wanted in. The four-year age difference between them was enough to make me nervous. It didn't take very long before I knew he was legit, though. Solid. For whatever reason, fate or circumstance or a fucked-up sense of responsibility, it was clear that Grease felt something really strong for my sister, and he just wanted to take care of her. He set her up on a pedestal and it didn't matter what stupid shit she did, he never let her fall off. Still, even though I trusted him and knew he was in it for the long haul, I didn't understand it.

Until suddenly, while I was sitting in a dive bar and holding a beer I wasn't legally old enough to drink, it became startlingly clear.

The girl was beautiful—blonde-haired, blue-eyed perfection. A messed-up, twisted girl wrapped in sexy packaging.

My sister's best friend. Farrah.

In less than a minute I wanted her, and seconds after that I learned she was taken.

Another girl with a man far too old for her. Fucking story of my life. His name was Echo, and he was big, scary, and wearing a leather vest that told me he belonged to the same motorcycle club as Grease. Farrah looked at him as if he were the answer to all her prayers. I made the decision then, watching her dance for him in the middle of the bar, that I'd do whatever I could to take her from him . . . even if he gutted me for it.

If I knew then what I'd find out later, I would have stepped up sooner than I did and saved her from the shit she'd have to endure. Life had a way of punching you in the throat when you least expected it, and to say we hadn't expected it would be an understatement.

Not long after I'd first really noticed Farrah, Callie and I were packing up her apartment, and Farrah was on her way over to help. I'd been in the bathroom, splashing my face with water and trying to not act like a complete pussy at the thought of seeing Farrah again—the girl who'd been starring in all my fantasies—when I'd heard a car backfiring outside my sister's apartment. It took me seconds, just seconds to realize that it wasn't a backfire, but that was too long. I'd watched Callie bounce out the door like a kid on a playdate less than ten minutes before, and my stomach dropped as I realized she and Farrah were outside.

Outside with a noise that sounded like a shitty car, but I instinctively knew wasn't.

I'd barely been breathing as I sprinted out the front door and down the stairs, and the scene I witnessed outside would be burned in my brain for the rest of my life. Farrah's man had been shot down in some fucked-up ghetto drive-by shooting, and by the time I got to her, she was practically covered in his blood. He was already dead, blood pooling around his body, as she kissed him. She'd kissed his slack mouth as if she were saying good-bye, as if they weren't covered in blood and he wasn't already gone. I'd wanted to fucking drag her away, to knock her out so she didn't see it, but the damage was done.

It was weeks before I realized it, but my grand plan to steal her away from him no longer mattered. It fucking sucked, but I didn't know the guy and couldn't find it in me to care about his death. The only thing I cared about, the only thing I could see, was the way Farrah had completely shut down after he was gone.

Stealing her away from Echo would have been a thousand times easier than trying to compete with his ghost.

Besides, there wasn't even anything left to steal. The girl I'd watched was gone. I never stopped wanting her, watching her as she spiraled, and silently willing her to get herself together, but it didn't seem to matter. Farrah was hell-bent on killing herself, drinking until she passed out or blacked out, tattooing shit all over her skin that I knew she'd hate if she ever snapped out of it, and piercing holes all over her body. She didn't want anyone's help, and was determined as all hell to keep everyone at a distance.

The more I saw, the more I understood Grease's overwhelming need to fix everything so my sister could breathe easy. I became Grease, but unfortunately for me, Farrah didn't become Callie. She didn't want anything to do with me.

The first few times I carried her out of a party, I'd followed her there, blending into the woodwork so I could keep an eye on her. After that, I'd get calls from different guys, mostly MC members that I'd met through Grease, who felt some sort of responsibility toward Echo's old girlfriend and knew I'd come get her after she'd gone too far.

On the occasions I'd dragged her home, she bit me and scratched me, kissed me, put her hand down the front of my pants, sobbed into my neck, and left the occasional hickey. I carried her out of parties belligerent, bubbly, weepy, horny, passed out, and resigned. I never knew what I'd be walking into, and I didn't care. I would have walked through fire for her—a woman who hated me for taking care of her. It was a compulsion I couldn't seem to get a handle on.

Farrah's downward spiral stopped abruptly when my sister's boyfriend was arrested and sent to prison for breaking his probation connected to an old assault charge. It was as if the moment Callie needed her, she snapped out of the fog and immediately went to work. The bond between the two of them was odd, but I didn't question it. I just continued to watch and wait, just as I'd done for so long.

By the time I headed back to school that fall, Farrah and I had formed an uneasy alliance, a quiet but important connection that I hated to walk away from, but I did it anyway. I took off for Yale and left her behind, relieved that she finally seemed to have her shit together.

I worked my ass off at school, writing papers for both my own classes and for pompous douche bags who'd gotten into Yale with their daddy's money, then used that same money to pay me to write their fucking essays. I didn't mind it, though; it gave me enough cash to fuck my way through sorority girls, and to go home to visit Callie and my grandmother whenever I could.

Along the way, I kept tabs on Farrah through visits home and phone calls with Callie, but we didn't talk, and I didn't try to contact her outside the times where it was impossible to avoid each other. She seemed embarrassed that I'd seen her at her worst, so I tried to give her space. I didn't want to be a reminder of that time in her life.

My IQ and numerous scholarships had gotten me sent to boarding schools across the country, away from my family since before most kids my age were wiping their own asses, so I wasn't homesick at college like many of my classmates. When I got to Yale I thought about Farrah every day, but life was simple for me at school—no drama or responsibility outside of getting my class work done on time. It was a bit of a relief.

I was used to being alone, the misfit, the scholarship student who wore plain Nikes in a gym full of whatever expensive brand was popular that season. I understood it; it was comfortable. So when I got a call from Gram telling me that Callie had been attacked and I needed to get back to Sacramento, I'd had no idea that I would never step foot on the Yale campus again.

By the time I was back with my family, Callie's body was healing but her mind wasn't. She was practically comatose, and Grease prowled around the damn hospital like a caged animal. There was nothing we could do for Callie; she had to work through the psychological damage left over from the attack by herself.

The man who'd attacked her belonged to the same gang that had killed my parents, and the correlation between the two events seemed to have been what pushed her over the edge—but thankfully not before she'd saved herself by killing him with one of

Farrah's handguns. His death left Grease and me at loose ends, and neither of us did the whole "helpless" thing well. Instead, we made plans to take care of the rest of the assholes who'd killed my parents and sanctioned the attack on my sister.

Then one day in a warehouse in San Diego, I turned my back on everything I'd ever known and fell in with a brotherhood that offered me the first place I'd ever felt at home. I fit there, in a lifestyle that I'd never imagined or understood. I'd somehow gained their respect with my ability to slide into any situation unnoticed. They compared me to a ghost, and started calling me by a new name. Casper. I became a prospect in the Aces motorcycle club, which worked like a probationary period in the club where I had to mostly stand around and clean shit up. Literal shit and vomit, and whatever other messes the patched-in brothers had made.

After a few months, though, I got a different job. I became a guard dog for the Aces vice president's daughter, Brenna. God, she was beautiful, the warm kind of beautiful that showed in the way she moved and smiled and listened intently when someone spoke to her. I sat outside her little house day after day, keeping an eye on things while her man, Dragon, did shit for the club. I saw shit that I wished I hadn't, but kept my mouth shut about it. And then one sunny morning, the threat I'd been watching for showed up.

I was only shot once, but for the second before I accidentally knocked my ass out on one of the posts of the front porch, it burned like the fiery pits of hell. By the time I woke up just minutes later, I'd lost quite a bit of blood, and I could hear Brenna's ex yelling at her and beating the shit out of her inside the house. I didn't know where her little daughter was, and I didn't know how bad off Brenna was, but I was determined to get inside and do something to help. I was bleeding pretty badly, and the porch was slick under my hands as I'd tried to pull myself into the house, using my boots for leverage.

God, I'd used everything I had to try to get in there, my teeth clenched in agony by the time I reached the door, but I failed. I failed her. I heard Brenna moaning and there wasn't a goddamn thing I could do about it. For the first time since I was fifteen years old, I felt my throat tighten and the back of my eyes burn.

I wanted to stand up and beat that fucker to death with my bare hands. I wanted to scream for Dragon. I wanted to tell Brenna that she was going to be okay, that I'd get help. And fucking hell, it made no sense, but before I passed out—I wanted Farrah.

Brenna survived, no thanks to me.

It took me months before I was well enough to ride my bike to California, even though my shoulder wasn't up for the long ride, but as soon as I knew I could make it, I took off. I hadn't seen Farrah or my sister since I'd been shot because Callie and Grease weren't speaking to each other at that point, and since the moment I'd woken up in the hospital, I'd been itching to head south. I needed to get to Farrah.

I parked at the apartment complex, the same complex where I'd watched Farrah's man bleed out on the pavement, and ran my hand over my shaved head. I knew the next few minutes could turn really fucking bad, but I was willing to take the risk.

I was done waiting for her to get her shit together. I was done waiting for her to get over the man who'd fucking left her to the wolves, but she mourned like he was fucking Gandhi. I was done letting her call all the shots.

And I was done pussyfooting around her like I hadn't wanted her for goddamn years.

Chapter 2

Farrah

I'd had a long-ass day. My best friend, Callie, had left that morning to force some kind of showdown with her man, leaving her two-year-old son, Will, with me. I loved the little bugger, but he hadn't been happy that Callie left, and it had been a rough day for both of us. I didn't mind watching him, though, even when he was being a pill.

When I was sixteen, I'd taken the Callie under my wing even though she was older than me, but it hadn't been long before those roles had become blurred. We'd gone through a hell of a lot since the day we met five years ago, deaths and attacks and the birth of Will, but somehow we'd come out the other side stronger. Her grandma had adopted me into their little family, and aside from the serious case of lust I had going on for her little brother, Cody, the bonds had formed with no cracks in sight.

I loved Callie, Gram, and Will more than I'd ever thought possible. And Cody? Well, I wasn't sure how I felt about him. Our relationship was complicated, dragged through the mud too many times to be clean or wholesome. He'd witnessed me at my worst, a situation that I didn't ever think I could be comfortable with, but there was still a pull there. We were like two magnets that snapped together whenever we were too close, so I'd spent the last few years making sure that we never were.

I finally dropped Will next door at Gram's house for the night when I knew he'd be falling asleep soon, and decided I deserved a little pampering after chasing him around the house all day. I was painting my toenails, watching *Almost Famous* play on the television, and wondering if I could pull off the beachy waves Kate Hudson was sporting when someone started pounding on my front door. It startled me so badly that I dropped the bottle of Purple Passion nail polish onto the coffee table and watched it splash in slow motion across the thighs of my favorite sweatpants. Mother. Fucker.

Whoever was on the other side of the door was going to die by nail polish wand in about two seconds. I stomped around the couch in that funky walk that only girls do, balancing on my just my heels as I tried to keep my freshly painted toenails pristine, and swung the door open expecting to see a religious nut trying to save my soul.

"I already bought my ration of Girl Scout—Cody?" I asked incredulously. What the hell?

It took me a minute to wrap my head around the fact that the one person I'd been simultaneously dying to see and trying to avoid was at my front door. I hadn't seen him in months. My gaze roamed down his torso, checking out his snug T-shirt and jeans before snapping back up to his face to catch him smirking at me. Smirking. I hated the word, almost as much as I hated the action.

"Callie's in Oregon," I said with a snort, once I'd gotten a handle on my eye-fucking idiocy. "She left this morning to see you."

I watched him closely as he stared at me, taking in everything from my messy ponytail to my bare feet, and I started to worry that I had food on my face or something because he didn't say a word. When he still didn't speak for almost a minute, I had to bite my tongue so I wouldn't chatter like a crazy person just to fill the silence. Cody had always had that effect on me, and it made my normally composed facade seem like a thing of the past.

Well, screw that.

I met his eyes with a droll look and spun around as gracefully as I could, pretending a nonchalance about his appearance at my door. "Come on in, if you want. I was just making myself pretty."

Cody's large hands gripped my hips from behind before I could get more than two steps into the room, and I stopped abruptly as I felt him step forward and press his body against me.

No, no, what was he doing? I couldn't think with his hands on me! We needed to keep a distance between us; it was in the damn unwritten rules we'd lived by for years.

I closed my eyes and vaguely noticed the sound of the front door closing as his breath fanned against the side of my face.

Oh shit.

"I'm not here to see Callie." He spoke quietly, bumping his nose against my ear. "I'm here to see you, and you're already beautiful."

Every muscle in my body froze at his sensual tone, at the memory that slammed into me from out of nowhere . . .

• • •

The apartment had been quiet that night as I'd tiptoed toward the living room to check the locks, but I jerked to a pause when I got there.

Cody had been asleep on the couch, his arms wrapped around a pillow with little pink flowers all over it. I couldn't help but smile; he looked like such a kid. When he was awake, the cocky way he carried himself belied his lack of life experience. It was only when he was sleeping that he looked so innocent.

The exact opposite of me.

My smile faded as I realized he was sleeping on top of my hidden stash of vodka. Why the hell wasn't he sleeping at his grandmother's? I clenched my hands at my sides and then needlessly flipped him off before spinning toward the bathroom in frustration. He really needed to stop sleeping in our goddamn apartment. This was a testosterone-free zone, damn it.

I made my way into the bathroom and closed the door before turning on the light. I avoiding looking in the mirror before dropping to my knees and opening the cupboard under the sink. Inside was a supersized box of tampons, scented ones that I knew Callie wouldn't try to steal. She made fun of me trying to make my vagina smell like a flower, but it was easy for me to laugh it off. I never actually used scented tampons.

The truth was that I never used any kind of tampons. When I'd started losing weight, my period stopped and it hadn't come back.

I quietly opened the box and pulled out a small bottle of whiskey, taking a large swallow before I'd even moved from my knees. It burned all the way down my throat, the bitter taste making my face screw up in what I was sure was a very attractive expression. I set the box on the counter and climbed to my feet, turning my head away so I wouldn't accidentally see my reflection.

By the time I got situated, curled up on the top of the closed toilet, I was feeling so much better. My hands were tingly, and the rest of my limbs felt loose and relaxed. Thank God. Alcohol was such a soothing thing, so much better than the sleeping pills the doctor had prescribed me after my "accident." I was enjoying my buzz, trying to decide if I should go back to bed, when I was startled by the bathroom door swinging open.

"Oh, sorry," Cody mumbled, rubbing his bare chest. "I didn't realize—" His eyes narrowed as he took in my tank top and shorts, and the nearly empty whiskey bottle resting between my knees.

I froze, my eyes wide as I tried to decide how I was going to explain drinking in the bathroom in the middle of the night. God, I was fucking pathetic.

But before I could say a word, he stepped inside, gently closing the door. "What the fuck are you doing, Farrah?"

"Having a drink!" I replied with a wide smile, toasting him with my bottle before raising it to my lips.

I would just have to brazen it out. Usually I could make a sarcastic or bitchy comment, and as long as I was safe in the apartment while drinking, it would be enough for him to leave me alone. But I'd barely tasted the booze on my tongue before he swiped the bottle out of my hand.

"You don't need this shit," he mumbled, twisting the cap back on the bottle. "God, Farrah."

"How do you know what I need?" I asked belligerently as I stood from the toilet, swaying as I stepped toward him and reached for the bottle he was holding out of my reach.

His entire demeanor pissed me off, with his gelled hair and fucking prep school clothes. What the hell did he know about anything?

"You think you know anything about me?"

"I know plenty," he told me seriously, reaching up to push my hair out of my face until I ducked away. "I was there too. I think it's easy for you to forget that, but I was there too."

I gasped and staggered back in shock. I couldn't believe he was going there. What a dick. No one dared to mention that day to me.

"Fuck you, Cody," I said with a sneer, my lower lip trembling. I tried to push around him but he held his ground, and I huffed in frustration.

"Let me out!" I said tightly, smacking him in the chest.

When I looked up to find him staring at me with kind eyes, although red around the edges, I lost it.

I slapped him again. I was sick and tired of him playing his knight-in-shining-armor games. I didn't need him stepping in all the time, treating me like a child. Fuck him.

I swung my arms, my hands alternately flat or fisted, and beat at his chest and arms. "Don't look at me like that! I'm fine! What, do you think you need to save me? Ha! Maybe I need to save you from those fucking polos and that ridiculous faux hawk! News flash, dickhead. If it's not an actual Mohawk, you just look like a douche!"

He took everything I had to give him and never once attempted to stop me. "Get it out, baby," he murmured, rubbing my back when he could reach it. It was extremely frustrating that he was trying to console me when I wanted him to hit me back. I wanted a goddamn fight.

What was wrong with me?

Eventually I was crying more than I was hitting, and that pissed me off even more. I fucking hated showing emotions. It made me feel like a drama queen, as if I were begging for attention. I dropped my arms to my sides and clenched my jaw, feeling overwhelmingly embarrassed for my freak-out. I pretended that tears weren't leaking from the corners of my eyes as I stared at his bare chest, now covered in red marks and scratches, and silently willed him to leave.

I was so focused on trying to get my shit together that when he wrapped his arms around me, I didn't even fight it. He pushed me back gently while I stared at the mole on his breastbone, and before I could snap out of my head, he sat down on the toilet and pulled me down with him so I was straddling his lap.

"I know you're hurting," he started, pausing when I scoffed.

"I'm fine."

"You're fine? That's why you're drinking Jack in the fucking bathroom at five o'clock in the morning?"

I didn't have a reply to that. It was ridiculous; I knew that. I just didn't have an explanation for it, at least not one that wouldn't make me seem even more pathetic. God, had I really told him he needed to be saved from his haircut? I could feel him looking at me, but refused to meet his eyes.

I knew I should get up and get the hell away from him. He was my best friend's little brother, and we were barely friends. But when my eyes began to grow heavy, and I hiccupped with leftover tears, he gently grasped the back of my neck, and I let him pull my face to his throat.

"It's okay, baby," he whispered gently, rubbing my back in slow circles. "Sleep, Farrah."

Strangely, I felt myself relaxing into his muscular body.

"Tomorrow, you can pretend this never happened," he told me seriously, his hand sliding down to grip my side, slowly burrowing under my tank top. He rubbed slowly on the side of my lower belly with his thumb, and I refused to acknowledge when he found one of my scars and paused. He turned his head and kissed my forehead gently, his thumb still resting on the small round scar burned into my skin. "Let me take care of you tonight."

I had fallen asleep that night to the gentle rhythm of his breathing, promising myself that I'd stay away from him from then on, thankful that he'd be leaving for school soon and I wouldn't have to see him again.

• • •

I snapped back into the present as Cody squeezed my hips once and stepped around me, headed toward the kitchen.

"You guys have any beer?" he called, as if I hadn't just zoned out for God knows how long, and he hadn't shown up on my doorstep like he freaking belonged there.

"Your sister keeps that piss you like stocked," I answered, rolling my eyes as I followed him. "I don't know why you drink that shit."

"I don't bitch about your beer, you don't bitch about mine," he warned, using the scarred countertop to pop the top off his beer bottle. "You in for the night?"

"Yeah. I had Will for a while, but he sleeps better at Gram's, so she took him a little while ago. For some reason, he refuses to sleep in his own bed when Callie's not here."

I watched him with confusion as he made himself comfortable in my kitchen, then I came to a decision. I grabbed a beer for myself from the fridge, then bumped him out of the way with my hip. If he was going to act like being here without Callie was no big deal, I'd do the same.

If anyone could pretend that a situation wasn't awkward or uncomfortable or just plain weird, it was me. I'd had years of practice.

"Hey, sweetheart, looks like you spilled some shit on your

pants," he joked, leaning against the countertop.

"Yeah, thanks for the flash, Gordon. I spilled nail polish all over the place when you started pounding on my door like the gestapo. You're buying me some new freaking sweatpants," I grumbled, opening my bottle. "I'm going to go change. Clean the shit off the coffee table, would you?"

I heard him bitching as I walked toward my bedroom, and grinned. He could take the blame for not being able to get that shit off Callie's coffee table. It was his damn fault it had gotten spilled in the first place.

Shit, my room was a disaster. I'd needed to go to the Laundromat last week, but with Callie waffling about whether she was going to Eugene or not, and trying to rearrange her schedule at the salon so her clients wouldn't revolt, I hadn't had time.

Shit.

The only clean pants I had were a huge pair of sweatpants that I wore to bed when I was having a bad night. They didn't stay up around my waist unless I tightened the drawstring as far as it would go and then rolled them like four times, but since the options were either the sweats or a tiny-ass pair of yoga shorts ... I stuck with the sweats.

If only I would have listened to Gram when she told me to stop throwing damp towels in with the rest of my dirty laundry, I might have been able to wear a semi-clean pair that actually fit.

By the time I made it back into the living room, Cody had polished off most of his beer and was grimacing as he rotated his arm slowly.

"Does it still bother you?" I asked, startling him as I rounded the couch.

"Nah, it's usually not bad. Long ride today, though," he answered, pulling a prescription bottle out of the pocket of his jeans.

"You've been drinking," I snapped dumbly as he dropped a pill into his mouth and washed it down with the last of his beer. "You better not be getting back on your bike tonight."

"That's funny, coming from you," he replied with a short bark of laughter, shaking his head.

I almost took a step back, the hurt flashing through me quickly at his comment, but I hid that small tell. It always came back to this—always—so I shouldn't have been surprised. I wouldn't let him catch me off guard again.

I turned my head toward the TV, refusing to look at him as I sat down on the far end of the couch. He'd seen me at my worst, and it seemed as if I'd never be able to escape that fact. It was why when I'd noticed him watching me over the past year, I'd ignored it.

Was I attracted to him? Of course I was. Cody was gorgeous, and he carried himself with a confidence that had become even more apparent as he'd found his place in the Aces. I couldn't help but be attracted to him; he was the embodiment of everything I'd ever looked for in a man—strong, kind, sexy, smart—but that didn't mean that I would ever act on it. There was no way I could ever move past the fact that he had kept me alive and in one piece more times than I could remember. It caused an inequality in our relationship that I hated.

The times that I could remember were bad enough; I wouldn't even let myself contemplate how bad the times I couldn't remember were.

"I shouldn't have said that," he said, leaning forward as if to touch my leg before I jerked away. "I wasn't planning on going anywhere, Farrah."

"It's fine." I laughed woodenly, staring with unfocused eyes at the television. "No harm, no foul. Let's not pretend that I should be making life choices for anyone."

"Fuck!" he said under his breath, surprising me enough to whip my head in his direction. "This is not what I planned on happening."

"What exactly did you plan?" I asked calmly, my mask firmly in place. "Your sister's not here, and your grandmother lives right next door. Why the hell are you still in my apartment?"

I watched as he ran his hands over the top of his head in frustration, and was about to climb off the couch to put some space between us when he reached over and dragged me toward him.

"You know why I'm here, Farrah," he answered quietly, turning sideways so he could settle me between his thighs with my back resting against his chest. "I gave you space, baby. I gave you thousands of miles of space, because I knew you needed it."

Cody tightened his arms around my torso as I scrambled to get up. He was going to get to me; he knew just what buttons to push, which words to use to get a reaction out of me, and he was going to use them. I could feel it.

"You weren't ready," he said. "I got that. I knew you needed time to get your shit together, to make a life where you could stand on your own two feet. But I'm done waiting, Farrah."

"I didn't ask you to wait!" I shot back, trying for boredom but sounding more panicked than I liked, so I decided to get physical and pushed on his arms. "What the fuck are you even talking about?"

Struggling to climb off his lap, I felt his lips drag softly over my shoulder, and I froze. It had been so long since I'd felt something like that. Drunken fumbling with strangers had happened occasionally when I was in the midst of my partying days, but even if they would have been inclined, I wouldn't have let them be tender with me. I hadn't been able to handle own emotions back then, much less someone else's.

My eyes drifted shut as he nuzzled against my neck. Had that ever felt this good?

"Do you know how beautiful you are to me?" he whispered, loosening his arms so he could run his hands up and down my belly. "Even when I was dragging you out of places, drunk out of your mind and pissed at everyone, you were still the most beautiful woman I'd ever seen. I couldn't get you out of my head, and then in the last year, there was just . . . so much more. You fucking light up, Farrah."

He dropped a kiss on my neck and lingered for a moment, inhaling my scent. "Your face was all I could think about when I was in the hospital—how your nose wrinkles when you scowl at me, the way you smile at Callie when she's being an idiot, that soft look you get when you're dancing with Will. *Fuck*, Farrah."

My throat tightened as I listened to him. His mention of the hospital and the way he was talking to me opened up the floodgates on emotions I usually kept locked tightly away.

Damn it, I *knew* it. I knew he'd get to me somehow.

"You were thinking about me when you were in the hospital?" I asked quietly, my body tensing.

"Constantly," he mumbled into my neck.

Before he could grab me, I was off his lap and standing next to the couch, trying to keep my nose from wrinkling as I glared at him.

"You're such an asshole!" I screeched, not caring that I sounded like a freaking lunatic.

"What the fuck?"

"Oh yeah," I said, working up a good rant as I yanked up my

sweats and paced in front of him, all of my protective filters deserting me. "You were just consumed with thoughts of me. Because I'm just *so* beautiful. What a load of horseshit!"

"What's your problem?" he shouted, climbing to his feet.

"You didn't even fucking call me when you were in the hospital!"

"I sent you a text!"

"Are you kidding me right now? You sent me one word, Cody! One! Do you remember what you said?" I watched him as he tried to remember, and my irritation ratcheted up even higher. "You sent, 'Alive.' That's it! That's all I got!"

"And?"

"You *cannot* be that stupid." I growled as his mouth curved up into a grin. "Do you know what that was like for me?"

"I knew you were with Grams. She was getting all the info you needed," he answered calmly, pissing me off even more with his logic.

"That's not the point!"

"Well, what the fuck is the point, then? Because it sounds to me like we're talking in fucking circles!"

"I was worried!" I screamed back, covering my mouth as soon as the words slipped out. I scrambled backward, my wide eyes meeting his as he stalked me toward the front door.

"You were worried?" he asked softly, his face softening. "I'm sorry, baby."

"Get the fuck out of my house!" I backpedalled, refusing to acknowledge my last words. Shit, I'd practically laid myself open with three freaking words. What the hell was I thinking?

But I wasn't thinking, and that was the point. *He* did this to me.

"Shut up," he said in a low growl as he advanced on me,

reaching me as my back hit the front door. "You were worried about me."

His mouth was on mine before I could reply.

Oh God.

He bit my bottom lip as I tried to turn my head away, but the gentle way his fingers brushed my cheeks was what stopped any idea of escape. This was *Cody*, and I had no defenses against him.

Before I could react he kissed me hard, then licked deep into my mouth as I whimpered and wrapped my hands around the back of his head to pull him closer. As much as I tried to deny it, to pretend like he was just an acquaintance, someone I had to deal with because of how entrenched I was with his family—it wasn't true. Not at all. I *had* been worried. I'd been scared out of my mind when we found out he'd been shot, unable to function until I'd gotten his text.

For the first time, my nightmares had begun to have a face. I'd woken up shaking and crying for a month afterward, my boyfriend's death playing over and over through my dreams, but it hadn't been Echo dying in those dreams. It had been Cody's face that startled me awake, leaving me covered in a cold sweat.

And now he was there, safe and wrapped around me in a way I'd never let myself imagine him. I inhaled against his throat, reveling in the clean scent of his skin as he lifted me against the door, and tried to wrap my legs around his waist.

"These have to go," he growled, pushing at the waistband of my sweats when the extra material kept me from getting as close as he wanted. They slipped off my hips and hit the floor just seconds before he successfully pulled my legs completely around his waist. "There you are," he murmured into my mouth as he used his hips to brace me against the door, then rocked his pelvis against me.

I could have sobbed with relief when his mouth met mine again. I knew my lack of baggy pants took away any chance of camouflaging how skinny I'd gotten, and for a second, I was terrified that when he saw me he'd be disgusted. He wasn't grossed out, thank God. If anything, my freshly waxed legs, no matter how slender they were, seemed to have lit a fuse in him that had him groping at them desperately.

I was sucking at his bottom lip, pulling his T-shirt up his body, when a knock at the door startled us both.

"You expecting someone?" he asked suspiciously as he set me down gently on my shaky legs.

"Yeah, maybe we can have a threesome?" I replied in a high-pitched voice, dramatically reaching up to twirl my fingers in my hair like an airhead. Then I dropped my hand and shook my head at him, scowling. "Don't be a dick."

The knock sounded again, and with one last glance he wiped a hand over his face before turning to unlock the door, pushing me cautiously behind him as he opened it.

"G-Gram," he stuttered, and I watched the back of his neck darken.

He didn't stop his grandmother as she used the palm of her hand to push the door wider, and I grimaced as she caught a look at me in all my whorish, half-naked glory.

"It's about time." She rolled her eyes. "Don't care what you're doing, but keep your voices down. The whole damn complex can hear you screaming, and if you wake up your nephew, I'll kill you."

She stepped toward Cody and reached around him, running her hand gently down my hair before giving my shoulder a small squeeze. "I'll see you both in the morning for breakfast," she stated firmly, catching my eye to let me know she wasn't going to let me skip out.

We stood there silently as she walked away, and as soon as we heard her apartment door shut next door, Cody turned toward me and closed the door.

"I'll get you some blankets for the couch," I mumbled in embarrassment, pulling at the bottom of my tank top as if to hide the plain cotton underwear I was wearing. No longer in the heat of the moment, I was rethinking the advisability of sleeping with my best friend's brother, especially with his grandmother next door. I took a step back, refusing to turn around and let him see my ass with the words YOU BOWL ME OVER written across my underwear, complete with little black bowling pins.

"Farrah," he said softly, refusing to move until I lifted my head to look at him. I tried to keep my expression neutral but must have been unsuccessful, because in the next moment he flipped the dead bolt and murmured, "Fuck it," as he lifted me up and carried me toward my bedroom.

Chapter 3

Farrah

Cody's lips never left mine as my back landed on the tangled sheets of my bed, and I squeaked in surprise when something dug into the back of my thigh.

"What's wrong?" He gasped as I tried to wiggle off the offending object, the breath from his words whispering across my skin as he moved his mouth over my jaw.

"Stop!" I yelped, pulling my face away.

"What?"

"Move!" I groaned, pushing him to the side as I scooted up the bed. "There's something digging into my ass."

"There's going to be," he said, waggling his eyebrows up and down.

"Shut up!" I giggled, reaching under me to pull out . . . a high heel? How the hell did that get there?

"Shit, Farrah. You're a little piglet."

He sounded surprised as he looked around my room at the

piles of laundry and miscellaneous junk that cluttered the floor. My face burned in embarrassment as I shrugged my shoulders and flopped back down on the bed.

"Tomorrow's laundry day," I grumbled, throwing my forearm over my face. What the hell had I been thinking, letting him into my room?

The bed dipped down and Cody straddled me on his knees, pulling my arm away to look at me.

"We're cleaning this shit up tomorrow," he told me with a smile, then ran his hands up my belly until he was cupping my small breasts in his hands.

"Cleaning is not an aphrodisiac, you lunatic," I huffed, retreating into my protective sarcasm as I rested my hands lightly on his thighs. Holy shit, the guy worked out.

"You're right, sweetheart, it really isn't," he whispered, leaning down until our faces were just millimeters apart. "But waking up with you in the morning *is*."

He ran his tongue across my bottom lip, completely distracting me from the conversation we were having, and I gasped as his fingers found my nipples and gently squeezed. Good Lord, it was like he knew exactly what to do to make me come unglued. We were both breathing heavily as the kiss grew frenzied, and I almost missed it when he began to pull the thin straps of my tank top off my shoulders. Almost.

The straps had reached the middle of my arms before sanity crept in, and I reached up to grasp the shirt at my collarbone as he began to drag it down. We played tug-of-war for a moment, a silent argument that didn't affect our kiss at all until he abruptly pulled away from me.

"What are you doing?" He leaned back until he was practically sitting on my hips, panting as he frowned at me.

Instead of explaining myself, I silently reached for my underwear, pressing my hands between his thighs as I pushed them down as far as I could. If I could just get him to the good stuff, we'd be in the clear. A guy couldn't resist a chick with no underwear, right? He didn't move a muscle above me, and I didn't meet his eyes as I tilted my hips, trying in vain to push them off the rest of the way.

"Farrah, baby, talk to me."

"I don't want to take my shirt off." I focused on his throat, unable to meet his eyes as I continued to tug at my underwear. All he had to do was shift just a little and I'd have them off . . .

His hand was gentle but firm as he tilted my chin up, forcing me to meet his eyes as he mumbled, "What's going on?"

"You don't want to take it off. Trust me on this. Can we just drop it?" I asked in exasperation, my hands moving from my hips to the button on his jeans. Maybe if I could get to the goods underneath, he'd forget the shirt. He was as hard as a rock underneath, and I couldn't help but get sidetracked, taking a small detour down the front of his zipper, causing him to suck in a harsh breath before he grabbed my wrists and pinned them above my head. Access denied.

"I *do* want to take it off," he answered darkly. "I want those tits. I've been dying to see how much of them I can fit in my mouth."

My jaw dropped in surprise, and I opened and closed it a few times before clenching it in frustration as I stared him down. He didn't seem to be changing his mind, and I debated putting a kibosh on the whole thing, but only for a moment. I'd never been more turned on in my life, and the thought of walking away was inconceivable. I didn't want to lose the chance of seeing him naked, especially because I had a feeling it would be a one-time deal.

"Fine," I said with a huff, relaxing my body onto the bed as my stomach clenched hard with anxiety. He was going to do it—take off what little armor I was wearing—and he was going to regret it, but there was no changing his mind. There was a reason I'd stopped wearing bikinis, choosing instead to wear pinup-style one pieces. I tried to catalog my swimsuit collection in my head to focus on anything but where I was and what was about to happen, but it didn't work. Once I'd given the okay, he released my wrists and swiftly pulled the shirt up and over my head.

I couldn't watch. I didn't want to see his reaction.

My eyes were shut tight and my hands in tight fists as his fingers traced lightly over my torso.

"Look at me," he whispered urgently, his tone relaxing me enough to look into his eyes. "Ladybugs . . . and a daisy?"

I nodded once, my throat tight with tears as he moved from one tattoo to the next with soft touches.

A few years ago, I'd had an accident—at least, that was what Callie and I had told the skeptical doctors. The truth? My mother had watched while her repulsive boyfriend beat me bloody and then proceeded to burn me with his cigar. Thankfully, I'd gone in and out of consciousness during the ordeal, so I only had vague memories. The scars, however, were not as easily forgotten. There were eleven in all, mostly scattered across my ribs, with a few on my breasts and one low on my belly.

It must have been a pretty long cigar.

I never knew what spooked them, why they'd hauled ass out of the house and left me in the middle of the living room next to the broken coffee table. It didn't matter. I was just thankful that after the last burn—the one right above my underwear line—he'd crawled off of me instead of pulling down my pants to inflict even more damage.

I lay there quietly while Cody ran his fingers over the small ladybug-covered scars peppering my body, and sobbed once in relief when he leaned down and swiped the daisy covering the scar two inches above my pubic bone with his tongue.

"Don't ever hide from me again," he murmured into my skin, his eyes meeting mine. "I'm all in, Farrah. There's nothing about you that would turn me off, okay?"

"Okay." I sniffled, nodding my head.

"Not sure how this is going to turn out," he told me seriously, causing my body to still. "But I've been covered in your vomit, and I still want you more than I've ever wanted anything in my life. That has to mean something."

"You just used the word *vomit* in a sentence and made it sound romantic," I replied with a shy grin. "I guess that means I'm all in too."

He wore a wide smile as he reached behind his neck with one hand, contorting his body to pull his shirt over his head and one arm, leaving it to dangle on his injured shoulder for a moment before he met my eyes and let it drop.

The scar from his bullet wound wasn't as bad as I'd envisioned, about twice the size of one of mine, but the reality of why it was there had my stomach clenching. It was so close, *too close* to where his heart beat heavy with adrenalin and arousal. It could have turned out so much worse. I couldn't stop the impulse that had me leaning up to caress the red skin lightly with my lips, and before I could pull away, I felt his hand tangle in the back of my hair to hold me in place.

"I'm sorry," he murmured quietly into the top of my hair. "If I could get rid of it, I would. I know it brings up bad memories."

I was startled by his comment, instantly remembering the

day Echo was shot. Honestly, I hadn't even been thinking about that horrible day; relief that Cody was safe and there with me overpowered any lingering memories of what had been the worst day of my life. I leaned my head against his chest, a mixture of guilt over my lack of reaction and relief that I hadn't reacted warring inside me as I breathed him in. Relief won.

"I don't want to think about it. Okay?" I told him quietly, kissing his chest. "I'm not really into threesomes. There's no room for him here."

I held my body still, waiting for his reply. Would he think I was a bitch for making light of it? Making flippant comments and poorly timed jokes was the way I made it through uncomfortable and painful situations, and speaking of Echo with Cody fell into both of those categories. I'd loved Echo, of course I had, but he died three years ago. At some point, after the downward spiral and subsequent come-to-Jesus meeting I'd had with Gram, I had to let him go. Whatever happened or didn't happen with Cody had to be completely separate from Echo.

I was cringing inside, waiting for him to call me out on my remark when he surprised me, using his hold in my hair to jerk my face up to meet his. I tried to read his expression, but didn't have the chance because his lips were on mine immediately, biting and sucking at them with an urgency that hadn't been there before. I kept my eyes open, reveling in the way his eyebrows drew down in the middle as if he was concentrating solely on me.

Just as my eyes began to grow heavy, my breath coming out in pants as his hands tightened in my hair, he pulled his lips from mine and let go of me completely.

Cody's eyes never left mine as he slid back off the bed and stood up, pulling his jeans, boots, and socks off before placing his hand between my breasts to push me back on the bed. Then he broke the connection to grab my underwear in both hands and yank them down my legs. I only had a second of self-consciousness about my pronounced hipbones and bony knees before he spoke, reassuring me with two words.

"Holy hell." He groaned when he realized that my legs weren't the only thing I waxed. "You're going to kill me."

"You're lucky, I just had my appointment last week. If you would have come here sooner ..." I shook my head in mock seriousness and giggled as his face lit up with humor.

What was this guy doing to me? I wasn't a giggler. Ever.

He growled and pounced on me as I howled with laughter, and I felt as if I were floating. Sex had never been fun for me before. It wasn't that I'd never liked it, but with every other guy I'd been with, I hadn't felt comfortable enough to let my guard down. It was serious business, sometimes frantic, other times slow and sultry, but never once in the years I'd been having sex had it ever been fun.

As I tried to crab walk away from him, he caught me by swooping down to pull my nipple into his mouth, and we both groaned as my back arched off the bed. I wrapped my hands around the back of his head, my knees gripping his sides as he moved back and forth, alternately kissing and sucking, pausing occasionally to detour to one of my ladybugs. Then he met my eyes with a wicked grin and leaned down to suck as much of my breast as he could into his mouth as his fingers slid between my legs.

The dual sensations had me scrambling as I tried to decide which to focus on, but as his fingers slid into me and his mouth popped off my breast, the decision was made.

"Condoms?" he asked desperately as his thumb started circling my clit while his fingers pumped slowly in and out.

Could your eyes *really* roll back into your head, or did they just feel that way? I couldn't figure out why he was bothering me as I chased my orgasm. Didn't he see I was busy?

"Condoms, Ladybug. Where are your condoms?"

I looked at him stupidly for a moment as his hand went still, then finally figured out what he was yapping about.

"I don't have any."

"What?" he practically yelled.

"Shut it!" I whispered back, afraid he was going to have Gram storming over from her apartment for the second time that night. "I don't have any! I don't have sex."

"W-what?" he sputtered as he wiggled his fingers inside me. "My fingers would beg to differ, sweetheart."

"I haven't had sex in over a year," I mumbled back. "Drunken hookups are pretty much nonexistent when you aren't partying anymore."

"Goddamn it." He groaned, dropping his forehead to my chest. "I haven't had sex in fucking *months*."

"Oh, poor you," I said sarcastically, the thought of him having sex with anyone else pissing me right the hell off.

My irritation was almost instantly forgotten as his fingers began to move slowly, as if he didn't even realize he was doing it, hitting the perfect spot inside me to have me crawling out of my skin. I whimpered deep in my throat and his head snapped up, his nostrils flaring as he took in my flushed face and clenched jaw.

"Fuck it. I'm clean," he muttered frantically, pulling his fingers from me to yank down his boxer briefs. "Please tell me you're clean and on the pill."

"I'm clean," I answered, staring at the *V* leading down to his thick cock, the hair trimmed short around it. "I can't get pregnant."

He reached out to spread my knees wide, and ran his finger

lightly from top to bottom before looking back up.

"What do you mean?"

"I haven't had a period in years, but there's nothing wrong." I paused, choosing my words carefully. "The doctors say I don't have enough body fat and it's messing with my cycle."

He watched me for a moment, his jaw tight, before dropping his hips to fit between my thighs.

"I'll buy condoms tomorrow," he assured me in a low voice, his hand cupping the side of my face gently. "But I can't wait."

With a swift thrust he buried himself to the hilt, and my face heated and tears blurred my eyes as emotion overwhelmed me. I didn't know if it was the fact that it was the first time in years I'd felt actual intimacy with another person, how incredibly good it felt to have someone connected to me again, or the fact that it was *Cody* inside me. Whatever the cause, I felt warm tears roll into the hair at my temples as he began to move.

He'd been braced with one hand above my shoulder, but at the sight of my tears, he leaned down until our torsos were flush with both of his forearms braced beneath my shoulders on the bed, his hands cradling the back of my head as if we were hugging.

He didn't say a word about my tears but paused, watching my face intently until I gave him a small, trembling smile.

"I'm good," I rasped huskily.

"You're beautiful," he said quietly, dropping his forehead to mine.

Then he began to move again, taking his time to find the things I liked, then using them until I was squirming under him and digging my nails into his back as I came.

Half an hour later I lay in his arms, listening to Cody snore quietly as I drifted off to sleep. I'd stopped running and I didn't regret it.

Later, I'd blame my mistake on all the fantastic sex endorphins.

Chapter 4

Farrah

I woke up at seven thirty the next morning to Cody's hand on my ass and my phone playing the Beatles' "With a Little Help from My Friends"—the Joe Cocker version—from somewhere in the mess on my floor. What can I say? I'm a fan, and Callie calls me the most often, so I picked a favorite for her ringtone.

"Noooo." I groaned, checking the clock before pulling my pillow over my head. We'd finally fallen asleep after round two only a few hours before, and I dreaded dragging my ass out of the cocoon that held the heat of Cody's body.

"Answer your phone, babe," he slurred sleepily, clenching the hand on my ass as the phone stopped ringing and then started up again.

"No way in hell," I mumbled back grouchily. "It's *your* sister. You get it."

I realized my mistake seconds later when the covers were whipped up on Cody's side of the bed, letting in the cold air I'd been avoiding, before I heard his gruff, "Hello? Yeah, you called Farrah."

"Shit! Gimme the phone!" I yelped, wrestling out of the blankets. He ignored my waving arms and shaking head until I overestimated the size of the bed while trying frantically to untangle myself. Instead of my hand landing at the edge, it hit nothing but air—propelling me ass over teakettle onto the floor.

"Goddamn it," I huffed out, watching him round the bed. "Give me my phone!"

"You okay, Ladybug?" he asked with a grin, the phone still pressed to his ear. "I thought you wanted me to answer it."

"Are you out of your fucking mind?" I growled, imagining the earful that Callie must be giving him on the other end of the line. "Give me the phone and put some fucking pants on!"

"Damn, baby, you always going to be this pissy in the morning?"

I dropped my head against the carpet and screeched in frustration. He knew exactly what he was doing by calling me pet names and insinuating that he'd be seeing me in the mornings. Any chance of keeping things quiet between us had just been shot to hell.

"Yeah, sister . . . Okay . . . I'll see you tonight, then. Here's Farrah." He ended his conversation, reaching down to help me up off the floor as I scowled at him.

"You're dead to me," I told him, grabbing the phone out of his hand.

"Get off the phone and come back to bed, Ladybug," he whispered loud enough for his sister to hear, then wrapped his long fingers around the sides of my head to pull me in for a deep kiss.

I stood there stupidly watching his bare ass cross to the bed and crawl back in, the phone forgotten in my hand for almost a full minute before I snapped back to reality.

"Why the hell are you calling me before the sun is awake?" I asked my best friend, propping the phone between chin and shoulder as I grabbed some underwear and my last clean sundress from the top of my dresser.

"Nice try, asshole. Why is my brother answering your phone?" she asked incredulously.

"He doesn't understand boundaries?"

"Why is he in our apartment before 'the sun is awake'?"

"Why are any of us here, Callie?" I asked rhetorically. "Why are any of us here?"

"Why isn't he staying at Gram's?"

"He was jealous because he assumed—correctly, I might add—that Will would steal Gram's attention away from him now that he's been usurped as the baby of the family?"

"You're an idiot." She laughed.

"Yeah, yeah, I've heard it all before," I said teasingly, grabbing a towel and turning on the shower before sitting down on the edge of the tub and dropping my head into my hands. "He came, he saw, he conquered."

"No!"

"Oh yes. Apparently your baby brother has a thing for me." I sighed, rubbing between my eyebrows with one finger to smooth the frown crease away.

"This is not news."

"It was to me," I grumbled.

"Does this mean—"

I cut her off. "No more about me. What happened yesterday? Did you see Grease? Did he freak out? Fall to his knees and declare his undying love? Or did he go the pussy route and cry?"

She laughed and kindly allowed me to change the subject without calling me out on it. Callie was one of the few people who could read me like a book, and she must have sensed I was freaking out.

"Yeah, I saw him." She sighed. "It didn't go so good, not at first, but we're solid now."

"How solid?" I asked cautiously.

Callie and Grease's relationship had gone through more ups and downs than any I had ever heard of. Up until the night before, they hadn't even talked in almost a year—a decision Callie had made while she was dealing with an assload of survivor's guilt and PTSD.

"Pack-your-shit-because-we're-moving-to-Oregon solid," she answered giddily.

"No fucking way."

"Yep. We want to move all of us up here this week." She spoke quickly as if worried I'd interrupt. "But before you freak, I want to tell you that if you changed your mind about moving or you don't want to go that soon, I won't be mad. I won't. I really want you with us, Farrah, and I hope that you'll come. We just don't want to waste any more time, you know?"

I sat in silence, weighing my options before speaking. I could drop everything and move with my family to Oregon, or I could refuse to go and be stuck in an empty apartment in a town where no one cared about me. I'd be alone and lonely. It was an easy decision to make.

"Well, I'll have to check my schedule . . . but I'm pretty sure I'm not busy next week," I told her flatly, pulling the phone away from my ear as she whooped.

"Okay, yes! We're leaving here in just a little bit so we can be home before Will goes to bed tonight. Asa is dying to see him, and we're just . . . we're ready to be a family. All in one place, finally." She sniffled, but the tone of her voice was pure joy. "So, I'll see you tonight!"

"Okay, sis. Drive careful."

"Nah, I thought I'd drive recklessly this time," she replied dryly, then her voice turned soft. "Love you."

"Back atcha, toots."

I hopped into the shower, already planning our move in my head. There was so much to do and so little time to do it. We needed to get boxes and tape, and we could probably use garbage bags for laundry and—shit! My laundry needed to be done before we started packing or I'd be screwed.

The news couldn't have come at a better time; it gave me a reason to think of something other than what the hell I was doing with Cody. My mind wandered as I soaped up and rinsed off, and for a while I completely forgot the man in my bedroom.

I was planning on wearing a vintage sundress circa 1970, so I took my time parting my hair in a severe middle part before putting hot rollers in it while I listened to music from the seventies. For some reason, I found that it relaxed me to listen to the era of the day's music while putting on my makeup and styling my hair. I hated looking in the mirror before I showered, or any time that I wasn't actually getting ready. It was a trigger for me, something I'd learned to recognize in the hours I'd spent in therapy. I didn't like seeing the barefaced girl with scars on her body and hollow cheeks—it reminded me too much of the day I'd walked to Callie's with a broken arm and oozing cigar burns—so I covered her up.

My wardrobe since high school had consisted of vintage clothing I found in thrift stores. The chain stores never had what I needed, but if I could find an old, musty, broken-down store in the middle of a dying strip mall, I usually hit gold. Some days, I was a fifties housewife with a demure little dress whose hemline floated just below my knees, and looked as if it were only missing a frilly apron. Other days, I was into nineties grunge and would wear a flannel shirt, jeans, and work boots, my hair in a messy bun. I also had skinny jeans and bell-bottoms, flat-soled Vans and platform sandals. I never stayed in a particular decade, choosing instead to dress according to my mood.

My clothes were my armor. They gave me confidence, a way to keep my head high when I wanted nothing more than to hide. I'd realized when I was young that if I didn't *try* to dress like everyone else—if I made my own style, attractive but completely different from the other girls—I would never look as if I were trying to fit in. It set me apart in a way that was *my* choice, the only way I could assert control in the life I'd been given.

After Echo was murdered, I'd even gone so far as to cover my body in piercings: septum, eyebrow, lip, belly button, nipples; I had piercings everywhere. I'd liked the way they made me look different—unapproachable—until suddenly I'd woken up sober for once and realized I looked exactly the same as every other emo teenager in my neighborhood. After that, I'd taken all of them out except for the one in my eyebrow. I still liked that one.

Thankfully, things had changed drastically in the last couple of years and I was able to make my own choices for the first time in my life. They weren't always the right ones, but they were mine. I'd grown up and left behind the girl who wanted to crawl inside herself and hide—my tormentors no longer had any hold on me— but I still loved the idea of being someone different from one day to the next.

I had all the my half-empty shampoo and lotion bottles lined up on the counter, letting my rollers set while I chose which bottles to keep and which to throw in the trash, when Cody scared the crap out of me by knocking on the door.

"Baby, you've been in there for like an hour," he called through the door. "I need to take a shower or I'm going to smell like sex when we head to Gram's!" He then jiggled the locked handle.

I swung the door open without glancing in his direction, then resumed tossing the bottles into the trash. I assumed he would just hop in the shower while I worked; it wasn't as if I hadn't already seen the goods. I'd sorted through a couple more bottles when I finally noticed that he hadn't moved from his place in the doorway, and turned to face him in irritation.

As I was about to snap at him to get going, the expression on his face stopped me in my tracks.

"Holy shit. I know it's weird, but you look hot as fuck in those," he rasped, motioning to my head.

"The curlers?" I scoffed, thinking surely he was joking.

"Shit, Ladybug." He stepped toward me, clenching his jaw. "We don't have time right now, but I need you to make me a promise."

"Okay?" I watched his face as he gripped my hips and pulled me closer, his erection pressing against me from beneath his boxer briefs.

"Promise me that you'll wear those for me—"

"Shut up." I felt my face heating as I realized he was serious.

"No, listen. Promise me that one day I'll come home and you'll be wearing nothing but those . . . and an apron."

"You're outta your mind!" I let out a laugh from deep in my belly, shaking my head.

"You promised!" he reminded me, then kissed me hard on the lips. He gave me one more squeeze, rubbing his hands lightly over my ass before pushing me aside to climb in the shower, mumbling under his breath, "Fuck, now I'm hard."

As soon as I heard the shower running, I couldn't help the wide smile creeping onto my lips. I couldn't believe he had a thing for my curlers. What a freak. I hummed quietly as I finished my work, and as I set down the last bottle under the sink, something dawned on me.

I'd just let Cody see me before I'd finished putting on my armor for the day, something I'd allowed no man to see since I was fourteen years old. I hadn't even noticed. I'd welcomed him into the room before finishing my most important ritual of the day, my few moments of complete peace before facing the world with a smug smile on my face.

I was bracing myself against the cabinet doors, wondering what the hell it meant, when I was rudely interrupted by Cody howling in the shower.

"Cold! Shit! Fuck! It's cold!" he yelled, slapping at what I assumed were the taps behind the shower curtain. "I've got soap in my hair! Shit! It's burning my eyes!"

"Sorry!" I called back, my smug smile finally in place as I looked in the mirror and started pulling out the rollers.

My smile widened as I added, "We run out of hot water at about, eh . . . one and a half showers."

Chapter 5

Casper

I couldn't stop staring at her.

We spent the morning with Gram and my two-year-old nephew, and watching the three of them together was a fucking revelation. I hadn't realized how tense it had become between Farrah and me until the tension was gone and I got to see her as she actually was.

The girl was funny.

The facial expressions I'd caught in the past were a small fraction of her arsenal. She had the most expressive face I'd ever seen, which was pretty amazing because she could also lock it down to the point that you wouldn't even be able to tell if she was happy or mad. For the first time I was inside the inner sanctum, able to gauge every reaction—but only because she was allowing me—and it was a hell of a place to be.

I guess Callie's call was about more than checking in. My sister had decided to finally move from Sacramento to Oregon to be with her man, so Gram and Farrah were in full-on planning mode, making lists and shit for all the things they needed to do. I knew Gram would follow Callie, but I couldn't help the smile on my face as Farrah told Gram she was going with them.

I caught Farrah's eye as we sat across from each other at Gram's scarred-up table, the shy smile on her face making my entire fucking day. I wanted to take her back to bed that very second, but even if we hadn't been in the middle of a conversation with my grandmother, the massive hard-on I was suddenly sporting wouldn't have allowed me to stand up from the table. *Goddamn.* The woman wound me up without even trying.

Farrah insisted on taking Will with us that afternoon to the Laundromat and to buy boxes from a moving company. There was something about the way she and the boy played off each other that had my chest tightening. It wasn't a maternal thing, really, but the way she loved on him and knew exactly what he needed and how to take care of him made me feel stupidly proud, really proud.

You could see the connection between them—not surprising since he'd lived with her his entire life—but it was more than that. Farrah would kill for him, and it showed in the way she held him protectively and watched him like a hawk. She loved that boy with an intensity that matched my own, and it made me dig her even more than I already did.

By late that afternoon, we'd finally made it back from our errands. I didn't know how she was so unruffled when I felt like dropping the baby at Gram's and taking off on my bike to get some quiet. Will was bouncing off the walls, exhausted because he hadn't gotten his nap, and asked every two seconds for his mom and dad. The poor kid had rarely been without both of them at the same time, and he'd finally reached his limit as we'd packed Farrah's clean clothes into the trunk of her car. He'd cried the entire way home, and when we got there, refused to stand more than a foot away from the front door, as if he was waiting for Callie to come through it. It was sad as hell ... and gave me a massive headache.

"Hey, Will! You want some Cheerios, dude?" Farrah asked calmly as she strode out of the kitchen holding a little bowl of dry cereal.

"Wan' Mama."

"Yeah, I hear ya, buddy," she told him with a sigh as she crouched down in front of him, the long skirt of her dress pooling around her on the floor. "Mommy and Daddy are on their way. You sure you don't want any of these absolutely scrumptious little o's?'

She popped a piece into her mouth with an exaggerated look of pleasure, and I couldn't help but smile when Will walked between her knees and laid his head on her shoulder, then grabbed a Cheerio from the bowl with his chubby little fingers.

"Only a little bit longer, bud," she murmured gently, kissing the top of his head.

She stayed that way, crouched down in front of him while he leaned his body into hers for a few minutes, before he scooted back to sit on one of her thighs. He was standing on her dress and as he moved, pulled the dress down until she dropped the Cheerios to the floor as she scrambled to catch her neckline before her tits came popping out. I watched the surprise on her face while Will pushed at her, and in what seemed like slow motion, they both toppled over and burst into laughter.

"My legs are like Jell-O!" she screeched at him, pulling him up so he was straddling her belly. "You're getting too big, Wilfred."

"No Wilfred!" he yelled back, giggling.

"Wilbur?"

"No!"

"Wilhelmina?"

"No!"

"Will-you-take-me-out-to-dinner?"

"No!"

They got louder and louder, completely oblivious to the world around them as Will belly laughed, bending at the waist like he couldn't hold himself up any longer, his sturdy little body shaking Farrah's underneath him.

"Well, what is it then?" she asked in mock exasperation, their faces close together.

"Willam Butter Hawtorn!" Will yelled back, spraying spit all over Farrah's face.

"Oh, right. Well, that's boring," she told him, rolling her eyes with a huge smile on her face as she nonchalantly wiped off the spit.

It was clear the argument was a familiar one by the way they each played their parts, and I watched in awe as Will's face relaxed for the first time in hours. He rubbed his eyes blearily before lying down flat on Farrah's chest and reaching up to grab one of her loose curls so he could run his fingers through it. They were flat on the old carpet that I knew Farrah hated, but she made no move to get up as she rubbed his back softly.

"My William." She sighed softly before she closed her eyes and began humming.

I hated interrupting because I knew she'd forgotten that I was even in the room, but I couldn't just stand there watching anymore. As I stepped closer to them, her eyes popped open and she gave me a sleepy smile. It was the most beautiful she'd ever looked.

I couldn't stop myself from reaching down and picking her

up, cradling her and Will at the same time and carrying them to the couch. Will had already passed out, and he didn't move a muscle as I pulled the cushions off the back of the couch so Farrah could scoot in, leaving room for me to lie down next to them.

"You gut me," I whispered as I wrapped my arm over the two of them.

"Because I pretend I don't know your nephew's name?" she asked with a smile, linking her fingers with mine as she closed her eyes.

I wasn't sure how to explain it, shit, *I* didn't even know what it was, so I kept my mouth shut as I watched her fall asleep. I finally closed my eyes, listening to Will's soft snores, and at some point I eventually passed out.

I woke up sweaty and hot as hell when I heard voices outside the front door, and watched sleepily as it unlocked and opened, Grease directing my sister into the apartment with a small slap on her ass.

"Shhh!" she whispered to Grease, catching sight of us on the couch. "They're sleeping. That's so freaking cute!"

I nodded my head at Grease, then glared at Callie as she whipped a camera from her purse and proceeded to take a shit ton of pictures.

"Pretend like you're sleeping!" she whispered, pausing in front of us.

I pulled my arm from Will's sweaty back, the kid was like a furnace, and rolled gently off the couch instead, leaving Farrah and the baby undisturbed as I pulled Callie in for a hug.

"I missed you, little brother," she mumbled into my chest, squeezing me hard.

"You too." I kissed her on the top of her head. "Will's getting huge."

"I know, right?" She leaned back to look up at me with a huge grin on her face. "He's a little tank."

"Not surprising since his dad's a fucking monster," I said, teasing her and enjoying the way her face lit up for the first time in over a year. "Everything good with you guys?"

"I don't know how he put up with my shit for so long," she said sheepishly.

"Bad shit happens, sis. It always will. But you've got a man that loves you, and after all this shit, you know he's not leaving. Just be thankful for that and stop worrying about stuff you can't change."

"When did you become . . . a man?" She searched my face in surprise.

"Last night," I answered with a dramatic leer, lifting my eyebrows up and down.

"You're fucking disgusting!" She laughed, pinching the skin on my side.

"Hey, Sugar, you have a phone charger?" Grease called quietly from her bedroom, taking her attention away from me instantly.

"I'm gonna go help him. You guys have dinner yet?" she asked, already walking away.

"No, we crashed a couple of hours ago. Have you seen Gram yet?"

"Yeah, we thought Will was with her so we stopped there first. She said she'd make dinner for everyone, someone just needs to go let her know." She paused outside her bedroom door, her gaze roaming over me. "I'm so glad you're here."

She spun around and entered the bedroom before I could reply, so I made my way into the kitchen. I wasn't sure if I should wake Farrah up or not, but figured I'd wait until I knew what

Callie's plans were. We'd barely gotten any sleep the night before, and Farrah needed the rest.

Thinking about her body needing rest brought to mind another thing that had been bothering me, but I knew last night hadn't been the time to say anything to her about it.

She was skinny.

For as long as I'd known her, Farrah had had a pretty slender body—small tits, very little ass, and a tiny waist. Her weight seemed to fluctuate pretty often, only a few pounds making a big difference in the way she looked, but this was the smallest I'd ever seen her. She didn't necessarily look sick, but it wouldn't be very long before she did.

I'd watched her as we had breakfast with Gram, and hadn't noticed anything off, but I had no idea what I was even looking for. She looked so delicate and fragile, completely at odds with her personality, and it freaked me out to the point of being nervous I was going to accidentally hurt her when we had sex. I didn't know what the fuck was going on, but at some point I had to say something to her about it, and I dreaded her reaction.

"Did Will do okay?" Grease rumbled quietly, jerking me out of my train of thought as he came into the kitchen.

"Yeah, he was fine. Farrah's good with him, and he does good with Gram," I answered, pulling two beers out of the fridge.

"I see your balls finally dropped," he said with a head tilt in Farrah's direction and a shit-eating grin.

"Fuck off," I shot back, then downed half the beer he handed me in one go. "She was dealing with a lot of shit. I was giving her some time."

"I know, brother." Grease's face fell. "Just fuckin' with you."

"You and Callie good?"

"Yep. Finally moving on, I think." He took a sip of his beer and sat down on the stool as Callie came into the kitchen.

"I'm going to go help Gram with dinner," she told us, leaning in to give Grease a kiss. "Wake Will up in fifteen, would you? If we don't, he's going to be up all night."

"Got it," he mumbled, pulling her in for another kiss that made my stomach turn. Fuck, Farrah was going to need to get her own apartment in Oregon so I didn't have to see that shit.

We were quiet as we watched Callie walk out, but as soon as the door closed, Grease's gaze came back to me.

"I'm gonna feel a hell of a lot better when her shit's actually moved."

I didn't blame him. Grease and Callie had been playing this game for a long-ass time, and the move had never happened. He'd been driving from Eugene to Sacramento for years just to spend little bits of time with her. Every time they decided she'd move north, something would happen to derail their plans. I didn't know if I'd be that patient in his position, waiting and waiting on the mother of my child to actually move in with me.

I was just glad I wasn't going to have to deal with that shit with Farrah.

Chapter 6

Farrah

"I have my own money, I don't need you to pay my moving expenses," I told Callie for the fourth time in an hour.

"But you're going to need that money to buy furniture and live until you find a job," she argued back, her eyes narrowed in defiance.

We'd gone back and forth since we'd sat down for dinner about how we'd split up the moving costs, and three hours later we were no closer to a resolution. The guys had taken one look at our stubborn faces and hadn't said a word as we'd argued in circles, and they'd eventually moved out of the danger zone to watch cartoons with Will.

I wondered how Grease felt about paying for even more of my shit, but I was sure he wouldn't have argued with Callie even if it bothered him. They'd finally gotten their relationship worked out, and I knew he wouldn't willingly upset the apple cart.

They were being super generous, offering to pay for the

moving van and gas to get us to Oregon, but allowing them to do it made me uncomfortable. No, uncomfortable didn't fully encompass my emotions on the subject. Frankly, it made me feel ashamed, like I was a charity case. For a long time I'd taken advantage of their generosity, living in their apartment and eating their food while I lost my damn mind, but that Farrah was gone. I made okay money at the salon where Callie and I worked, and I'd been paying my half of the expenses for a while now. I was proud of the fact that I could pay my own way, and she was embarrassing me by acting like I couldn't take care of myself.

"Why don't Farrah and I share an apartment? That way she doesn't have to worry about furniture and all that nonsense just yet, and I'll have some company." Gram spoke up with a reassuring pat on my hand, trying to defuse the tension at the table.

"No."

My head spun so fast toward Cody, I must have looked like that chick from *The Exorcist*.

"Why the hell do you think you get a vote?" I asked incredulously as he and Grease stood up and came toward us.

"You're not sharing an apartment with Gram," he said, obviously unconcerned with my attitude.

"I'm pretty sure you're not a part of this conversation," I said with a sneer, turning away from him in dismissal.

I caught Callie's wide eyes as she looked back and forth between us, and wanted to hit something as speculation showed clearly on her face.

"Yeah, that probably isn't going to work, Farrah," she told me apologetically, as if trying to find a diplomatic way to tell me I was crazy. "Aren't you guys together now? I mean—"

"No!"

"Yes."

I whipped back around to find Cody glaring at me.

"Wait, but I thought—" Callie's words were quieted by Grease as Cody stalked toward me, and I realized we probably should have discussed whatever it was we were doing before airing the dirty laundry in front of our family.

"Farrah and I are going to bed," Cody told everyone, his face emotionless as he picked me up and threw me over his shoulder. "We'll finish this shit in the morning."

I buried my forehead against his back in embarrassment as he carried me out of Gram's and over to my apartment. But as soon as he set me down in my bedroom, I let loose.

"What the fuck are you doing?" I hissed, overly aware of the group of people next door, probably waiting silently for a chance to hear our fight.

"Why the hell would you say we aren't together?" he bitched back, sitting down on my bed to take his boots off.

I walked to my dresser, pulling my dress off as soon as I reached it. "Just because we had sex once or three times doesn't mean we're in a relationship," I informed him snottily, choosing a large T-shirt from my pajama drawer. I pulled it on and spun around, stalking toward the bed as he undressed silently beside it. "We never said anything about being together. You said I was pretty, kissed my neck a few times, and we had sex. That's it! That doesn't mean you can make decisions or have any say about where I freaking live!"

We crawled into bed from opposite sides, and I made a big show of pulling the blankets all the way to my neck before turning my head to look at him. He was lying on his back, one arm behind his head and the other resting on his chest, seemingly relaxed.

"Say something!" I hissed, and smacked the bed between us

in frustration.

His head slowly turned my way, and he was completely calm as he rolled the rest of his body toward me until half of it was pinning me to the bed.

"I didn't say you were pretty. Lots of girls are pretty, Ladybug, and they're nothing special. You're fucking beautiful, inside and out."

My breath stuttered at his intense look, and I swallowed hard.

"And I know you're mine," he continued. "You were bitching about how we weren't in a relationship, spouting bullshit about how it was nothing but me sweet-talking you into sex, but the moment we got in this room, you started getting ready for bed and crawled in here beside me like we've done it a thousand times before. That's not a woman having casual sex."

My jaw dropped as realization dawned, but he wrapped his arms around me before I could bolt out of the bed.

"We may have just started *this*, but you can't pretend that this is where *we* started. We've been building on this shit for years, and I'm not going to pretend that you're just a random fuck to me. I don't care if that pisses you off." He leaned down to bite my neck lightly before lifting his head again with a small smile. "You living with Gram would seriously fuck with our sex life. You really want to fuck me with Gram in the next room blaring Dwight Yoakam?"

He was right; living with Gram really would mess with whatever we had going. I just wasn't sure that I was ready to live alone, so when Gram offered, I'd jumped at the chance to share a place with her. Deciding to get my own apartment just because I wanted to get freaky with Cody didn't seem like the smartest plan, and I felt my panic begin to rise as my comfortable life seemed to drift further and further away. I wanted comfort, and after growing up the way I had, I needed it.

"I don't know if I can do this," I warned him quietly, my heart racing. "I don't think I can."

"Ladybug, you don't need to do anything." He tipped my face up to his and brushed his lips lightly over mine. "This is just you and me. There's no big agenda or reason to put labels on shit. It just *is*. You're already doing it."

I didn't answer him, my throat tightening in panic until he leaned down again to kiss my lips, then slid his tongue into my mouth with a low growl. His touch worked like the best anti-anxiety meds I'd ever taken, instantly relaxing me.

I didn't know if it was because I knew from experience that he'd never hurt me, or if it were just instinct, but for some reason he was one of the few people I trusted implicitly. But even though I knew he was trustworthy, it didn't stop the big red sign in the back of my mind from flashing DANGER! over the situation we were in.

Cody's hands skated under my T-shirt, pulling it farther and farther up as he smoothed the tips of his fingers over my torso, and before long he pulled it over my head and dropped it off the side of the bed, leaving me in nothing but my panties.

I heard Callie and Grease come in the front door as he leaned down to pull one of my nipples into his mouth, and the pressure of trying to stay silent while he pulled and tugged with his teeth created an intensity that I had no hope of controlling. I ran my fingernails up his back as he switched to the other nipple, and as soon as he let it pop out of his mouth, I pushed his head away from my body so I could scoot down enough to reach his boxer briefs.

"In a hurry?" he asked jokingly, breathing heavily.

"Are you complaining?"

"Fuck no. Take 'em off."

We laughed quietly as we scrambled with the last pieces of clothing keeping us apart, still snickering as we tore into the box of condoms Cody had bought earlier in the day, finally growing serious as he lay down on his back and pulled me on top of him.

"Ride me," he rasped, his hands moving from my hips to my throat and back again. "Hard and fast, Ladybug."

I nodded once before reaching down to position him. *This* I could handle. Sex between us was fantastic; it was all the other stuff that had me worried. I steadily pressed against him, feeling my muscles inside adapt to his size, but I wasn't quite ready for him so I only made it halfway down on the first stroke. I didn't want to say anything, knowing from experience that within two more passes I'd be wet enough for things to feel great, but Cody must have noticed because he grabbed my hips and stopped me before I could drop down a second time.

"Fuck, I'm sorry," he said, letting go with one hand to put two fingers in his mouth. "I'll get you ready."

I jolted as his slick fingers swept between my legs, rolling around my clit in slow circles as if he wasn't in any kind of hurry. I was quiet as I watched what he was doing to me, and it only took seconds before I was beyond ready.

"Now," I mumbled frantically, reaching back down to position him. "Please."

He dislodged his cock and slid his fingers into me once before a low sound of approval came from his throat, then he pulled his hand away so I had room to maneuver.

Once again I positioned him and dropped down, this time taking him to the hilt in one long glide. We both moaned louder than we should have at the sensation, and it wasn't long before he was staring at my breasts as I bounced above him.

"Son of a bitch." He groaned, one of his hands dropping to

my clit so his thumb could rub gently, matching the rhythm of my movements. It took me a while to come, it always did, but he kept up the pace and didn't give up until I was coming apart above him as he watched me. As soon as I was done, he used both hands to pull me down as his hips thrust up off the bed, his jaw clenching, nostrils flaring, and a quiet grunt leaving his throat when he came.

We had to make a very uncomfortable trip to the bathroom, hearing Callie and Grease's low murmurs from her room as we passed it, but soon we crawled back into bed together, all embarrassment forgotten in exchange for exhaustion. He pulled me so that I lay on top of him, and I listened to his heartbeat and breathing slow as he fell asleep, my stomach a mass of nerves.

If we did this—if we tried to make it work and became a couple—I'd eventually screw it up. I knew with certainty that for one reason or another I wouldn't be able to keep him. What made it even worse was that I wouldn't be able to keep *them* either. Cody's family were the only real family I'd ever known, and I was risking losing them in order to have him.

Falling in with Cody was like playing with a fire that could burn my family's house to the ground, yet I continued to move closer and closer to the flames.

Chapter 7

Farrah

Callie and I quit our jobs at the salon, which made my anxiety skyrocket, but I had little time to think about it as we packed up the apartments and left for Eugene, Oregon, five days later.

It was amazing how little we were leaving behind, especially me, who'd lived in Sacramento for as long as I could remember. Leaving the city was actually the least of my concerns, though. I was glad to be making a clean break from all of it, both the memories and the people. I didn't plan to ever go back.

Grease must have talked to Callie, because she'd come to me in the middle of packing up the kitchen to let me know that they decided I could pay a third of the moving expenses. She reasoned that I really had very little to move in comparison to her, Will, and Gram, so she couldn't let me pay half. It galled her to do it, her body was stiff and her jaw tight as she told me, but there was compassion in her eyes. She understood me in a way that no one else ever would, and even though it killed her to do it, she'd conceded.

Grease and Cody pulled strings with some people they knew up north—they seemed to know everyone—so by the time we got there, Gram and I had apartments in the same complex just a few doors away from each other. It was comforting to know that she would be close by when everything else seemed to be changing at the speed of light. Grease had rented a newer house in a subdivision a few blocks away for Callie and Will, and both Callie and I had cried when we'd finally finished unpacking and it was time for them to go home.

It was the end of an era. I'd lived with Callie, or practically lived with her, since I was sixteen years old, and the thought of living without her was scary as hell. We'd held each other up for so long; it was heartbreaking that she no longer needed me for that. The hardest part, though, was saying good-bye to Will that night. He'd come home as a newborn to our little apartment, and there had never been a day that I hadn't changed one of his diapers or shared a cup of Cheerios with him.

As irrational and unfair as I knew it was, I couldn't help but feel a little resentful that Grease was taking them away from me. I'd never say anything, because underneath it all, I was beyond happy for my best friend.

I just wished that everything didn't have to change.

Once Cody and I helped Gram get her bedroom situated so she'd have a place to sleep, we hugged her good-bye and walked to my apartment for the night. The apartments were right down the sidewalk from each other, but the two doors between them felt like a hundred miles after being so close for so long.

By the time we walked inside my apartment, I felt the creeping tightness in my chest that signaled an epic panic attack. I tried to use my breathing exercises, repeating over and over in my head that I was fine and it was just my mind playing tricks on me, but it didn't seem to help. Finally, I squeezed my eyes closed in defeat, begging my body not to break down in front of Cody.

But it was no use.

My fingers began to tingle as I stumbled toward my bedroom, and I barely heard Cody's voice asking me what was wrong before I started panting. I wheezed, unable to get enough air, and dropped to the floor to grab the garbage bag holding the quilt from my bed. I just needed my quilt and I'd be okay. Someone had tied a knot in the top of the bag that I couldn't pry loose, and I felt tears running down my face as Cody knelt down beside me to still my frantic fingers.

"You're scaring me, Ladybug. What's going on?" he asked urgently, turning my face up so he could look at me.

"Need my blankie. In the bag." I continued to wheeze as more tears poured from my eyes. Oh God, I needed my blanket.

"Okay, babe, I got it," he said, reassuring me as he dug his fingers into the bag to rip open the sides. I made a soft noise in my throat as I saw the familiar wedding ring pattern, and reached my hands into the open bag next to his, the sight and feel of the soft stitching promising relief. We pulled it free together, and I was sobbing and shaking as I hurriedly unfolded it. Once it was opened up between us, I lay down on my side and pulled it over my entire body, covering myself from head to toe.

The shaking stopped almost instantly, fading to small tremors, but it took a while for my breathing to get back to normal. I lay inside my safe place, soothed by the feel of Cody's hand rubbing comfortingly up and down my back. Finally exhaustion set in, and I got enough air in my lungs. We were quiet for a few moments, relief palpable between us, before I saw his hand grab the side of the quilt as if to pull it away.

"Not yet!" I rasped insistently, pulling back at the cover.

"Okay," he said softly, and relaxed his hand.

He was quiet for a moment before he shifted, and then suddenly he was under the blanket with me, pulling it over his head so we were face-to-face, cocooned in darkness.

"This okay?" he whispered.

"Yeah." I sniffled once and wiped the back of my hand beneath my nose.

"What was that, Ladybug?" He reached out a hand to cup my cheek, and the soft gesture almost had me sobbing again.

"A panic attack," I said quietly. "Why are we whispering?"

"I don't know," he said, a little louder. "How often does this happen? Why the hell would you have a panic attack?"

I debated trying to play it off, but knew he'd see right through any smoke screen I threw up. He always had.

"It doesn't happen very often. A few times a year, maybe? It happened a lot as a kid, but they aren't as bad since I moved in with Callie."

"How did I not know about this?"

"I don't think anyone knows except for Gram. She found me freaking the hell out one day, and she used one of the quilts your aunt Lily made to cover me up."

"This quilt?"

"Yep, she gave it to me after that. I had my own blanket when I was a kid, but after I . . . left my mom's, it was gone. I'm not sure how Gram knew to cover me up, I was pretty out of it by the time she'd found me."

"I think one of my uncles had panic attacks as a kid."

"Makes sense," I murmured as he laid his arm out in front of him so I could snuggle against his chest.

"Why would you have a panic attack, Ladybug?"

"Good question," I joked dryly. "I'm not real good with change. I think maybe moving and all of this shit just caught up to me. I'm sorry."

I hated calling attention to myself. No, that wasn't true. I hated *inadvertently* calling attention to myself. I had no problem stealing the attention of a roomful of people, putting on a show, but I hated being the center of attention if I wasn't able to control it. Panic attacks were the ultimate loss of control and I loathed them, especially when someone witnessed them. After Gram had caught me during one of the worst ones I'd ever had, I was so embarrassed I'd stopped talking to her for a week.

"Don't say you're fucking sorry. *I'm* sorry. I should have figured out how to help you instead of standing there with my dick in my hand like a fucking idiot."

"You did exactly what I needed you to do," I told him with a kiss. "And now I'm ready to get up."

We decided to take a shower and head to bed, both of us exhausted from the long drive and unloading boxes all day, and I didn't once question if he would be staying over. We were in his city and he had his own place to sleep in, but it honestly never crossed my mind to ask him to leave. I hated how quiet the apartment was, and I was happy that he was going to be there with me all night. Like Scarlett O'Hara, I told myself I'd deal with the empty apartment tomorrow.

We'd christened the shower and fallen into bed naked, choosing a soft bed and clean sheets over going through the boxes and bags in my room. I was almost asleep when Cody leaned up on one elbow to look at me.

"You're sleeping naked from now on," he ordered me quietly.

"You're getting spoiled because I can't find my box of clothes. Don't push your luck," I mumbled back, my cheek pressed into the pillow.

"Ladybug, if I'm here, you're sleeping naked. You can argue all you want, but you know I'm just going to strip you down anyway." He leaned down to kiss my bare shoulder, running his tongue to the back of my neck. "What's this?"

"My tattoo. You've seen it."

"No, I remember when you got it, but your hair's usually down or you've got a scarf on. What is it?" he asked, running his tongue along the back of my neck, causing my tired body to clench weakly in pleasure.

"An echo," I answered sleepily, my eyes popping open as I felt his body go stiff beside me.

"You tattooed an echo on your fucking neck?" he yelled, his anger completely baffling me.

"That's what I said," I answered sharply, rolling over and scooting into a sitting position to hide the offending tattoo. "What's your problem?"

I was being a bitch. I knew it as I spit the words at him, but I couldn't help myself. For some reason, I was feeling really embarrassed about him finding fault with something on my body. Even though it had nothing to do with my shape, it still caused my insecurities to flare up like a bottle rocket. And when they did, I had my own way to deal with it. I didn't do insecure; I did smug disinterest.

"Are you fucking kidding me right now?" he mumbled under his breath in frustration, pinching the bridge of his nose. "You know what, I'm gonna head out."

"What?" I almost gasped, but held it in by sheer force of will. I wasn't going to give him that power—not ever. My emotions belonged to me and no one else. He'd never know that his words were like a slap across my face.

"I'm gonna head to my place at the club and make sure everything's cool. I haven't been there in a while and I need to check in." He spoke easily as he pulled on his clothes and boots, but his frustration was evident as he moved around the room, his movements sharp and jerky as he refused to look at me.

I hated the thought of him leaving, not only because he was so obviously angry, but also because I was nervous to stay in my new apartment all by myself. I didn't say a word as he grabbed his wallet off the floor and headed to the door, though. I'd long ago promised myself that I'd never again beg anyone for anything, and that was what I knew it would be—me begging him to stay. If he wanted to leave, I wouldn't stop him. They all left at one point or another; maybe it was better that we hadn't gotten any deeper into whatever we were doing.

So I watched him stonily, building my internal defenses against Cody as he turned his head to nod good-bye, and without a word was gone.

I sat in bed for a few minutes, calmly trying to figure out what had set him off, but the only reason I could come up with was some odd jealousy. It didn't make any sense that Cody would feel jealous of a tattoo in memory of a dead man. It wasn't even a big tattoo, just an eraser-sized circle on the left with half circles to the right, starting small and growing steadily larger. It was shorter than the pinky on my left hand; I'd measured it.

I thought about crawling under my quilt, but refused to cower just because he'd left. That wasn't me. Instead, I started going through all my boxes until I found the one holding most of my clothes. Once I'd dressed in my pajamas, though, I wasn't sure what to do with myself. It was silent in the apartment aside from the humming of the refrigerator, and it felt like the walls were closing in on me as I grabbed my phone out of my purse and checked the time.

Ten o'clock. Not too late, thank God.

"Hey, Gram." I smiled when she answered, hearing music playing softly in the background. "Want some company?"

She didn't ask where Cody was when I got there, and didn't say a word about why I wasn't in my own apartment. Instead, after a long look at my face and a squeeze on my bicep, she put me to work unpacking dishes and utensils into her kitchen cupboards while she bustled around setting out canisters and a bread box on her counter.

Gram kept me busy until I felt ready to drop, then without any discussion turned off the lights and led me into her box-filled bedroom. We climbed into her bed together, each of us rolling to face the outside of the bed—our backs almost touching—and fell asleep like we'd done for months after Echo was killed.

It was only a few hours later that I woke up to someone lifting me from the bed. My heart began to thump loudly in my ears as I wondered what was going on, but my sense of self-preservation kept my limbs relaxed. I opened my eyes into slits to see the shadow of Gram standing in the doorway, and I suddenly recognized the scent of the person who'd picked me up.

"Taking her home," he whispered, leaning down to kiss Gram's forehead as he passed. "Thanks, Gram."

I was still pretending to be asleep as we reached the living room, but I felt tears begin to form as Gram called out quietly to Cody.

"You wanted this, Cody. You waited her out and you chased her, now you've got her. But you need to remember that she's a lot softer than she lets on. Today's been a hard day for her, moving into a new place without Callie and Will. She's dealt with a lot in her lifetime, spent years protecting herself from people she shouldn't have had to. It takes quite a bit for her to trust someone." She paused for a moment, the air heavy with tension. "It doesn't take much to break that trust, son. You keep that in mind before you go leaving her again when she needs you."

"I won't do it again," he answered quietly, tightening his hold on me.

"See that you don't."

Chapter 8

Farrah

The next morning I was up early, the sound of Cody's soft snoring irritating me like nails on a chalkboard. I tried to stay in bed—the early morning hours were no friend of mine—but soon realized it was a lost cause. His body heat and the heavy arm draped over my waist felt as if they were suffocating me.

He'd been right that night when we'd argued about my living arrangements. Our relationship *had* started long before we'd started having sex. We'd begun some strange cat-and-mouse game years before, both of us pushing and pulling at each other until neither of us knew which way was up. I never knew if he would ignore me or be in my face, but I always knew that he would be there, watching and waiting for his moment. It was something I'd foolishly grown to count on.

Now, though, the chase was over. He'd gotten what he wanted, and I didn't mean the sex. He'd somehow convinced me to start a relationship—not that I'd taken much convincing—and we were sleeping in the same bed and spending time together. The lines of where I ended and he began had become blurred.

I'd had my own life in Sacramento with a job, apartment, friends . . . and now my world seemed to revolve around Cody. We were making plans dependent upon what the other person wanted to do, eating our meals together, visiting Gram together. It was beginning to feel like too much.

It had only been a few days, I knew that, but that was exactly why I was having such a hard time. Before, when he'd leave, I knew he was coming back. There was no reason for him not to come back. We'd been friends, and any spats we'd had were forgiven and easily forgotten. But I knew now that we were trying to be something more, life would no longer be so simple.

As I quietly unpacked my toiletries and the few household items that didn't require me to walk back into the room with Sleeping Beauty, I came to the realization that I was completely and utterly fucked. After less than a week, I'd been ready to curl up in bed and cry like a little girl because Cody had gotten pissed and left. If I continued on the path we were racing down, losing him would break me in a way that I might never come back from . . . and I knew I'd lose him. The only question was when.

My normal beauty routine didn't calm me like it usually did as I got ready for the day, my elaborate victory-roll hairstyle and flawless eyeliner failing to take my mind off the man sleeping in my bed. I had to make a decision, and whatever decision I made could potentially change the entire course of my life. How did someone deal with crap like that at nine in the morning? It was unnatural.

So instead of making a decision and standing by it, no matter how bad it hurt or how much it scared me, I decided to take the coward's way out and do nothing. I'd continue on as we were, having fun and ridiculously good sex, with one small difference.

I had to push my guard back into place. I'd been foolish to drop it around him, letting him see too much. That was going to change today. When he left, I'd be prepared. It was the only way I could carry on with whatever it was we were doing without losing myself entirely in the process.

"Can't believe you woke up before me," he called from the bed, startling me as I slipped into a pair of powder-blue cigarette pants and a short-sleeved button-down blouse.

"Yeah, I couldn't sleep," I answered, keeping my eyes averted from the bed as I started unpacking my bedroom. If he was already awake, there was no reason to avoid the room anymore.

"I was a dick last night."

"No, just pissy," I reassured him with a fake smile. "Not a big deal." I blew off what sounded like the beginning of an apology with the wave of a hand. "I hung out with Gram and we got a ton of her kitchen stuff put away, so it actually turned out good that you left."

I was using all the bravado I could muster, talking to him over my shoulder as I unpacked, and it seemed to be working. He didn't say anything more as he got up and walked out of the room, and my shoulders dropped in relief when I was sure he couldn't see me.

I could do it. I could brace myself without causing some huge argument, I just had to be stealthy about it, and when he left me I wouldn't say a word about it. Things could go back to how they were before, without any drama or fanfare, and I'd be able to keep my little adoptive family.

It could work.

I turned to him when he came back in the room, and

couldn't help the way my gaze roved over his mostly naked body. He wasn't huge but his muscles were evident, with a six-pack that showed up when he flexed, and strong, defined thighs. I hated when guys had a ton of upper-body strength, but their legs were as skinny as mine. It looked ridiculous.

Cody wasn't lanky, but he wasn't big and beefy either. He was streamlined, muscular, but more compact than a guy who spent all his time at the gym. I wondered if it was just good genes that gave him that body.

"Do you work out?" I mumbled, never taking my eyes away from his chest and the small sprinkling of hair there.

His laughter snapped me out of my fog, but not before I realized he'd grown hard as I was staring.

"Yeah, I run and lift some weights. Don't do it as much as I should, though, haven't had the time lately." He crossed the room until he was standing right in front of me, and I didn't stop him as he slowly unbuttoned my shirt. "You like what you see?"

"Eh, it's okay," I answered with a shrug, the hitch in my breath completely belying my words. "I've seen better."

One eyebrow rose as he pushed my shirt off my shoulders, his jaw clenching as he saw what I had on underneath. I wasn't wearing a bra—I didn't really need one—just a small camisole edged in lace that I'd found in one of my favorite thrift shops. My hard nipples were on display through the pale blue silk, and I shuddered as his thumbs immediately ghosted over them as he wrapped his fingers around the sides of my chest.

"You've had better?" he asked softly, unfastening my pants and pushing my underwear with them to the floor.

"Seen." I cleared my throat in nervousness, his expression no longer playful as he grabbed a condom off the dresser. "I've *seen* better." I didn't know why I was pushing him; my joke had taken on a completely different tone by that point, sounding like a challenge I hadn't intended.

He grabbed my wrist as he spun on his heel and stalked toward the bed, dragging me behind him until he'd sat down and scooted up against the headboard. His body was tight, all the muscles I'd been ogling on full display as he pushed down his boxers and rolled on a condom, and I'd started to quietly back away when his head snapped up.

"Get over here," he growled, making my heart race.

I moved forward cautiously, climbing onto the bed and moving toward him on my knees, but apparently I wasn't fast enough because as soon as he could reach me, he dragged me over his lap.

"On your knees," he rasped, turning me to face away from him so I was straddling his thighs.

"Cody—" He was beginning to make me nervous, and while I knew he'd never hurt me, I'd never reacted well to the unknown.

"Quiet, Farrah." The intensity, the raw *need* in his voice caused my mouth to snap shut in surprise. "Down on your elbows."

When I hesitated briefly, he pinched me lightly on the ass—startling me into submission, which pissed me off. Why was I letting him talk to me like that? Before I could turn around to bitch him out, his hands were on my ass cheeks, pulling them apart.

"Don't ever compare me to anyone else, Ladybug," he ordered, leaning in to run his tongue lightly from the top of my clit all the way back to right before the pucker of my ass. "You've never had better than me. You'll never *have* better than me. I've taken care of you for goddamn years, watching you do your thing and getting nothing out of it except for the peace of mind of knowing you were safe."

His tongue burrowed inside me and my whole body clenched, my hips arching back toward him as I dropped my head to the bed between my hands. I couldn't get close enough to him, scratching against the soft sheet beneath us with my fingernails as I pushed back against his mouth. His hands were firm on the back of my legs, his thumbs framing my pussy as he held me still.

"I've always taken care of you, Farrah," he rasped with a small bite to my lips before focusing on my clit. He licked in small circles almost leisurely while I panted and mewled into the bed, acting as if he had all the time in the world, until suddenly he started rubbing up and down fast and slipped first one, then the other thumb inside me. I lost it, screaming into the bed as I came.

I barely noticed as he pushed me forward, pulling his body up and over me from behind. He braced himself above me, tilting my hips to get the angle he wanted as he used the stubble on his chin to push my curls over one shoulder, leaving my back bare above the silky camisole. He paused for a moment, leaving me panting and tilting my hips up just a little farther in anticipation, but his next words made me freeze.

"Nobody will ever take care of you as good as I do. No one will ever fuck you as good as I do. I'm it for you, Ladybug. Now, scream my name so I know you heard me," he instructed in a gravelly voice.

He bit down on the back of my neck and shoved forward, seating himself in me on the first thrust. I yelped and tried in vain to pull my hips forward as he pulled halfway out and thrust again, so sensitive from my orgasm that the feeling was almost painful, but he didn't let me move. Instead he tempered his thrusts, going easy until I was ready for more, then picked up the pace as I started moaning beneath him, his teeth never leaving my neck.

As he came, I realized two things. There were going to be bruises in the shape of teeth marks on my neck, directly over Echo's memorial tattoo. He'd covered up Echo's mark with his own.

As much as I wanted to keep my distance, Cody was just as determined to break through.

Yeah . . . I was completely and utterly fucked.

Chapter 9

Casper

Farrah tried to play off the night before as if it hadn't mattered, but I knew it did. I'd fucked up, overacting about that fucking tattoo and then leaving her after she'd already had such a shitty night. I'd been so pissed that she'd tattooed something on her body for him, I was afraid I'd do something I'd regret—like telling her what a piece of shit her precious Echo was. So I'd left instead, which I realized later was just as bad.

I'd gotten on my bike and gone to the club, checking in with the brothers to make sure I was still good for some time off. I hadn't thought my trip through, in more ways than one, and running into Slider when I hit the bar was weird as fuck for both of us. He'd known I was going down to knock some sense into his daughter, and there was a good chance I'd be coming back to Oregon with her, but he probably hadn't thought it would actually work.

Slider's relationship with Farrah was pretty nonexistent;

they'd only met when Grease had put some shit together after he'd realized Farrah's mom was a bitch that Slider used to fuck at the club. Slider had known about his daughter, there was no question about that, but he'd ignored her for years because he didn't want to mess up shit with his old lady. The man came through, though, when he found out Farrah was being abused. He'd gone to Sacramento and dispensed his own brand of justice on Natasha and her fuckbag old man, but by then it had been too late for Farrah to ever want anything to do with him.

It was a shitty situation and I could see both sides of it, even if I didn't agree with either one. I couldn't imagine leaving one of my kids, especially with a bitch like Natasha, but I hadn't been around then, and I had a feeling there was more to the story than what we'd been told. It seemed like Farrah was being pretty stubborn about the whole issue, though. The man had raced to her rescue as soon as he'd known she was in trouble, taking out the fuckers who'd hurt her—one of them an Ace—without batting an eyelash. That had to count for something, right?

He'd been pissed when I claimed her at the club, making sure everyone knew she was mine, but he hadn't said a word. What could he say? She didn't want anything to do with him, and if he didn't want to alienate her further, he'd have to keep his mouth shut. Even if he hated it.

Most of the boys had been in the clubhouse last night, and I'd had the chance to shoot the shit with Dragon for a while. I hadn't seen him since the night he'd gotten out of jail, and at that point he'd been too interested in getting to Brenna to say anything to anyone. The man was doing good, happy to be home and excited as fuck that he'd knocked Brenna up again. By the time I left to get back to Farrah, he'd invited both of us to a barbeque at his place with Tommy Gun's family, and Grease and Callie.

So this morning I lay in bed as Farrah went to clean up and do all her girly shit again, debating how I'd ask her to go with me. She wasn't going to be down with driving to the club, and it wouldn't matter that Dragon and Brenna's house was set apart from it. We'd still be on club property, and since Brenna was close with Slider's old lady, Vera, there was a good chance one or the both of them would show up at some point.

It was a recipe for disaster, but if Farrah stayed in Oregon, I wanted her to have a network of people she could reach out to if she couldn't get to me. Before long, I'd be heading out on runs, and I needed to know that if something went down while I was gone, there were people in the club that she knew she could trust.

"Hey, Ladybug?" I called out as I climbed off the bed. Shit, I needed a shower. I was pretty sure I smelled like sex and sweat.

"What's up?" She walked in looking as perfect as she had before I'd pulled her into bed, and I wanted to pull her back in so she had that just-fucked look again.

"You got plans today?" I asked as I pulled clothes out of my duffel bag. Shit, a shower and then laundry. Thank Christ these new apartments had a washer and dryer in them. I hated the fucking Laundromat.

"No. I think Gram and I were going to see if we could find me some cheap furniture, but nothing definite. Why?"

"Got invited to Dragon and Brenna's for a barbeque today." I watched her closely for a response but got nothing, her face devoid of emotion. "Callie and Grease are gonna be there."

"Okay, what time?"

Although her eyes were steady on mine, she'd swallowed hard after she asked, her nervousness apparent if I watched carefully.

"Dragon said one o'clock, so we've still got a few hours to

kill," I answered slowly, waiting for any other indication that she was going to balk.

"Okay, I'm going to head to Gram's for a bit then. See if she needs any more help." She grabbed some earrings off the top of the dresser, looking at the floor as she put them on. As soon as they were in, her shoulders straightened as she met my eyes. "The dick and his bitch-face wife going to be there?"

"Not sure yet, babe. D didn't say anything about them, but there's a good chance."

She nodded as I spoke and then spun toward the door, stopping at the threshold as I called out to her.

"Come kiss me."

"I'll be back in a little bit," she answered quietly, never turning around.

"Come kiss me, Farrah." I wasn't going to let her walk out without reminding her what I was to her. She wasn't in it alone anymore, and by the way she was acting, I knew she needed some reassurance.

She took a deep breath before turning around and making her way back to me, her shoulders still straight and proud as if she didn't have a care in the world. She rose up on her toes to reach my face, and I didn't help her as she brought her mouth to mine. Her hand slid around the back of my head, her nails scratching lightly against my scalp as she puckered up and gave me a soft peck, but it wasn't what I was looking for.

As soon as she pulled away, I followed her, leaning down to push my tongue between her lips in a rough kiss, ruining her bright red lipstick, but being careful not to fuck up her hair again by keeping my hands gripping the cheeks of her ass.

"Don't forget your shoes, Ladybug," I told her as I let her go, stepping around her to head toward the shower.

As soon as I heard the front door shut, I turned on the shower and stepped into the hot spray. I hadn't planned on her agreeing to the barbeque so quickly, but I really shouldn't have been surprised. Farrah didn't back away from anything, especially a challenge, and she knew if I'd canceled on Dragon, everyone would have known it was because of her. Her pride wouldn't have been able to handle that type of blow, so she'd agreed to visit a place she hated and spend time with people she didn't want to know, just to save face.

I was both proud of her and irritated as hell that she hadn't told me how she really felt about it. If I was going to be her man, I needed to know when something was bothering her. I couldn't do shit to protect her if I didn't know there was a problem. If I hadn't been watching so closely and known her so well, I would have missed the subtle tightening of her throat as we'd discussed it, and I'd have been walking into the situation blind—which worried the shit out of me. Her armor was already clicking back into place after I'd fucked up the night before, I could see it, and there was fuck all I could do to stop it.

I'd been ready to talk her into it, convinced that it would be good for her—for us—but as I stepped out of the shower into the quiet apartment, I had a really bad feeling about the fucking barbeque.

Chapter 10

Farrah

I talked Gram into going to Dragon and Brenna's house with us. I knew Callie would be there; she was the type to join the crowd and make friends, but she'd be with Grease and I didn't want to rely on her to have my back if I needed her. At least with Gram there, I knew there was someone who wouldn't be distracted. If Gram was nothing else, she was a fierce protector of her kids, and somehow I'd become one of them.

As we pulled in the gate and drove slowly down the gravel driveway in Gram's car with Cody leading the way on his bike, I felt myself begin to sweat. I needed to get my shit together before we arrived if I had any hope of leaving again unscathed. I was under no illusion that the people at the barbeque would like me. After all, I was the bastard child of a man whose wife they were really close to; I didn't belong there.

We climbed out of the car in front of a small house, and I shifted Gram's potato salad in my arms. I hadn't thought to bring anything with me, and I'd been silently freaking the fuck out until Gram pushed it into my hands. I couldn't take credit for it, but at least I wouldn't have to walk in empty-handed. Gram must have read my mind because she'd made a big show about how her arthritis was so bad she couldn't carry it . . . and then insisted on driving.

Cody ushered us up the steps of a small covered front porch, practically pushing us inside. I couldn't figure out what the hell he was doing at first, since his movements were jerky as he opened the screen without knocking and quickly ushered Gram inside. My hands had grown a little sweaty, though, so I'd glanced down at the salad bowl to rearrange it in my arms, and saw what he'd been trying to shield us from. A huge bloodstain sat directly to the right of our path, faded a darker brown than the weathered boards surrounding it.

He made a noise in the back of his throat as I stopped short, my stomach dropping. *Oh God.* It was Cody's blood.

I was frozen, unable to look away from it when he grabbed my chin hard and jerked my face toward his.

"It's over, Ladybug. Don't look at it, baby. Don't think about it."

I nodded mutely, my heart thumping in my chest as we followed Gram into the house. I wasn't sure how I'd get that stain out of my head. I knew he was protecting Brenna when he'd been shot, but I never imagined that I'd face such a stark reminder. Why the hell hadn't they replaced those boards?

There was no one in the house, so we followed the noise of people into the backyard. It was open, only a couple of trees between what they used as a yard and the huge field beyond it, and was filled with kid stuff.

I pushed my sunglasses on to hide my reaction and take in

the crowd before me. A small plastic pool sat off to the left, a little girl and boy playing in it with Barbies and plastic dinosaurs floating around them. Another little girl screamed as she ran through a sprinkler just past the pool, her hair a tangled mess of curls. And two more little girls sat in the grass, picking dandelions and throwing them in the air.

Holy shit, these people were like rabbits.

Grease was standing next to the barbeque with two other men, one deeply tanned with long black hair, the other with light brown hair and a slight beer belly. No sign of Slider yet. At the edge of the yard under the trees were three women, one of them Callie, who had Will on her lap.

They all stood up to greet us as we made our way outside, and I felt my hands tremble as they started walking our way.

"Gram and Farrah, that's Dragon and Tommy at the grill. The pretty redhead is Brenna—" Cody said, his words cut off with a growl from the black-haired man. "Obviously Brenna belongs to Dragon, and the brown-haired sweetheart is Trish, Tommy's wife."

I could see why Cody was accepted so easily into the little group. He utilized a perfect mixture of teasing and charm, and it was a side of him I'd never seen before. He was working the people staring at us like a pro.

Different hellos were called out as the women reached us, and my hands started to shake as Brenna leaned up to kiss Cody's cheek, her eyes on me.

"Hey, Casper. You've been ignoring us," she teased.

My back snapped straight at her insinuation, and it took all I had to keep a pleasant smile on my face.

"Had some things to deal with," he replied, wrapping his arm around my waist.

Just as she was about to say something else, we were

interrupted by a small body wrapping itself around my legs.

"Auntie!" Will yelled, his face covered in something red and sticky.

"Hello, my William." I'd never been so thankful for the kid's lack of respect for personal space.

"Will! Let go of Farrah, you're gonna get shit all over her pants," Grease called out from across the yard.

My head snapped up in surprise at his tone, and in my peripheral vision I saw Callie's had as well. My stomach burned, resentment building as I looked up to meet Callie's apologetic eyes. It killed me that he had the right to warn Will away from me as if I were a passing acquaintance. I turned my head slowly toward Grease, and it took everything I had not to tell him to fuck right off as Will silently let go of my legs.

"You're okay, Wilfred," I said calmly, placing one of my hands on his head. "I can wash these pants, buddy." My eyes never left Grease's, the sunglasses not shielding any of my feelings as we stared each other down. The yard was silent until he nodded and turned away, and I knew I'd made my point.

"Nice to meet you, Farrah," Trish said. She was nervous, her fingers fiddling with her hair as she pushed it behind her ear, and I instantly liked her.

"You too," I replied.

Cody's hand squeezed my waist before he pulled away, and I watched him walk toward the men, patting backs and giving weird handshakes as he reached the group. The women around me were speaking, but I ignored them. I was uncomfortable as hell, and wished I were anywhere but there when I heard my name.

"Are you here long, Farrah?" Trish asked.

"Actually, I just moved up here."

"Oh, to be with Casper?" Brenna interjected.

I couldn't decipher the emotion in her voice, but something in it rubbed me the wrong way. What the hell was her problem?

"No, actually to be with Callie," I joked back, my smug smile in place. I wasn't going to let her get to me, even if she was studying me like a bug under a microscope.

"Farrah and I shared an apartment before we moved here," Callie informed them as we walked back toward their chairs. "I begged her to move with us. Will and I would be lost without her here."

I smiled at my best friend, grateful that she'd jumped into the conversation. She was the yin to my yang, the calm to my storm. Sometimes I forgot for a while, taking her friendship for granted, but it was times like these that I remembered why we fit so well.

Grease came up and took the forgotten potato salad from my arms as we sat down. His face was blank, no emotion in sight, but I knew why he was there.

"We cool?" he asked softly.

"This isn't the place," I answered. The conversation was flowing around me, but I knew that everyone was listening. I wasn't about to give them a show, especially since I knew it was stupid to be pissed at him.

"Still . . . sorry about that, Farrah." He turned and walked away, giving a chin lift at the guys as they came to sit with us.

The men sat in front of their women on the ground, all of us facing the kids as they played in the water. Pretty soon we were listening to Tommy tell a story—who was kind of a dumbass but actually super nice—when the little girl who'd been running in the sprinkler ran up and plopped down on Dragon's lap. The resemblance between the girl and the fierce biker was uncanny.

"Let's sing our song, Papa," she said.

He ignored her for a moment, still caught up in Tommy's story, but eventually had to pay attention when she wrapped her hands in his beard and pulled his face down to hers.

"Let's sing our song, Papa!" she repeated.

"Not now, Trix," he snapped, untangling her fingers from his beard. It sounded harsh, but I couldn't really blame him for snapping. Those little fingers in his beard must have hurt like hell.

The child's lower lip trembled, but she didn't make a noise as she nodded and leaned her head on his shoulder. He rubbed her back as she sat there, quiet as a mouse. She didn't look chastised or afraid; she looked embarrassed as she glanced around at the adults surrounding her.

"Dragon," Brenna said curtly as she flicked the back of his head.

"The fuck?"

"Look at your daughter."

His chin dropped down to glance at Trix, and his gaze softened as he met her eyes. He looked up at us, obviously uncomfortable as hell, but he still whispered something to her, making her whole face light up. She leaned back on his knees, grabbing his leather cut in both hands as she started to sing.

"All my life has been a series of doors in my face, and then suddenly I bump into you!" she belted out, startling most of us.

I had to bite my lips to keep the laughter at bay when she started swaying to the song, but what happened next wasn't funny. With an extremely embarrassed but bravado-filled glance at the adults, Dragon began quietly singing back to her.

I didn't know what the song was, but it was pretty clear that they'd sung it before, because Dragon knew exactly when to cut in for his part of the duet. We couldn't really hear Dragon, his voice was too low, but the picture they painted was enough. Dragon and

Trix watched each other as they sang, and Brenna sat behind them, a smile on her face and a hand resting on the small swell of her belly.

As we took in the scene, Cody leaned his head back into my lap and I ran my fingers over his shaved head, relaxing us both. It occurred to me that if the way she looked at her family was any measure of Brenna, maybe I'd judged her wrong.

A while after Trix had scrambled off and the men decided that the burgers were done, my original opinion of Brenna was proved right as she got up from her chair and stopped in front of me.

"Hey, Farrah? Can you help me get the rest of the food out of the fridge?" she asked.

I barely knew her, even less than the other women in the group, but she'd still asked *me* to help her. *Shit.* I was seriously rethinking my decision that she was halfway decent.

I caught Gram's eye as I moved past her back into the house. We both knew Brenna was trying to get me alone, and a small shake of Gram's head indicated she wanted me to stay calm. Easy for her, I thought, as I braced for the confrontation; she wasn't the one in enemy territory.

"Here, let me set it all out on the counter and we can just dish up in here," Brenna said as she leaned into the fridge. "It was nice of you to bring something, you didn't have to."

"I didn't," I replied flatly. "Gram made it."

"Oh." She looked surprised to find me standing right behind her, still wearing my sunglasses inside the house.

I moved past, careful not to brush against her as I grabbed Gram's bowl and set it on the counter behind her. I wasn't going to play into her shit or give her an inch. She'd asked me to go inside with her for a reason, and I just wanted her to get to the point.

"Look, I know you don't know me, and I almost didn't say anything, but I just wanted to tell you that Casper is really important to me. To us. I know you're friends with his sister and her loyalty is probably split, which complicates things..."

"Stop right there," I ordered coldly. "You don't get to say anything to me about Cody... or Callie, for that matter."

"Actually, I think I do. He almost died trying to protect me. We're close. So I just wanted to warn you that we're behind him one hundred percent. I'm not sure what game you're playing, but he showed up at the club last night, and there was obviously something wrong..."

My blood ran cold and I slid my hands into my pockets to hide the way they shook. Her insinuation that he'd been complaining about me was like a bucket of ice water thrown in my face. I shouldn't have been surprised, but I was. Cody knew how I felt about them, and how uncomfortable I was with the entire situation.

"You don't know shit about our relationship. Nothing. You call him *Casper*, for Christ's sake." I worked hard to keep my voice from breaking, but I felt like I'd been blindsided. "Keep your fucking opinions to yourself. *You* got him shot, but I'm the one fucking him. You don't have shit on me—"

"Farrah!" Casper's angry voice cut me off, and it was the impetus I needed to snap my shield of complacency back into place.

I stood silently, getting my emotions in check as he walked around me. Thank God he'd come in when he had, before I'd really lost my cool and did something stupid. I almost sighed in relief as I waited for him to back me up, to stand up for me, but as he stepped close to Brenna and glared at me, my heart sank.

"Take those fucking sunglasses off. What the fuck?"

No.

No.

And just like that, I was done.

I reached up and pulled my shades off, calmly folding them and tucking them into the neck of my shirt before I raised my eyes to his face and looked right through him.

Fuck him and fuck her and fuck the entire thing. I'd been so worried about how much I'd let him see in the last week, my shields dropping more and more as I desperately tried to reinforce them. I really should have thanked him because he'd finally done what I couldn't. He'd built them back up for me. Standing there in Brenna's kitchen, I was once again a blank slate, my armor fully in place.

His eyes grew wide with comprehension. "Farrah—" he whispered.

"Thank you for inviting me over," I told Brenna coldly, my eyes meeting hers. "But I just remembered I had something else planned today."

With a small nod of concession in her direction—she'd won, after all—I slowly turned and walked back out the back door. They would not see how bad it hurt for him to take her side, especially right after I'd told her that I was more important to him. I was an idiot and I'd let her get to me. Damn it, I'd let them both get to me.

I'd never let it happen again.

I returned to the backyard and made my way toward the women, catching Callie's stricken look when she saw me. I shook my head at her. She needed to fit in with these people; I couldn't pull her into the drama.

"Gram, can I use your car?" I asked woodenly, stopping next to her. "I need to get out of here."

Her worried eyes searched my face, glancing between me

and the house before she answered me.

"Sure, baby. I'll go with you," she replied.

Gram rose from the chair before I could stop her, and just when I thought things couldn't get any worse, Slider and his wife walked out the back door with Cody and Brenna.

"I wanna go *now*, Gram," I told her under my breath.

Then I called out to Will across the yard. As anxious as I was to get away from there, I couldn't leave him without saying goodbye. He came running toward me dripping from the kiddie pool and I swung him up in my arms, unconcerned that his wet shorts were soaking my clothes.

"Hey, Wilfred. I'm gonna go, but I'll see you soon, okay?" I said, rubbing his nose with mine. "Be good."

We left without any fanfare; the group watching us go without a word, assuming I was dodging Slider. I let them think it. But the truth was, I could have faced him. I could have made nice, been respectful to his wife who probably hated me, and kept things civil. As long as I had Cody there, I was sure I could have done it.

It wasn't Slider I was running from as Gram drove us home; seeing him had actually seemed pretty anticlimactic. It was Cody that I had to get away from. He hadn't said a word to me as I left the house, ignoring me completely as he'd chatted with the guys.

All of it was too much for me—the bloodstain on the porch, the bullshit with Grease, Brenna thinking she could warn me off, Slider showing up, Cody's giant fuck-you as he'd sided with his little girlfriend. I wasn't equipped to handle it, so I shut it down.

Fuck him. I didn't need this shit.

Chapter 11

Farrah

When someone started pounding on my door later that night, I was expecting it.

Gram had taken me to a discount store on the way home from the barbeque, using some bullshit reason that she needed to stop. She'd ended up buying nothing, which hadn't surprised me, but I'd come home with a new and inexpensive kitchen table and a shit ton of other household goods.

I'd felt better as we left the store, anxious to get my things home and start setting up, and I was pretty sure that had been Gram's plan. She'd set out to distract me and it had worked, but only a few hours later I was done washing my new dishes and putting together my furniture, and the distraction had worn off.

So I sat down in one of my new chairs to wait. I'd been there for almost an hour when he finally showed up.

"Hey," I said, swinging open the door and taking a step back as he reached for me. "Come on in."

"What the hell happened, Farrah?"

I made my way to the table, the only furniture in the apartment aside from my bed, and sat down, motioning him to the chair across from me. I didn't want him close; I couldn't bear for him to touch me when I felt so raw.

Cody looked puzzled as he took in my newly furnished kitchen, but quietly sat down, leaning forward on his elbows to watch me closely.

"Brenna asked me what game I was playing," I started softly, knowing that sentence would grab his attention. "I hadn't known what she was talking about at first. When we got there, it seemed like everything was fine. We'd arrived as a couple and I assumed that everyone would respect that."

"Farrah—"

"No, let me finish," I said, cutting him off. "I didn't know what she was talking about until she mentioned you going to the club last night, complaining about me."

"That's bullshit!" His chair slid out from behind him as he stood from the table, anger tensing the muscles in his neck and jaw. "I didn't even see Brenna last night, and I sure as fuck never complained about you."

"It doesn't matter, Cody!" I raised my voice above his ranting, my face a blank mask of serenity. "Can you just sit down?"

"I didn't say shit, Ladybug, I swear to God. I wouldn't do that," he replied adamantly as he sat back down.

"It doesn't matter. It doesn't matter if you said anything." I looked down at the table, trying to focus. The next words were harder to say than I thought they'd be. When I looked back up to meet his eyes, he was staring at me in disbelief.

"She asked me what game I was playing, and I didn't understand it at first, but now I do. We *have* been playing, playing at a relationship, playing house, playing like this could actually work. It was reckless and stupid, and I don't want to play anymore." I swallowed hard, hoping he wouldn't notice. "I fold."

"No, fuck that. No. You don't," he said.

"I'm done."

"Because you got in a fucking fight with Brenna? That's why you don't want to be with me all of a sudden? That's bullshit, Farrah!" he shouted. Then he grabbed my brand new ceramic fruit bowl from the center of the table and threw it against the wall.

I watched it shatter, barely flinching at the noise before I stood.

"If you're going to throw a tantrum, could you do it somewhere else?" I asked flatly.

"Why are you being such a fucking cunt? I didn't do anything wrong, Farrah! I'm in love with you!" He reached across the table and grabbed me by my arms, pulling me over it as I scrambled to find purchase with my bare toes. "I'm in love with you," he repeated softly, his face close to mine.

"I'm sorry for that," I whispered back.

It was a direct hit, just as I'd known it would be. His eyes widened for a moment, but instead of the resignation I'd been expecting, something else filled his gaze. He took a step away from me, running his hand over his face as if to calm himself. After a few deep breaths, I watched in panic as his eyes narrowed to slits and he reached for me again. He wrapped his hands around my arms in a gentle but uncompromising grip as his lips pulled back in a menacing grimace.

"You love me," he whispered harshly.

"Of course I do," I told him sincerely, trying to defuse the situation. "I love all of you. You're my family. You guys took me in—"

He shook me once, barely restraining himself, and leaned down into my face. "Bullshit. You're in love with me. Don't even try that shit. You want me to be your man so much you can *taste* it. You want me inside you, wrapped around you, sleeping in your bed."

"No," I whispered. This wasn't going how I'd planned, and I felt tears of frustration burning my eyes. Why couldn't he just leave? I didn't want to argue, I just wanted things to go back to how they were before. Safe. Calm. I needed him to leave so I could start to put my life back together.

"You're so fucking afraid of your own shadow, you can't see what's right in front of you," he said.

"Fuck you, I'm not afraid of anything," I argued, my hackles rising even though I knew there was truth in his words. I realized he was getting to me, he was doing what I'd sworn just hours ago that I wouldn't let happen again.

My mask, cracking and peeling but still intact, fell back into place. "You need to leave."

"I'm not going anywhere, Farrah," he replied, letting go of my arms to take a step back. "I'm gonna grab something to eat and head to bed, and you're going to come with me."

The mask slipped. "You're insane!"

"I'm pretty sure I'm the only one in this situation acting even remotely normal." He chuckled dryly, pulling his T-shirt over his head as he walked toward the fridge.

I was stunned.

He was *laughing* at me. It was too much. The mask dropped completely.

"Get the fuck out of my apartment!" I screamed at the top of my lungs, my face turning beet red and the veins in my neck bulging. "Get out!"

He didn't move from the kitchen, but spun back toward me with a calculating look. "It looks like zombie Farrah has left the building."

"Get out!" I screeched again, the tears I'd been holding back finally falling from my eyes as I clenched my fists against my thighs. My heart thundered in my ears, pounding wild and heavy as I tried without success to calm myself down.

"You want to try and make me?" he asked in a bored tone, one eyebrow raised in question.

"Fine!" I shouted. "If you won't leave—I will."

I'd barely gone two steps before he was standing in front of me, blocking my way. "You're not going to Gram's."

My entire body stilled and I closed my eyes, taking deep breaths through my nose as I struggled to control my rioting emotions. I was stiff, my muscles so tense they felt locked in place.

"Come on out, Ladybug," he taunted with a bitter laugh. "Aren't you frustrated, baby? I'm ruining your plans. You set up this whole scenario so I'd walk away, you were so sure I'd leave. Come on, you want to hit me?"

I opened my eyes to find him watching me with a fierce look. I took a step back, not realizing how close we'd become when he swung his hand out and hit himself hard in the chest.

"Come on, Farrah, fight!" He hit his chest again. "If you want me to leave, then you're gonna have to make me believe it, baby." He hit it again.

He raised his arm yet again and I'd had enough. "Stop it!" I screamed, flying at him when the latest blow came way too close to the bullet scar on his chest. He braced his feet as I moved, and when I reached him he used his hands to grip my hips, hoisting me up until my arms and legs were wrapped around him.

My fingernails dug deep into his back as I held him to me,

pulling and grabbing as if I couldn't get close enough. God, what was I doing? I was so confused I was shaking, the adrenaline from our fight making my body tremble as he started walking toward my room.

"I hate you," I whimpered into his neck.

When we reached the bed, he peeled me from his body, dropping me. "No, you don't. You love me, and it doesn't matter how much you push, Ladybug. I'm not going anywhere," he growled, unbuttoning his jeans and shoving them and his boxers to the floor. "You try that shit with me again, you'll get the same result."

My breath caught as he stripped my pants and underwear down my legs. His hands were gentle but his words were not, and I was having a hard time keeping up with what was happening. I'd been so sure that I'd be able to shut it down, so sure that I could chase him away with a few precisely chosen words, that I no longer knew what to do with myself. He was lovingly stripping me bare as if I hadn't just tried to break up with him. My head was spinning.

He crawled onto the bed, our bottom halves fitting like the pieces of a puzzle as he braced himself above me, meeting my eyes with a tenderness I hadn't seen before.

"You took her side," I whispered, hating myself for sounding like a whiny little girl, but unable to let it go.

"Won't happen again," he promised. "My loyalty is to you, even when you're being a bitch. It's always you, Ladybug. Forgive me?"

"I wasn't being a bitch," I replied sullenly.

"She was trying to protect me, baby. Her heart was in the right place," he told me gently, but my body still stiffened beneath his. "Let me finish. Her heart was in the right place, but it won't happen again. She knows not to do that shit again."

"Yeah, because I'd fucking lay her ginger ass out," I huffed, refusing to meet his eyes as he barked out a laugh.

"I have no doubt you would," he said. "But you won't need to—I made that shit clear after you'd left. You gotta understand, Farrah. She feels responsible for me after everything that happened. Not saying that's right or wrong, it just is. And I haven't talked about you, so me moving you up here was a surprise."

"You didn't move me up here. I moved up to be with Callie. Plus, it's not like you had anything to say about me anyway," I grumbled.

"I had plenty to say, just didn't say it. Shit was too weird with us then, the back and forth, barely seeing you. I didn't want them asking about us when I wasn't sure if you'd even let me in here."

"I was so mad at you today," I confessed.

"I knew that when you turned into a zombie," he replied, brushing my hair gently from my face. "I didn't know what was going on and you were spouting off nasty shit, so I just reacted. It won't happen again, Ladybug. You come first, always."

"Please don't leave me alone with them again," I asked in a shaky voice.

His nostrils flared, his eyes filled with remorse. "I won't, baby, I promise."

He climbed off me and reached for my hand as he sat up against the headboard. He leaned over and grabbed a condom from the nightstand, somehow opening it with his teeth and rolling it down his length with one hand. We held hands as I scooted over to rest my ass on his thighs, and eventually his other hand rose to cup the side of my face.

"Things aren't always going to be easy, Ladybug," he told me quietly, our eyes meeting in the dark room. "I'm going to screw up and you're going to piss me off. Stop trying to walk away. Stop trying to push me out. I'm not going anywhere, okay? I don't want to be anywhere but right here." He let go of me to maneuver my body, and soon he slid inside me until we were fully connected. Then he stopped.

His fingers slid into my hair to hold me in place as I wrapped my hands around the sides of his neck. "I need you to fight for yourself, baby," he whispered against my lips. "I need you to fight for us."

"I'll try," I replied. Then I began to move.

I pulled myself up and dropped back down, over and over until my thighs burned. His hands were everywhere—sliding down my back to grip my ass, wrapping around my waist, cupping my breasts, gripping my hair. They didn't stay in one place for long; just when I'd start leaning into what he was doing, he'd stop and start somewhere else.

When we were both sweaty, our breathing fast and heavy, he reached up and grabbed my hand, pulling it between us.

"Get yourself off." He was panting, his eyes wild. "I want to watch."

I was too far gone to feel any sort of self-consciousness, and immediately started rubbing my clit in small circles, my orgasm rushing in within minutes. I couldn't stop the moans that poured from my throat, and barely heard his words as he talked dirty in my ear.

When the orgasm finally ebbed away, I could no longer continue riding him. My body was boneless as I slumped against his chest, my arms barely able to hold on as he flipped me onto my back.

"I love you, Farrah," he said into my shoulder. His face was buried in my neck as he raised my hips and thrust hard a few more times, finally coming with a low grunt.

It wasn't the first or the last time that Cody would completely derail my plans, but whether that was a good thing or a bad thing remained to be seen.

Chapter 12

Farrah

"**W**hat about this one?" Cody asked, running his fingers across the script tattoo on the side of my right thigh. "*All the reading she had done had given her a view of life that they had never seen.*"

"Did you ever read Roald Dahl books in school?" I asked.

"Sure, *Charlie and the Chocolate Factory*."

"Right. This tattoo's from *Matilda*. I loved that book growing up. Her parents sucked too."

He ran his tongue over the letters. "You like to read?"

"I love it, always have. We didn't have a TV when I was a kid, but I could always check out books from the library at school. That's probably why I have such an addiction to them now."

"Me too. I haven't had time to read in a while, though," he replied.

"I always read, I feel weird if I haven't read in a while, like jittery and shit. The only time I wasn't reading a bunch was when I was drinking all the time. It's hard to read when you can't focus on the words."

"Not too drunk to get tattoos, though, huh?"

God, the smirk on his face *killed* me.

"Never too drunk for that," I joked, "as long as you can find a tattoo guy that doesn't give a shit."

"How many are there? Maybe I should count them," he mumbled against my skin, running his lips across the tattoo again.

"Twenty." I laughed as his face lifted in surprise. "I have ten ladybugs, though, and my flower."

The mood in my bedroom turned somber as my last sentence sank in. We'd been lying in bed for hours, dozing and talking. We were both trying to keep things simple, coming down from our earlier fight, but the reminder of my scars was like a bucket of cold water thrown over our bodies as we relaxed in our afterglow.

"I wish I could have killed him for you," he told me seriously, resting his chin on my belly.

"Well, thankfully that ship has sailed."

"How long was he with your mom?" he asked nonchalantly. His hands had started trailing over my tattoos again, but he couldn't hide the tension in his shoulders.

"They got together when I was twelve." I didn't want to tell him. I wanted to forget everything that had happened before I'd been taken in by Callie, but I found myself speaking anyway. "At first it was okay. My mom was always a junkie, ya know? So when I was little, there were all of these tweakers in and out of the house. It freaked me out. When she got with Gator, that shit stopped, and I was fucking relieved."

Cody kissed my hip and moved himself up the bed to lie next to me, gently pulling me on top of him, our bodies aligning from toes to chest.

"Keep going," he said.

I laid my arms across his chest, resting my chin on them as he played with my hair. "So, yeah, at first I was stoked. I didn't have to deal with all the creepers anymore. Mom and Gator were barely ever home, so that was a plus. It took a couple of years before he started creeping me out, though. Like, this one time, he came up behind me in the kitchen and sort of pulled my hips back against his, and his tiny dick was hard. I was, what, fourteen? Yeah, I think I was like fourteen by then, because it was the summer before high school. Anyway, it was fucking gross, and he tried to play it off like he'd thought I was my mom or some shit. But then he started talking about my boobs and how I'd filled out, blah blah blah."

I shuddered in revulsion, feeling Cody's body jerk. What I didn't tell him was that was when I'd started deliberately losing my curves.

"Did he touch you?" he asked, his voice deep and rough.

"No, no. He never got far. By then I'd started hanging out with some people outside of school, so I wasn't around much," I assured him, trying to hide the lie.

There had been one other time, after I'd met Callie and had started hanging out at her place more than I was home. Gator had stopped making excuses for touching me, and one night he'd thrown what little control he had out the window and attacked me.

I'd fought him—hard—and he hadn't gotten what he wanted, but it had started a chain of events that I could have never imagined. I'd wondered back then if I would have just let him, if I'd just lain back and pretended I was anywhere else, if my life would have been easier. I remember scratching up his face, pulling at his hair, and finally kneeing him in the balls to get him off me. When he'd let me run out the front door, I thought I'd won.

What a joke.

Gator had left my mom after that, telling her that he didn't want to be around me because I was disrespectful and rude. He'd talked around her, stroking her bruised ego by telling her that he'd been drawn to her because she was such a good mom, but he just couldn't handle me anymore. It had left my mom in a situation she didn't want to be in. The man she'd depended on for years left because of me, but she couldn't kick me out because the reason he'd liked her in the first place was her mothering skills. It was a complete crock of shit, but it had worked, just like he'd planned.

After he left, my mom became the partier she'd been before, with people in and out of the house at all hours, and random men stopping by as they got off their shifts at work. The indifference she'd treated me with before turned into hatred so vile it made my stomach turn to be in the same room with her. That had also gone exactly how Gator planned it would.

It had been a simple yet brilliant plan, and I'd been surprised that an idiot like Gator had manipulated the situation so well. He'd left blaming me, cutting off all contact with my mother including the drugs he'd been supplying her with, but he'd made sure that she couldn't kick me out. So when he decided that maybe I wasn't so bad and decided to come back, my mother was willing to back him on any situation concerning me. I'd been a lamb in a house of wolves, and they'd nearly devoured me.

I swallowed the bile in my throat from the memory and smiled at Cody, who was watching me closely. "What about you? What's your story?"

He laughed a little and shook his head. "No story. Grew up with two parents and Callie. I was fifteen when my parents died, and Gram became my legal guardian. Now, here we are."

"I know all that, dumbass," I told him, rolling my eyes.

"What about the rest of it? Weren't you away at school most of the time? How the hell did you wind up with the Aces?"

"Yeah, I got sent to a private boarding school on the East Coast when I was seven."

"Holy hell!" I gasped. I hadn't realized that he'd left home so young. It made my stomach cramp to think of Will moving that far away in only five more years.

"It was all right. I was way ahead of all the kids in public school, and my parents couldn't afford to send me to a private school in San Diego." He shrugged, and pulled me higher on his chest. "My mom came from Mexico, hoping to go to college up here, so when they knew I was really smart, she started applying for all these scholarships and shit. School was really important to her, and she wanted to make sure that Callie and I got every advantage. It turned out that the one scholarship I was accepted for was set up by this old dude who didn't have any kids, and wanted to send one to all of his old prep schools on the East Coast."

"That's crazy. I can't imagine sending my kid across the country."

"Yeah, I wouldn't do it, but I can't really complain. I had it a lot better than a bunch of other kids in the world, you included."

Cody looked uncomfortable at the thought of comparing our childhoods, and it made me feel like shit.

"It's not a competition, handsome," I told him, leaning up to give him a slow kiss. "I hit the shitty parents jackpot, but that doesn't mean yours were saints."

"Yeah, well, they weren't bad."

Silence fell as we looked at each other, and for once, I wasn't sure what to say. I couldn't understand how we'd ended up where we were, lying together in bed and sharing secrets. I'd never talked to anyone about my mother, ever. I hadn't even told Callie about the stuff I'd dealt with growing up, and she'd never pressed for information. I had a feeling that would not be the case with Cody.

Eventually, he'd learn all my secrets and I'd be screwed.

"So, how'd you end up with the Aces, then?" I asked, changing the subject.

His gaze moved from me to the ceiling and he let out a heavy sigh. "That's a story for a different day, Ladybug."

Chapter 13

Casper

Farrah was driving me insane.

After her big blowup, things had been better for a while. Once she knew I wasn't going to take off, it seemed like she'd gotten a little more comfortable with the situation. Comfortable with Farrah wasn't the same as comfortable with anyone else on the planet, though. I wasn't sure if she'd ever lean on me the way I wanted her to.

Don't get me wrong, I fucking loved it that Farrah could take care of herself. I'd been with chicks who played like they couldn't change a lightbulb, and it had been irritating as shit. I was glad she could handle herself in most situations, but it was the situations that she should have called me and didn't that pissed me off.

She'd found a job working at a little salon not far from her apartment, and she seemed to dig it. Instead of getting a job with Farrah like they'd planned, Callie had decided to stay home with Will for a while, and I knew Farrah had been really nervous about going it alone. She'd never said anything, though, and after a week, her natural bravado had relaxed into actual confidence.

One night I'd gone to Farrah's place after working on shit with the club for a couple of days, and her car was in the lot, but she didn't answer her door. I was leaning on her hood, wondering where the hell she was, when I saw her coming down the sidewalk. On a fucking skateboard. Turned out, her car hadn't started for the past two days and instead of telling anyone about it—like maybe the guy she was sleeping with who had access to a state-of-the-art garage—she'd started using a ratty-ass old skateboard to get there.

I would have laid into her—it was stupid as fuck that she hadn't said anything—but goddamn, she looked sexy as hell. She was wearing some loose Dickies, red Vans, and a tiny-ass white tank top, and it was like looking at my dream girl at fourteen. Instead of yelling at her, I'd rushed her into the house and banged her against the front door.

She dropped her guard during sex. It was one of the only times that I could get a read on her, so I used it to my advantage. It seemed to calm her down, at least for a while, and I really dug the relaxed Farrah.

There were a ton of things about Farrah that drove me up the wall, but she'd still come a long way from the girl I'd first met. She rarely drank anymore, she found a good job that she seemed to enjoy, and even though we argued about it, she wouldn't let me help pay any of her bills. She was acting like an adult—doing her thing without using Callie as a crutch, and there was nothing sexier than a woman who had her shit together.

She'd also gained back a little of the weight she'd lost. I still couldn't figure out why she gained it and lost it like she did, but I was happy as hell that I'd never had to say anything about it. Her collarbone and hip bones weren't as prominent anymore, her elbows and knees losing a little bit of their sharpness. She was beautiful before, but goddamn, she was a knockout when she gained a couple of pounds.

Shit was good. We'd settled into life and I was practically living with her, which she didn't seem to mind. All the pieces were finally falling into place—Callie and Grease had settled into living together for the first time, Gram had found a senior center to hang out in when she wasn't helping with Will, and Farrah was working and feeding her book addiction every time I turned around.

If a man who did what I did for a living could be content, that would be the word that described me.

But I should have remembered that the minute you settled in and thought things were good, that was when shit happened. Life was once again about to punch me in the throat, and I didn't even see it coming.

I was on my way to the club after leaving Farrah exhausted in bed. She still refused to have anything to do with that part of my life, and I had to admit, it made things a little tense. I had to spend a shit ton of time there. I wasn't trusted enough to go on any important runs yet, but I was making small trips for information and doing daily club shit.

I was also expected to be at the parties for members, and there were so many of them that there were parties all the fucking time. I wanted her with me at the parties, and asked her to go every time, but her answer was always no. Almost four months later and she still wasn't over the shit that happened at Dragon and Brenna's.

Poet had called and told me to get my ass to the club early, so I was surprised when shit was quiet as I pulled up. A new recruit was at the gate, and it was a little weird when he started scrambling to open it for me. We were both prospects, but the guy treated me like I was his boss. Idiot.

None of the bays were open, and it was silent as I hit the door to the main room. I took a quick look around, and for the first time since I'd been hanging around, there was absolutely no one inside. I almost turned around and left when I heard voices coming from the room off the back of the bar. It was a room the boys called "church" and I'd never been allowed inside—yet another thing I wasn't trusted to be a part of.

I debated sitting down at the bar to wait, but as I walked toward the bar, Poet stepped into the doorway, his face emotionless.

"Come on in, kid." He gestured with his hand and stepped back into the room.

I really didn't want to. Shit, I wasn't getting a good feeling about the entire scenario. My mind was racing, trying to figure out if I'd done something to piss them off, but I couldn't think of anything.

Poet, Slider, Doc, Grease, Dragon, and an old-timer named Smokey sat around the table, their faces drawn and tight.

"Hey, brother, we've got a situation," Grease said quietly as his eyes met mine across the table. "Sit down."

I made my way to the only open spot at the table, and was glad as hell that I'd already pulled out my chair when Poet started speaking, because if I hadn't, my ass would have been on the floor.

"Early this morning, Tommy Gun's woman was attacked," he said. "Someone lit their fucking house on fire." He paused to clear his throat and run his hand over his hair, from his forehead to the end of the long red braid hanging down his back. "Kids and Trish slept on the top floor. Didn't make it out."

The men were emotionless as they watched me take in the news, and as much as I wanted to pretend like it didn't have any effect on me, I couldn't hide it.

My head dropped forward as I squeezed my eyes shut. *Fuck*.

Trisha and Tommy had been together since they were fifteen years old. It was kind of crazy how well they balanced each other. They were both quiet—didn't really get into any of the drama at the club or any of that shit—but anyone could see that Trish was Tommy's North Star. She kept him grounded, stopped him from doing stupid shit without thinking it through, and gave him a reason to keep his shit together and come home. She'd given him five kids; the oldest was eleven and the youngest was three. Three girls and two boys. All gone.

Holy fuck.

"Where's Tommy?" I asked Slider.

"Got home this morning from Portland, found the house and called us. He's in his room. Fucker's huge and we could barely corral him, had to have Doc knock him out," he replied.

I paused for a minute to let it all sink in. They'd obviously wanted me there for a reason, but I couldn't figure it out. I couldn't even think about it. My head was too busy sorting through memories of Trisha and the kids.

Their oldest, Cameron, had a serious case of hero worship for me, and the kid followed me around whenever Tommy would bring him to the club. When Curtis, their five-year-old, was there, the worship was multiplied by two—he loved his older brother and if Cam wanted to be just like me, then Curt did too. Fuck me. I hadn't had much contact with the girls, but what I'd seen of them, they were sweethearts. Little replicas of their mother, one of the sweetest women I'd ever met.

This was going to rock the club's foundation, no doubt about it.

Shit, I was going to vomit.

I stood up and took quick steps to the outside door, losing what little was left in my stomach from the night before.

"You ready to come back in, brother?" Grease asked after I'd stopped dry heaving.

"Yeah. Be right there," I replied.

When I got back into the room, the guys were speaking quietly to one another, but with one hand gesture from Slider they all fell silent.

"Tommy took some boys up to see what was going on with one of our suppliers in Portland. Name's Thompson. The guy's a pussy, but he's been a solid contact for almost twenty years, so when he called saying he couldn't do business with us anymore, I figured something or someone was fucking with him. Sent the boys up to give him protection if he needed it, or some incentive if that was the case," Slider informed me.

"Turns out the man was already dead," Poet added. "New gang up there took out his family and took over their business. Real shady shit."

"Why am I here?" I asked, gesturing to the room we were in.

"Need you to go do your thing in Portland. Find out who these guys are and what they're doing. Don't ride your bike—we'll give you one of the cars in the shop. Wear some of those college-boy clothes you have, get in and out," Slider replied. "Need to know if they're behind this shit with Trish, and if they've got any more plans to fuck with us before we retaliate."

"I can do that," I told Slider confidently. "Leave today?"

"Yeah, within the next coupla hours," he said. "Don't worry about shit down here. I'll keep an eye on my daughter, and Grease is takin' care of Callie and your gram. Just do your job and get your ass back here."

"Will do." We stood up from our chairs, and with a nod I left the room. I had a ton of shit to get ready if I was going to leave in two hours.

First on the list was Farrah.

With Tommy and Trish heavy on my mind, I started up my bike and headed toward home. I needed to see my woman and get lost in her for a while.

I had a feeling shit was going to get a whole lot worse before it got any better.

Chapter 14

Farrah

For most people, a day off work would mean a chance to sleep in until noon and lie around in their pajamas all day, but I couldn't do it. I tried to find things to do when I wasn't scheduled to work, so I wouldn't have to sit alone in the apartment. It was still too quiet without Callie and Will, and it made me antsy.

I still saw them a lot. We spent time at Gram's or brought Will to the park, but it wasn't the same. Callie's inner circle had widened; she was having playdates and shit with other women from the club, and even if I'd had kids, I wouldn't have been a part of it. I'd been steering clear of all of them except for the few times Trisha had brought her kids over to Callie's.

Even though it was my choice to stay away, I still couldn't shake the feeling of being left out of their little group.

I'd made plans to go garage-saling with Gram, and we wanted to hit all the good ones early. There was a science to it that Gram had mastered before I was born, and she'd been slowly letting me in on the secrets over the past couple of years. I think she was afraid that if she told me everything at once, I'd start going without her. She hadn't realized yet that I didn't really need any secondhand tablecloths or clothes hangers—spending time with her was the draw.

If you were looking for the good stuff, you always went as early as you could on the first morning the garage sales were open, usually Friday. It was imperative to get there before the hordes descended and all that was left were some mismatched McDonald's collector glasses and an old recliner that smelled like buffalo ass. On the flip side of that, if you just wanted the really cheap stuff, you'd go Sunday afternoon when the sale was ending and the seller just wanted the shit out of their driveway. They'd be selling their stuff for a dollar or less, just so they wouldn't have to haul it away. Sometimes we went crazy and showed up on both days.

I finished getting ready—it was a 1950s housewife kind of day—and was packing up my purse when Cody walked in the front door. I knew immediately that something was wrong. When he closed the door behind him, he locked the dead bolt with more force than was necessary, then pulled on the doorknob as if checking to make sure that the lock was in place. His broad shoulders were tight and his body was jittery as he turned to face me.

"Hey, handsome," I called quietly. "Thought you had to go to the club this morning?"

He didn't answer. Instead, he stomped toward me, the usual grace in his movements completely absent. I wondered if I should call Gram and ask her to come over—he was acting really strange—but before I could even finish the thought, he was in my space and lifting me up. I wrapped myself around him, wondering what the hell was going on, but stayed silent as he shuddered against me.

"You going to work?" he asked into my neck.

"No, I was going to run errands with Gram," I answered, running my fingers around to scratch the back of his neck softly.

"Grab your phone and text her, Ladybug. No errands for a while," he ordered.

"What's going on, Cody?" I whispered, my stomach churning at the emotion in his voice.

"Text Gram," he repeated.

I leaned down to the back of the couch where I'd left my phone, and sent a quick text to Gram letting her know I wouldn't be able to go anywhere, and that Cody said we shouldn't be running errands for a while. I didn't understand what that meant, but Gram must have, because all she did was text back "OK," which was actually pretty damn good since she usually couldn't remember how to reply. As soon as I was done, Cody snatched the phone out of my hands and tossed it.

He pulled back his head and smashed his mouth onto mine before the phone had even landed on the couch. I jerked as he bit my lower lip and sucked it into his mouth hard, letting go of my ass to slide under my dress, his hands desperate and wild on my skin.

It didn't take long before his desperation was feeding mine; it seemed as if every time he put his hands on my skin lately, I was ready for him. Like some kind of Pavlov response, I'd been trained by months of incredible sex, so the instant he touched me, my body started winding up.

I never understood the whole "panty-ripping" thing in romance novels; it seemed like that would leave freaking fabric burns on your hips, but maybe I was just wearing the wrong kind of underwear. The thought flashed through my mind as Cody reached between my legs to rub over the crotch of my underwear, but before I could debate the merits of flimsy underwear, he'd pushed it to the side and thrust his fingers inside me.

"Hold on, baby," he whispered huskily as my back made contact with a hard surface. It must have been a wall, but I wasn't sure which one since my eyes had closed and my head had fallen to his shoulder as his fingers pumped in and out. He fumbled with the button on his jeans, and his fingers halted.

"Don't stop!" I murmured frantically.

"I'm not. I'm not," he mumbled before pressing his mouth against my shoulder and biting down. He must have gotten his pants undone and pushed out of the way, because before I could complain again, I felt him against me. "Guide me in, Farrah."

I lifted my head, our gazes meeting from only inches away, and I swallowed hard. His eyes were red and watery, and his jaw was tight as he stared at me, waiting for me to follow his direction. He looked at me like I could save him, but I had no idea what I was supposed to be doing. Normally I didn't walk away from emotions, I ran, so for a split second I thought about making a smart remark, just to break the tension.

But for the first time ever, I couldn't do it. I couldn't think of a word to say because I knew I had go against all my instincts and comfort him. I had no other choice; there *was* no other choice. I tentatively leaned forward so our noses were touching, then rubbed mine up the side of his as I reached down to move his cock so we were lined up. Before I could move my hand back around his neck, he slammed inside me.

There was no finesse to his movements, no thoughtful glances to see how I was doing, or lingering touches to make sure I was climbing with him. He was oblivious, grinding and thrusting and holding me close as his breath stuttered shakily in and out. He felt good inside me, really good, but I knew I wouldn't orgasm. I needed more than I was getting to find release, but surprisingly, I didn't care that he'd forgotten. In some perverse way I was glad that I wasn't going to orgasm, because this time wasn't for me. For some reason, he needed me to hold him—to get as close as we possibly could—and I'd never refuse him that if I could help it.

His hips started to slow, and he groaned low in his throat as he pulled me away from the wall. My hands had been soothingly running over his shaved head as he pounded away, but I paused when he came to a complete stop. I wrapped my arms around his neck as he carried me into the bedroom, still planted deep inside me, and unzipped the back of my dress with one hand.

"I'm sorry, Ladybug," he crooned as he lay me on the bed, pulling out to strip my dress over my head. He ran his hands from my shoulders to my hips, then with a sigh, he rested his forehead on my sternum.

"That's okay," I reassured him, leaning up on my elbows to watch him nuzzle my belly. "What's going on, Cody?"

"Nothing."

"Bullshit. What's wrong?" I asked, rubbing my hand down the side of his face.

"Just some shit with the club," he replied, his face losing its vulnerability as he leaned up and flipped me onto my belly. "On your knees, Ladybug."

We'd done pretty much everything we could do in bed, and I trusted him implicitly with my body, but something felt off. I couldn't see his face anymore, and it scared me that he seemed to be hiding it as his body covered mine and he pushed inside me, hard. I yelled out in surprise and dropped to my forearms when I was suddenly supporting all of his weight. His chest was heavy on my back as one of his hands found where we connected, then rubbed quickly at my clit as his other arm wrapped around my chest, his fingers reaching for my breast.

He rode me hard, more aggressive than he'd ever been. I'd have normally been frustrated as hell because I'd never been able to orgasm in that position, but before long, my hips were pushing back into his and I was coming. It went on for what felt like forever, his thrusts fueling the fire until I thought I'd pass out.

When his fingers finally stopped their movement, I collapsed. My hands slid forward until my chest was taking my weight, and I barely had enough strength to push my face to the side so I could breathe. His arm was trapped beneath me, but he yanked it out as he leaned back, and then both his hands were on my hips, pulling me into him. I watched the wall blearily as he pumped a few more times, feeling satisfied and spent.

It would have been the best sex we'd ever had, but after he came with a shout and all was silent, he rested his head on my back and I felt something warm and wet run down my spine.

With a small kiss between my shoulder blades, he left me on the bed. My body felt boneless but my mind was churning as I rolled to my side and flipped the quilt over me.

Was that a good-bye fuck? Had he finally decided to leave? No, no, things had been fine that morning, hadn't they? It must just be something with the club that was bothering him, like he'd said. But why wasn't he telling me what was going on? Something big was obviously happening if he was that upset, but I couldn't figure out what it could be.

Fifteen minutes later, I finally pulled my awesomely sore body from the bed and stretched my limbs. I found my towel from this morning hanging over my footboard and cleaned up, and then shuddering, I rolled the towel into a ball and set it in the corner. I didn't want to accidently use it again thinking it was clean.

Without bothering to put underwear back on, I grabbed a summer dress off the floor and took a quick sniff. Yep, it was clean. I needed to be dressed if I was going to figure out Cody's shit; I only wished he wasn't in the bathroom so I could touch up my makeup and hair. I'd feel so much more comfortable if my armor were in place.

I was sitting on the bed cross-legged when he finally came back in the room.

"I'm heading out on a run, Ladybug," he told me as if nothing out of the ordinary had happened. "You still got that box of shit I asked you to store for me?"

"No," I replied slowly. "I threw it out a couple of minutes ago when I realized you were going to keep telling me nothing was wrong."

"Babe." He shook his head. "I'm gonna be out of town for a few days, maybe a week. I wanted to see you before I left."

"Is 'see you' a euphemism for rough sex? Because I've been using that phrase all wrong if it is."

He froze, a look of horror on his face as his gaze ran up and down my body. "I hurt you, Farrah?"

"No, you didn't hurt me!" I shot back, frustrated as hell that he wouldn't tell me anything. "It was fine! I came, you came, then you cried! Everything is just hunky-fucking-dory!"

His worried face turned cold, and I knew then that I should have kept my mouth shut. "I wasn't crying."

The Cody glaring at me wasn't anyone I'd ever met before. Even when we were fighting or I was trying to kick him out of my house, he'd never used that tone of voice with me. Like I was beneath him. Like I was nothing. All of a sudden it was clear why he fit in so well with my biological father's club, and I hated it.

"It must have been sweat," I whispered back, my nose

stinging with unshed tears. "Your box is in the back of my closet."

He pulled his plastic storage container out of the closet and stuffed collared shirts, jeans, and a fucking hipster cardigan into one of my duffel bags. I almost opened my mouth to ask what the hell he was doing when he packed a pair of lace-up Vans sneakers, but the scowl on his face stopped me. I could feel myself beginning to shake as he put the box away again, considerably lighter than when he'd pulled it out.

"I'll be back next week," he told me, then kissed me quickly, rubbing his hand up and down my arm briskly. "You cold? Put a sweater on."

He walked out the door, asking me over his shoulder to let Gram know he'd be out of town, and within a minute I heard his bike start up outside. Just like that, he was gone.

For a few moments, I'd turned back into that girl I'd been before—willing to let a man talk down to me just so I'd know that he was coming back. After Echo died, I promised myself that I'd never let anyone treat me like that again, yet I'd just let Cody do it. I'd even placated him, pretending I'd been mistaken so he wouldn't stay mad at me.

What the hell was I doing? He left me shaking, sore, and close to crying in the middle of my bed. I'd let him use me like a random fuck, mistakenly thinking I was doing some selfless deed to comfort him.

He didn't even ask me if he could borrow that fucking duffel bag.

I ran to the bathroom and barely made it to my knees before I started vomiting.

Chapter 15

Farrah

I took a little time to get myself together before walking over to Gram's. I sure as shit wasn't going to stay in the apartment, licking my wounds. I was both pissed as hell and disappointed in myself, frustrated that I'd seemed to have fallen back into old patterns. If it were three years ago, I would have found someone to party with after I'd gotten into it with whatever guy I was seeing. But since I hated the thought of that even more, I chose to play dice and eat Gram's banana bread instead.

I tried talking Gram into hitting some garage sales despite what Cody had ordered, but she wouldn't hear of it. She'd spent a lot of her life listening to her man and her sons tell her not to do things, and she told me she knew when to listen and when to ignore it, something about a feeling in her gut. Apparently this was one of the times her gut was telling her to listen.

We'd played a gazillion dice games called Ten Thousand and were hanging in the living room watching *Matlock* when Grease,

Callie, and Will came in the front door. We rarely knocked at Gram's, so the fact that they hadn't didn't surprise me, but the way they came in was just slightly off. It was too fast and loud for a normal visit, too urgent. The look of devastation on Grease and Callie's faces had Gram and me jumping to our feet.

Oh God. Cody.

"Cody?" Gram croaked, her arthritic fingers rising to her mouth in horror.

"No! No, Gram. He's fine!" Callie turned her head to Grease. "He's fine, right?"

"Far as I know, Sugar," Grease answered.

I didn't like his answer.

"What's going on?" It felt like déjà vu as I glanced back and forth between them, neither of them giving me a fucking thing. "Someone better tell me right now what the fuck is going on. Shit. Sorry, Wilfred."

"Iss okay," Will said, walking toward the toys Gram kept for when he came over.

"Now, Callie." My voice was almost a growl as I glared at her.

Grease answered for her, pulling Callie into his side. "Tommy's wife, Trish, and the kids were killed in a house fire this morning."

"Oh shit." I sat down hard on the couch, the morning's events becoming so much clearer. Oh, Cody. Goddamn it, why hadn't he said anything?

"I'm sorry, baby girl," Gram said to Callie, walking over to wrap her in a tight hug. "I know she was one of your friends."

"Yeah." Callie sobbed quietly into Gram's shoulder as I sat on the couch, stunned.

Grease stepped away as Gram ushered Callie away from Will and into the kitchen. He dropped down on the other end of the sofa and leaned forward so his elbows rested on his knees.

"I'm so sorry," I said. I didn't know if it was the right thing to say or if I sounded like an asshole, but this whole comforting-people-who-weren't-Callie thing was hard.

"Thanks," he replied, watching Will build a tower with Legos. "You saw Casper this morning? He seem okay?"

"No, he didn't, and he wouldn't tell me what was going on," I said as I watched Will paw through the toy box.

"Yeah, he probably didn't want to say anything until the rest of the brothers had called their families. We've spent the last two hours trying to calm Tommy down." He paused and cleared his throat. "Been a shitty day."

"I bet," I whispered.

I'd liked Trisha. She'd seemed sweet as hell when I'd been around her, and her kids were freaking adorable, at least the ones I'd met. The oldest was a little too old to hang out with the little ones, so I'd never been around him. God, I couldn't believe they were gone. Poof. Just like that.

"Why would Slider send people out on a run with all of this stuff happening? It seems like you should be circling the wagons or something."

Grease looked at me in surprise. "We're all staying pretty close to home, if we can. Don't think anyone's leaving."

"Cody left this morning," I replied slowly, trying to read him but his expression had gone blank. "So, not everyone is home. Where did he go?"

"Club business, Farrah." He dismissed me with a flick of his hand, stood up, and walked away.

I should have known he wouldn't give me a straight answer, but I was going to go crazy trying to figure it out on my own. Why would Slider send Cody out by himself? He was a prospect, could barely wipe his ass without one of the brothers telling him to do it. It just didn't make sense.

"Auntie! Come play!" Will called from the floor.

He was just what I needed to snap me out of my conspiracy theories. They could wait, and lately, time with Will was something I didn't get very much of. The thought was frightening as I remembered a few kids I'd never see again.

"Okay, dude. What are we playing?" I asked as I lay down beside him on the carpet.

We played on the floor of Gram's living room for over an hour before Will started to get cranky. I was trying to give Callie and Grease some time with Gram, but the kid didn't want to hang with me anymore, he wanted his mom or dad.

He must have known something was going on. There was no way he'd missed the way his parents were barely holding it together. If you didn't look very closely it seemed as if Grease was unaffected, but Callie was no good at hiding her emotions, she let them fly. Both of them were hurting, that couldn't be ignored, even by a two-year-old. *Especially* by a two-year-old.

It felt like sadness was sucking all the air out of the apartment as I watched Gram stand behind Grease, rubbing his back and speaking to him softly. He was nodding, his head bowed to the table in front of him, and beneath the table I could see Callie's hand gripping his thigh. I hurt for them.

I followed Will into the kitchen and watched as he climbed onto Grease's lap, laying his head against the leather-clad chest as Grease wrapped his arm around Will's back. In that moment, I was suddenly really, really glad that my best friend and her son had finally gotten their happily-ever-after. Even if it wasn't very happy at the moment, their bond was a sight to see. Maybe it was the time I'd had to get used to things, or the way Callie immediately stood from the table and wrapped her arms around me, assuring me that she still needed me, but my resentment was gone.

I held my best friend close, letting her cry into my shoulder, and wished that I hadn't craved her attention. It wasn't the way I'd wanted her to need me.

"When do you work this week?" Grease asked me as I let go of Callie and started following Gram around the kitchen.

It looked as if Gram was prepping for Armageddon as she pulled jar after jar out of her fridge and cupboards, getting ready to throw together a whole basket of food for Tommy and the guys at the club.

"Monday, Tuesday, and Thursday," I replied, widening my eyes at Callie as Gram continued to pull food out.

"I'll come and give you a lift."

"Nah, it's okay. Cody got my car fixed, so I'm good," I answered offhandedly, oblivious to the way everyone had grown quiet.

"I'll drive you to work, Farrah." Grease's tone had me spinning to face him. "We're being careful. None of you are going anywhere without one of the boys."

"What the hell?" I asked, my voice breaking at the end. "What are you guys not saying?"

"Not sure how that fire started yet—"

"Holy shit."

"Just taking some precautions," he assured me.

Wait a second . . .

"Where the hell is Cody?"

"It's club business, Farrah. Your man didn't tell you, you don't rate the info," he replied unapologetically.

"That's bullshit!" I yelled.

"Farrah!" Gram hissed at me. "Knock it off. You know how those boys work. Quit harping on Asa."

"Et tu, Brute?" I gasped, glaring at Gram. "Screw this, I'm outta here."

I was too pissed off to notice or care that I was being an ass to Gram. I felt for them, I did, but fuck if I would just go blindly along, minding my business, with no idea where Cody was or what the hell was going on. It wasn't like I was going to go all vigilante and do something stupid. I just wanted to know where we stood in the shit storm that seemed to be billowing up around us.

I slammed out of the house as Grease ordered me to stay in the apartment, flipping him off as I went. My apartment was close and I got there within seconds, but I didn't realize that there was someone sitting at my doorstep until I was almost on top of him. My heart stuttered in my chest as I stumbled to a stop.

I began to take a step back, Grease's warnings blaring in my head, when the guy pushed his hoodie off his head and looked up at me. What the fuck?

"Who the hell are you?"

Chapter 16

Farrah

"Are you Farrah?" the kid asked, climbing to his feet. I took a step back as I realized he wasn't as small as I'd thought, and looked at him suspiciously.

"Who . . . ? Oh shit, you look just like your dad," I whispered.

"You know my dad? I tried to go home and—" His voice broke and his hands clenched into fists. "Our house was gone. Can you call my mom?"

"What's your name?" I asked again, horror building with a sense of recognition.

"Cameron," he answered. "Is Casper here?" He leaned to look over my shoulder, but I knew no one was behind me.

Holy shit. Holyshitholyshit.

"He's not here, dude," I told him, the words coming out garbled as my mind raced. "I don't have your mom's number, but Grease is a few apartments down. Why don't you come in and I'll call him?"

He stepped aside so I could move into the recessed doorway, and my hands shook as I fit my key into the lock. What was I supposed to do? In a few minutes, this kid's entire world was going to implode and he had no idea. Shit, how old was he again? I couldn't remember, but I knew that he must be big for his age. He couldn't have been older than twelve, but he was already a little taller than I was.

"Come on in." I waved my arm toward the living room, and with no hesitation Cameron walked in and dropped down onto the couch. "You want something to drink?"

"No, thank you," he replied in a careless show of manners. "I like your place. Casper said you haven't had time to make it girly, but I think it's nice the way it is. My mom has—" His voice cracked for a second time. "—h-had a ton of pillows and stuff."

The boy was acting as if he wasn't scared out of his mind, but his hands rubbed over his thighs over and over as if he couldn't sit still. I was completely out of my element. I'd always had an easy time comforting Will, but this kid was different. He was too old to comfort with a bowl of Cheerios.

"I'll just, uh, call Grease, okay?"

He nodded, not saying a word, and I walked quickly into my bedroom.

It only rang once before Grease picked up.

"Dude. You need to get over here, pronto," I growled through my teeth.

"You okay?" I could hear Grease moving around on the other end of the line. "You just fucking left."

"Yeah, yeah, I'm fine. But okay, so, I walk home, right? And I don't notice anything at first—"

"Get to the fucking point, Farrah."

"CameronishereloookingforCody," I told him in a rush. "I

don't know what the fuck to do!"

"What?" he whispered back in disbelief.

"Tommy and Trish's son Cameron IS IN MY APARTMENT!" I yelled, then immediately covered my mouth with my hand, looking toward the bedroom doorway. I was trying to keep my shit together, but seriously, it was like fucking Lazarus rising from the dead.

"Holy fuck. You sure? I'm almost there." He hung up before I could reply, and I made myself walk calmly back into the living room, even though I wanted to run.

"So you've been here before, huh?" I said, startling the poor kid so badly, he jumped up off the couch and whirled to face me.

"Yeah, I was with Casper when he stopped to pick something up," he answered nervously. "I didn't hang out here or anything!"

"Hey, no sweat, man. *Mi casa es su casa*. You can hang here whenever you want."

We were both babbling, and I had no idea what had just come out of my mouth. Did I really just tell some kid I didn't know that he could hang out at my house? *Shit. Fuck.* I didn't know what to do! Where the hell was Grease?

Cameron seemed to relax a little at my words, so I couldn't take them back. I would have done anything at that point to calm the poor guy down. He wasn't going to come hang out anyway, so I didn't know why I was even thinking about it. *Shit.* We watched each other, standing at opposite ends of the room, and I sighed in relief when Grease came barreling in the door.

"Cam!" he shouted, practically running to where Cameron was standing so he could wrap his arms around him in a huge hug. I felt like I was intruding as I watched Grease grip the back of Cameron's neck and kiss the side of his head. "Hey, bud, you okay?"

I didn't hear Cameron's answer, but I did read Grease's lips as he raised his head and asked me to call the very last man on earth I'd ever want to talk to. Goddamn it. It wasn't like I could tell him, "No, thank you. I pretty much hate him and would rather have an apartment full of snakes than that asshole in here," when I had a preteen in my living room who had no idea most of his family was dead.

For the second time that day, I walked quietly into my room and fought the bile in my throat as I scrolled through the contacts list on my phone. Cody had programmed quite a few numbers into it when I'd moved here, so I couldn't even use the excuse of not knowing the freaking number.

"Slider," he answered, making my stomach knot up.

"It's your wayward daughter," I replied sarcastically. "You need to come over to my apartment."

There was an awkward pause, neither of us comfortable with my request, but eventually he spoke again.

"To what do I owe this invitation?"

Was that hope in his voice? It took all that I had not to hang up. Fucking douche. Like I'd really invite him over to hang out.

"Cameron's here," I answered flatly. "He went home this morning to a burned-down house and came looking for Casper."

His voice grew dark. "Farrah, if this is some game you're playing . . ."

"I'm not an asshole, apparently that *isn't* something you can inherit. He's in my living room with Grease."

"Good Christ," he muttered quietly.

"See you soon, Pops." I hung up and stood silently in my bedroom.

My hands shook and my chest felt tight at the thought of my father walking into my apartment. I didn't like him, I didn't want to see him, and I sure as hell didn't want him there. The apartment was my space. Mine. I was finally able to sleep there alone, which I knew I'd be doing for the next week, at least until Cody came home. I was afraid the minute Slider walked in the front door it would be tainted, turning it into yet another place where I didn't feel comfortable.

After the mess with Cody that morning, finding out about Trisha and the kids, the fight with Grease, Cameron showing up at my apartment, and now my father on his way, I was at my breaking point. I sat down heavily on my quilt, rubbing my fingers along the stitching. I could call Gram, but I knew she had her hands full with Callie and Will, and we sure as shit didn't need all of them traipsing into my apartment.

Were they going to tell him here? Shit! I hadn't even thought of having to deal with the fallout of that scenario. I felt like the walls were closing in around me, and I seriously considered hopping out the window in my room.

I needed to get it together, and I could only think of one way to calm myself down. I lay down on my bed, pulled the quilt up and over my head, and called Cody.

He didn't answer.

Of course he didn't. He was on some super-secret mission for the club; he didn't have time for my emotional inadequacies. I spent a few more minutes breathing deeply inside my little cocoon before tossing the blankets back. I could do it. I could walk out into the living room and deal with the drama that I knew was coming. I'd handled far worse, hadn't I? I just needed to make sure I was presentable, flawless, and then I'd deal with it.

After giving myself a pep talk in the bathroom as I made sure my hair was in place and my makeup was okay, I headed to the living room. Slider hadn't arrived yet, and I was relieved to hear Grease and Cameron speaking quietly from the couch. There hadn't been any yelling or sobbing. I was in the clear, at least for a while.

The relief left me in an instant when I saw how the two were sitting. Grease's back was against the couch cushions, his shoulders tight and his feet flat on the floor, and Cameron was sitting almost in his lap. The poor kid's chin was tucked into his chest and his arms were crossed in front of him, a pose that would have looked petulant if it wasn't for the way he was huddled under Grease's massive arm, tears rolling down his face. When I walked toward them, both heads snapped up, and the agony in their expressions was overwhelming.

"I stayed the night at my friend's house last night and my house burned down. My mom and my sisters and brother are dead," Cameron told me, lifting his chin. He looked at me in defiance, too proud to admit that he was upset. For anyone else, he might have been hard to read. The scowl on his face was as bratty as I'd ever seen, impressive really, but with a closer look, there was no way to hide the complete lack of hope in his eyes.

I knew that face.

I'd worn it for years.

He expected me to baby him and was warning me off. He didn't want my pity. I respected that in a way he'd never understand.

"Yeah, dude, I heard," I answered calmly. "I'm really sorry."

His shoulders slumped and he leaned back into Grease. Just then, there was a knock on the door, and I opened it up to Slider and Poet—my father and his vice president. I watched them as they took in Grease and Cameron, their faces moving from disbelief to joy within seconds as they stood frozen just inside the door. Poet moved first.

"Cameron, it's damn good to see you," he announced roughly, stepping over to the couch to pull the kid up from the couch and into a bear hug. "So good to see you, boyo."

"Where's my dad?"

"He's at the clubhouse," Slider answered, finally making his way into the room. I took a couple of steps away from him, the apartment already feeling too small. "Didn't want to get his hopes up."

"Nice." I scoffed, shaking my head. He hadn't believed me. My gut burned, and I knew I had to get out of there before I said something and made the situation infinitely worse for everyone. I turned to Grease and met his eyes. "I'm going to head over to Gram's. You guys stay as long as you need to. Lock up behind you."

At his nod, I spun toward the door.

"Thanks for helping me, Farrah," Cameron called out quietly, his manners still intact even after having a life-changing bomb dropped in his lap.

"No problem, Cameron."

I turned my head to see him standing under Poet's arm, the entire group watching me leave. Seeing him there looking so small and broken reminded me too much of things I was trying to forget, and I had the unwelcome urge to hug him. I wanted to take him away from all of it, I wanted to go back twenty-four hours and warn his mother, and I wanted to do anything to ease the ache in my gut at his obvious misery. Instead, I said something that would change both of our lives.

"You're welcome here anytime, little dude."

Chapter 17

Casper

I spent four days in southeast Portland before I got a hit. The night I'd gotten in, I realized that my clothes weren't going to work unless I wanted to call attention to myself. These people weren't polos and skinny jeans, they were worn-in work boots and baggy jeans falling off their asses. I'd stopped at Wal-Mart and bought some clothes, running over them with my car in the gravel parking lot next door to give them some wear. That seemed to have worked.

    I finally found the boys we were looking for in a shady strip club. Shit was all spread out in the side of town I knew I'd find them, and it was hard as hell to hit as many places as I could in a day without looking suspicious. I'd had to make my way around, asking guys on the street about jobs and spare cigarettes, striking up conversations that led to where I could get a beer. I knew they'd be holed up in some piece-of-shit bar, somewhere they knew they'd get the respect they wanted.

Small-time assholes always went to the shadier parts of town, the ones that were down on their luck, with wannabe gangsters on the corner who thought they were hard but weren't. That was where they'd find their power, in a place that had a hell of a lot of followers but no leader.

The women dancing looked barely old enough to be legal, and the entire club reeked of stale smoke and feet. It was fucking disgusting, but I clocked the two men I was looking for right away. Two men, midforties, one with a mole next to his nose and the other with a patchy chinstrap beard. Their backs were to the wall, placing them right next to each other, and they were the only two smoking in a club with No Smoking signs on every wall.

Bingo.

They were ruling their shitty little kingdom from the back corner of a strip club covered in ratty red shag carpeting left over from the seventies. Fucking tools.

I'd been sitting near them, watching the dancers for almost an hour before I heard the word I'd been both hoping and dreading.

Aces.

I spent another hour listening, regulating my breathing and keeping my body relaxed and seemingly focused on the dancers, before I dropped a couple of bills on the stage and left. I had what I needed.

I didn't even stop at my hole-in-the-wall hotel before heading south on I-5 toward Eugene. I'd never wear any of the clothes again anyway, and I'd kept all of my stuff from Farrah's in the trunk of the small Honda that Slider had given me for the trip. I was practically vibrating with the need to turn around and kill the motherfuckers sitting in the strip club. If I didn't get out of there soon, I knew I wouldn't be able to hold back.

It only took me a couple of hours to get back home, and when I pulled into town I had to force myself to go to the club first. I wanted to pack up Farrah and Gram and get them the fuck out of there, then make my way to Callie's, but knew I had to speak with Slider and Poet first. They were going to be livid, and we needed to plan. My family wasn't the only one that needed protection.

I walked into the club and made my way over to the couch where Slider and Vera were groping each other like a couple of teenagers.

"Boss?"

"Fuck," he hissed into Vera's mouth, pulling his hand out of the back of her jeans. When he finally looked up and met my eyes, recognition dawned and he jumped up from the couch. "Club business, baby. Be back in a while," he said to Vera, who only nodded with a small smile at being interrupted.

"Poet! Call Dragon and Grease and have them get their asses here. Doc! Smokey! You're with me."

We followed him into the back room and once again sat down at our places at the table. The other brothers had watched me with a mix of hostility and confusion as I'd followed them in, and I almost groaned at the fucking pecking order that assured I'd be cleaning bathrooms for the next month. They didn't understand why I'd been allowed in, and they weren't happy about it.

Fuck me.

I started to talk as soon as we sat down, but Slider put one hand up to silence me before I could say much. "We'll wait for the boys," he said, "so we're all hearing it at the same time. Makes shit easier."

I nodded and sat back to wait, fidgety and uncomfortable with the eyes in the main room I could feel on me through the open door. By the time Dragon showed up, I was clenching my jaw and had moved to popping my knuckles. Grease walked through the door, shutting it firmly behind him.

"You got what you needed in four days? Any problems?" Poet asked.

"No problems. Found the brothers in a titty bar in Southeast playing kings of the fucking castle. Took me a while to find them, working my way through the guys out of work or homeless on the street." I cleared my throat, feeling a little uncomfortable with all of the eyes on me. "Found out what they're planning and headed out straight from there."

"Is it something we can handle?" Slider asked quietly.

"They're small. Nobodies. No competition if they were doing shit on the up-and-up," I answered, meeting his eyes. "They won't be. Their next hit is another family. Not sure which one, they weren't specific, but it was clear they wouldn't be hitting us directly."

"Motherfuckers."

"Goddamn it."

"Son of a bitch!"

"Fuck!"

The faces around the table had gone from questioning to livid, and I was glad that I was on their side. They were scary as all hell. As Dragon stood up, looking like he was going to kill someone with his bare hands, Slider started barking orders.

"Poet, you get the men with families in here. We'll let them know what's going on. Find anyone that's sober and supply them with some cars, the drunk fuckers aren't going to be able to go home to get their women alone. Who the fuck knows if they'd get there in one piece or what they'd be walking into." Poet stood up from the table, clapping Slider on the shoulder as he walked out of the room.

"Dragon," Slider continued, "you and Brenna should be good. We're going to lock down the gates and you're already inside them. See if your woman has some extra shit she can spare or any room, the clubhouse is gonna be over-fucking-flowing. You take one of the cars if Poet needs a hand."

Dragon left next, veins popping in his neck as he slammed the door closed behind him.

"Doc, make sure you've got enough shit on hand in case things go downhill. Order anything you need and get it out here tonight. Once the gates are closed, we aren't opening them. Smokey, make sure the bitches are out of my clubhouse before the wives get here. Tell April and Jenny to stay, they've both been around a long fucking time and have enough of a reputation that they could be targets. Those picky whores have only been fucking a couple of the boys anyway, no one with wives. Everyone else, out." With a nod, he dismissed the old-timers.

"Grease, go get your woman and her grandmother. Make sure she's got everything she needs for your boy. Stop at the store if you need to. Know this is her first time, so make sure you got enough diapers and all that other shit that you could need. Nothin' goes in or out until we get this shit taken care of."

After Grease left, Slider and I were the last ones left sitting at the scarred table. It sounded like chaos out in the club, with bikes roaring out of the lot and girls bitching that they had to leave early, but it all faded out as Slider watched me.

I didn't know if I'd done something wrong, if I should have stayed in Portland to get more intel, or just called Slider to relay what I'd heard. The seconds ticked quietly between us until suddenly he spoke up.

"You did good, kid. Now go get my daughter."

I was up and out the door before he'd finished his last

sentence.

Chapter 18

Farrah

I was on the couch watching *Pulp Fiction* with Cameron—who I thought was too young for it before he told me he'd already seen it—when I heard the lock of my front door turning noisily.

Our eyes met, wide and nervous. *Shit.* His eyes weren't just nervous; they had a look I'd seen before. He was going into that protective mode that I'd seen on both Cody and Grease's faces throughout the years. God, how early did it start with these guys? The little shit was only eleven!

I laid a hand on his shoulder and shook my head at him sternly to keep him seated as I stood up. He could scowl at me all he wanted, but he'd better keep his ass on the couch.

It was late and I wasn't expecting anyone. I'd realized as a child that nothing good ever came from late-night visits, and at an early age had learned how to protect myself. I hadn't been prepared when I'd needed it—those particular attacks had come in the middle of the day—but I'd learned my lesson. I was never unprepared again, and no one was getting into my apartment unless I let them, especially with Cameron there.

I walked to the side table and opened the drawer, quietly pulling my revolver out. By the time the door opened, I'd checked to make sure it was loaded and was standing in the entryway, the gun hanging loosely at my side. I really hoped the little shit would stay where he was, partially hidden by the couch.

As Cody stepped inside, I felt my entire body relax.

"Hey, Ladybug." He looked at me curiously. "You okay?"

"Yeah. Shit." I sighed, emptying bullets into my palm. "You fucking scared me."

"I'm sorry, baby. I missed you," he replied, stepping forward. "Some shit's going on at th—"

Just then Cameron stood up from the couch, interrupting whatever he'd been about to say. It was like a scene from a movie as Cody's eyes widened and he stumbled to the wall, barely catching himself with one arm. He looked like he was going to pass out.

"Cameron?"

"Hey, Casper." The little dude was nervous, though I didn't know why.

Cody gasped. "Holy fuck. What? How?"

"I'm guessing no one told you," I remarked quietly as Cody got his shit together and literally jumped over the couch to reach Cameron.

They both laughed as Cody lifted him off his feet in a hug, and I swallowed hard at the sound. It was the first time I'd heard it in the two days Cameron had been hanging out at my house. I wasn't sure what was going on with Tommy, but Grease had dropped Cameron off both times, so the club knew where he was. I wanted to ask what the hell was going on, but kept my mouth shut.

The kid wanted a safe place to hang out? I wasn't doing anything after work, and I kind of liked the company anyway.

"You've been hanging out with my woman?" Cody teased, pulling my attention back to him as he ruffled Cameron's hair. "How the hell did that happen?"

His gaze came to me and I shook my head slightly. I didn't think it was something the kid would want to go over again. It had been hard enough to live it.

"So, you're back now?" I asked, wrapping my arms around my chest. I was fighting tears at their reunion and it pissed me off. I didn't cry at happy things. That was ridiculous.

"Shit, yeah, and we need to talk. You okay out here? We'll be right back." He looked at Cameron, slapping him on the shoulder and giving it a squeeze in one of those weird male rituals. Then he ushered me into my room.

"I really hope you don't think we're having sex with an eleven-year-old in the living room," I said, coming to a stop at the end of my bed.

"Seriously?" He rubbed his hand over his head. "I can't believe that shit. How the hell is Cam—what—? Fuck, I'll figure it all out later. We've got some shit happening at the club and we're locking it down. You need to pack a bag."

I looked at him incredulously. He must be out of his mind.

"Um, no."

"Farrah, I didn't ask you. I told you," he replied, looking for a bag in the closet.

I wanted to stomp my foot like Will did when he didn't get his way.

"You took my only bag, remember? When you took off and didn't tell me that Trish was dead or what you were doing or where you were going or what the hell was the matter with you." With each word my anger mounted, but he was too distracted to notice.

"Fuck. I'll grab a garbage bag. Start grabbing the things you'll need. Enough for a while, we aren't sure how long this shit is going to take." He paused to take a deep breath and I wanted to scream as he ignored my comments about the last time I'd seen him.

"I'm not going to your club," I told him again. "No, thank you."

He was wound tight as hell, I'd noticed it when he'd walked in, but once he'd seen Cameron it had seemed to evaporate. Unfortunately, the minute we hit the bedroom, the tightness of his muscles and the stress in his eyes had shown back up.

"I am not fucking playing with you, Farrah," he enunciated clearly. "Get your shit or I'm taking you without it. I don't give a fuck if you spend the entire time wrapped in your fucking quilt because you don't have any makeup."

I inhaled sharply at the low blow. Using my odd need for things to look just right against me wasn't even a little bit okay. I wanted to argue with him, be a bitch and make him pack my things himself, but I caught myself just before I did something stupid. I'd known there was something going on, but it took me a moment to catch the inflections in Cody's voice instead of just the words.

He wasn't being a dick.

He was scared, and that scared me, so I sucked up my attitude.

"I have a suitcase under the bed," I told him quietly, walking forward to wrap my arms around his waist. I hadn't seen him for days, and before we left the house and our lives became a complete clusterfuck, I needed to feel him. Just for a second.

"I'll get that, you get all your shit," he said, kissing my head.

He ran his hands up my arms and around my neck as he tipped my face to his. "Hurry, Ladybug."

We packed in record time, with Cameron helping me put all my toiletries into separate ziplock bags. He grumbled about it, but I think he was glad to have something to do. All of his things were at the club now, mostly clothes that the old ladies had pitched in and bought him. If Tommy was helping with anything, I hadn't heard about it, and it pissed me off. I liked the fact that Cameron came over to hang out, but was concerned that he felt the need to spend time away from his only surviving family member. Something wasn't right there.

It took us about twenty minutes before we were out on the road, Cody leading the way to the club with Cameron and me riding in my car. Gram had been staying with Callie, and apparently Grease was making sure they got to the club too. I hoped that they were there before I was. The entire situation was scary, not only packing and leaving in the middle of the night, but also the fact that I was going to be surrounded by people who didn't like me. I needed to know my family was safe, and I wanted them with me.

My hands shook and grew sweaty on the steering wheel as the guy at the gate checked inside my car and trunk with a flashlight. It didn't even matter that I was the president's daughter and had Cameron with me, he still checked everywhere. By the time we parked in the grass to the side of the club building, I could feel sweat gathering on my top lip. Really fucking attractive. I'd never been so glad for the tissues I kept in my glove box, even if Cameron was looking at me like I was crazy as I blotted my face.

I popped my trunk open and took a deep breath before climbing out of the car. I could do this; I just needed to stay near my family and I'd be fine. Piece of cake. Cameron flew out the door as soon as I stood up and disappeared into the darkness, and I almost jumped out of my skin as Cody came up behind me.

"You're staying in my room," he informed me, pulling my suitcase out of the trunk. "I know you're freaked out, but you're with me and you've got Grease too. No one's going to mess with you."

I nodded, taking a deep breath as we made our way through the tall grass. I could see Brenna and Dragon's house in the distance, every window lit up, despite the late hour. Their lives had been interrupted too, even though they lived in the compound.

The thought made me pause. Is this really the life I wanted? Running out of the house in the dark, frantically choosing what I could stand to lose? What if we had kids? I'd have to hustle them out of their beds, scare them.

Before I realized it, we were walking into a massive room with a bar on one side, and couches and a pool table on the other. A bunch of adults and kids were talking in quiet voices around the room as women laid out sleeping bag after sleeping bag on the floor. I scanned the place, looking for Gram or Callie, and after a few seconds I saw them walking out of what seemed to be a hallway off the back wall.

"There's Gram," I told Cody with a tilt of my head. No one had noticed us yet, and I was afraid if I pointed or looked too closely at the other occupants of the room, someone would realize we'd walked in.

"Wonder where Gram's staying tonight?" Cody murmured.

He grabbed my hand and pulled me through the room as I kept my chin high and my eyes on his back. I wasn't going to cower, fuck that, but I refused to see the look on people's faces when they recognized me.

"Oh, Farrah! Thank God you're here," Gram exclaimed,

pulling me into her arms. "All my babies are in one place."

"Hey, Gram," I murmured into her hair. Just the smell of her calmed me down.

"Where are you sleeping?" Cody asked.

"Oh, Poet says I can sleep in his bed," Gram replied, and Cody began to sputter. "Oh, get your mind out of the gutter. He's sleeping on his daughter's couch."

I laughed a little at the relief on Cody's face.

"Hope you cleaned that fucking disaster you call a room, brother," Grease commented, pulling our attention from Gram to see him standing with one arm around Callie's shoulders. "Farrah's gonna leave your ass, you expect her to sleep in it."

My nose wrinkled at the thought of Cody having a messy bedroom. I couldn't imagine it, but my head snapped up to stare at him when he replied.

"Had April clean the shit while I was gone." His hand squeezed mine, but I couldn't read his expression.

Who the fuck was April?

Chapter 19

Farrah

"**I**'ve got a bathroom in here, so you won't have to share," Cody told me, dropping my bag just inside the door of his room. "It's not huge, but at least we won't be crowded into the main room."

"How'd you score a room?" I asked, looking around at the bare walls and the plain black comforter on his bed. I'd seen the number of men in the main room, and the number of doorways in the long hallway off the back of the club. That shit didn't add up.

"Some of the brothers don't keep a room here," he said with a shrug. "That's why they're all camping out on the floor. If I didn't have an old lady, I would have been expected to give up the room, but since I do . . ."

"Wait, what?" I turned to look at him in horror.

"What?"

"You're talking about me?"

"Oh, fuck me. Are we really getting into this now?" he asked in irritation. "Of course I'm talking about you. When the fuck would I have time for someone else, and why the fuck would you be in this room if you weren't mine?"

I spluttered, trying to find the words to blast him. He was irritated? Fuck that! He was the one who'd promised we weren't putting labels on shit! We were as good as married in the club's eyes, and I'd had no fucking idea.

"Who's April?" I asked stonily, not willing to give an inch.

"The bitch that cleans the fucking club. You're being an idiot."

"Fucking fantastic, Cody," I mumbled, yanking my suitcase farther into the room. Once I'd opened it up and found the makeup case I was looking for, I met his eyes. "You can go."

"Why are you being such a bitch?" he asked, reaching behind him to lock the door. Good, at least when I beat the hell out of him, no one could come in to save his ass.

"You said no labels!"

"I told you that *you* didn't have to label it. I never said shit about claiming you at the club," he growled back.

"Semantics!" I argued, my voice even. I didn't want everyone to hear us fighting, but my tone was scathing. "Echo never—"

He tackled me onto the bed midsentence, knocking the makeup case across the room. I found myself glaring at his face as he straddled my belly and captured my hands above my head.

"Echo was a fucking pussy," he said with a sneer, so close I could feel his breath on my face.

"Shut up! You didn't know him!"

"I'll say whatever the fuck I want." He punctuated his vow by squeezing my wrists. "He didn't take care of you."

"Yes, he—"

"No. He didn't."

"Let me talk!" I screeched, bucking my hips in an

unsuccessful attempt to move him.

"No. I'm talking now," he said menacingly. "I watched you lose your shit when he died, and I didn't say shit because I knew you couldn't handle it."

"Fuck you!"

"But we're going to get a few things straight, right now. Echo was a fucking pussy who didn't take care of you. He didn't say shit when you were fucking wasting away. He didn't do shit about your parents fucking beating on you and making your life miserable. He was too concerned with his own ass to make sure that yours was safe. He didn't deserve your tears. The guy deserves to be dead."

"No, he doesn't." I sobbed, barely able to catch my breath as his words pummeled me. He was relentless, pushing and poking at every memory I had of the first man I'd thought loved me. I slammed my eyes shut and fought the memory of the day I'd locked myself in my bedroom, calling Echo over and over until Gator had finally broken through the door, my phone and any chance of escape lost.

"Don't," I cried out. "He was good to me. You don't know what you're talking about."

"Listen to me." He shook me gently. "Look at me!"

I opened my eyes to meet his, and my stomach dropped.

"I am in love with you," he said. "There is not one thing I wouldn't do for you. I'd kill for you. I'd die for you. No hesitation, no question. Do not ever compare me to Echo again. That man is dead, and he isn't worth the dirt he's buried under. Do you understand me?"

"He wasn't—"

"He wasn't anything, Farrah. He didn't claim you because he wasn't worth shit. You were my old lady from the night you pulled into town. I claimed you, even knowing you would be pissed. You know why?"

I sniffled, my breath hiccupping in my throat. Tears were still rolling down the sides of my face, and I hated him for making me cry in front of him. "No."

"Because I would do anything to keep you safe." He leaned down, pressing my hands into the bed, and kissed me hard. "Even if you hate me for it."

His tongue pushed into my mouth, and he let go of my wrists to grip my head. I slapped at his chest even as I kissed him back, my emotions too strong to contain. I wanted him and loved him and hated him as I fought against his words. I was so afraid that what he was saying was the truth.

Our fight turned to desperation as I tore off his cut and the T-shirt underneath, scratching his back with my nails. He yanked my shirt over my head, and instead of unsnapping my bra, pulled out a knife from his jeans and flicked it up from between my breasts, cutting the bra in half.

We pushed and pulled and rolled around the bed, at one point almost hitting the floor until Cody caught us, using one arm to push us back up. He bit me and I bit him, our bodies red and sweaty by the time we'd stripped our bottom halves.

"Brace your hands on the wall," he ordered as he knelt above me, his chest heaving. Without thought, I followed his direction, placing my hands on the cold concrete above my head.

"Brace 'em, Ladybug," he repeated.

As soon as I'd locked my elbows, he pulled my hips from the bed and slammed inside me. My head flew back, the tendons in my neck straining as I held back my cry. I was still conscious of the people outside his room, but I wouldn't be for long.

His fingers dug into my hips, pulling me toward him as he snapped his hips forward again and again, and soon I was moaning with every thrust. Then he let go of one of my hips and ran his fingers down the length of my chest, from my neck to my belly button. He wiped away the sweat that had been beading on my skin, and my entire body clenched as he lifted his fingers to his lips and licked them clean.

"Tastes good," he rasped.

He pounded in again before pulling out with a muffled curse, then flipped one of my legs over the other so I was lying with my bottom half twisted sideways.

"Keep those arms up," he reminded me as he pushed the top leg until my thigh was resting against my chest.

Without any warning, he pushed slowly back inside me. The change in angle and the tight feeling of his entry had me gasping, the sweat on my hands making them slip against the wall. He leaned down so one of his forearms was braced beside me—his fingers wrapped gently around my upraised arm—and rested his chest against my torso, bringing the other hand up to rub up and down my bent leg, keeping it in place.

"Oh my God." I groaned, clenching my teeth as he started to move faster.

He made a noise against my collarbone as he grasped behind my knee and rotated his hips just a fraction. I was so immersed in him—the way he smelled, the taste of his skin, the sound of his voice in my ear—that by the time he let go of my thigh to reach down and pinch my clit, hidden under my drawn-up thigh, I was so close to orgasm I detonated on contact.

"That's my girl," he whispered in my ear. "I take care of you, don't I?"

I moaned high in my throat as the orgasm went on and on until finally my body relaxed. As soon as it was finished, his hand slipped away from where we connected and grabbed the opposite arm. Without slowing his thrusts, he turned me fully onto my side. When I was exactly how he wanted me, he leaned down to tenderly kiss my lips, and then used my hair to jerk my face away from him.

Breathing heavily, he came, biting down on the back of my neck.

He summarized his point by once again covering Echo's mark with his own.

Son of a bitch. I was too tired to argue anymore.

Chapter 20

Farrah

The first few days at the club actually weren't that bad. People seemed to give me a wide berth, which suited me just fine. I wasn't there to make friends, and if it had been up to me, I wouldn't have been there at all. I was pretty small potatoes when it came to club politics, and I doubted anyone would have even connected me to the Aces, but Cody was adamant that it wasn't safe for me outside the barbed wire fence that surrounded the grounds.

I didn't fight him on it. I'd felt like shit when I had to call in to work, but when I'd told the owner that I had a family emergency, he'd been super cool about it. At least I didn't have to worry about losing my job. I could live with being cooped up with a bunch of people I didn't know as long as my family was around.

I spent most of my time hanging outside with Callie, Will, and occasionally Cameron. Gram had found her way into the kitchen and was schooling all the other women on how to feed an army, and Cody was mostly off doing shit for the guys in the club, so I didn't see them as much.

After the first day, the adults had realized that it was insane to try to keep the kids locked inside, so they set up some water games and yard toys in the field behind the building. The old ladies were comfortable with each other, and they took shifts slathering the kids in sunscreen and watching them run wild, but none of them ever made their way into our little group.

I felt bad that I seemed to be alienating Callie from the women she had so much in common with, but it really couldn't be helped. They didn't want anything to do with me—my reputation must have preceded me—so even if I'd smiled at them and tried to play nice, they wouldn't have given us the time of day. We were interlopers, and by the strain on Callie's face by the end of each day, I knew it was weighing on her.

By the fifth day of confinement, I made myself cut her loose. I knew that while I was around she wouldn't make any of the friends that she quite obviously wanted, so instead of following the crowd outside after breakfast, I told her I wanted to spend the day reading in Cody's room. It was a bit disturbing the way her eyes lit up before she deliberately gave me a disappointed look, but I let it go. I understood, as much as it irritated me.

If I'd known what I was getting myself into, I would have gladly tagged along with Callie and kept her friendless.

I'd been in Cody's room for about an hour when there was a soft knock on the door. Thinking it was Gram or Callie, I climbed off the bed and swung the door open, immediately wishing I could slam it closed again.

"Hi," she said nervously, her voice rough and deep. "I'm Vera. Slider's wife?"

"Is that a question?" I asked flatly, my asshole persona falling flawlessly into place.

"No." She scowled. "I just wasn't sure if you knew who I was."

I looked her over slowly, taking in her slender body covered in a Harley Davidson tank top and low-cut jeans designed for someone half her age. Every life choice she'd made seemed to have made itself known on her features, from her overly tanned skin to the wrinkles around her lips from puckering a million times around a cigarette. Yet, there was still something oddly beautiful about her.

"Yeah, I know who you are. Can I help you with something?" I was praying to any god that could hear me that someone, anyone, would walk in and interrupt us.

"I just wanted to talk to ya for a minute," she said, stepping into the room without invitation, forcing me to take a step back.

I stood silently with a polite look of disinterest on my face and fought the panic building in my chest at our proximity as she looked me over. I'd been avoiding her for days, and just my fucking luck, the minute I got comfortable, there she was.

"You're so beautiful," she said softly. "I knew you would be."

She reached up to touch me and I flinched away violently, my mind racing. What the hell was she doing?

"Um . . ."

"You've been giving your dad such a hard fucking time," she said, gently scolding me with a shake of her head as she pulled a pack of cigarettes out of her pocket with shaky hands. "It's—"

I cut her off midsentence. "He's not my dad."

"Honey, your birth certificate didn't lie, and neither do those eyebrows and that chin you've got pointed to the sky. Hell, you looked just like him when you were born, though you've got the look of your mother now."

"What?" I asked in confusion. Was I in the fucking twilight

zone? She'd seen me as a baby? I couldn't grasp what she was trying to say, and my fingers began to tingle.

Oh shit.

She looked around the room, almost as if she couldn't meet my eyes as she started to speak.

"I was pissed as hell when your dad told me he'd knocked up some club whore. God, I could have shot him with his own damn gun. Ya wanna sit?"

I shook my head woodenly as I locked my knees. No, I did not want to fucking sit.

"I'm gonna sit," she told me with a nod, perching on the side of Cody's bed. "Story's a fucked-up one, but I think you need to hear it. Your dad sure as shit will never tell ya, and even though he never says nothin', I know he worries about ya. He's always worried about ya."

I fought the lump in my throat, determined to stay standing and coherent as she sat awfully close to my wedding ring quilt. If I hadn't been so afraid to get near her, I would have snatched it off the bed before her vanilla perfume could contaminate it.

"Knew your mother. Didn't like her. She always hung around back then, scoring coke off the boys however she could. Didn't know she was fucking my husband, not until later, but I knew something was off about her. Something was missing."

"Don't touch the fucking coffee table, Farrah! You knock any of my sugar off the table, I'll beat your ass!"

No. Nonononono.

"When I found out she was pregnant, I wanted to kill her. Seriously considered it a time or two. But your father, well, we'd been trying for a long-ass time by then, and still no babies. He tried to act like he didn't care, but I knew a part of him was a bit excited by the whole thing. Couldn't help himself."

"That's your daddy in the picture. See him, Farrah? Handsome motherfucker, huh? He didn't want you, so he sent us away. Like we were trash, just tossed us out like garbage. Shoulda never gotten pregnant."

"As much as I wanted him to, he couldn't ignore what was happening. He was afraid your mother'd keep you coked outta your brain and starvin', so he set her up in a little house on the other side of town. Paid her bills and shit, made sure she was eating, and tried to keep watch on her through the boys so she couldn't go out and score." I vaguely registered her voice catching on the last word. "Eventually she realized Slider wasn't going to leave me for her, even though at the time, shit wasn't good between us for obvious reasons."

"Coulda stayed with your daddy, you know. He didn't want kids, though, so once you came along I was screwed. Hand me mama's dollar over there, yeah, that one. You remember that, Farrah, I chose you. So you be a good girl and don't you make me regret it."

"She told us that we could adopt the baby, and for a price, we'd never have to see her again."

Vera sniffled, but I still refused to look at her. My vision was starting to have little spots in it as I tried to quietly pull air into my lungs.

"It wasn't easy for me, I want you to know that. I didn't want nothin' to do with her kid at first, the proof of my husband fucking around on me. But eventually I seen what it was doing to Slider, and I knew that I had to dig deep down inside me to find if I was willing to overlook a baby, the man I love's baby, just for the sake of pride."

"Your daddy's cunt wife was gonna kill ya, Farrah. I saw it. I knew if I didn't get you away from there, she'd do it and she'd

get away with it. She wanted you dead, I had to protect ya."

"Less than a month before you were due, we agreed to take you." She made a hoarse sound deep in her throat, making me cringe. "I loved ya before you were born, knowing you were gonna be mine. Haven't loved anyone more in my entire life, and that's the God's honest truth. By the time you came, I had a little room all set up for ya, lots of clothes and toys you wouldn't be using for months. I got everything just perfect."

My breath was wheezing past my tight throat as I listened to her bullshit, and almost overpowering my fear was the absolute certainty that she was lying.

"We only had you two months before she took you back."

My ears started ringing.

"Didn't trust lawyers back then, hadn't signed adoption papers or any of that shit, so when your mother came with the police saying Slider'd kept ya against her wishes, we had no choice. Then she just ... she just disappeared and took you along with her."

"Had to flee in the night like one a those Lifetime movies. Just like it. Your daddy woulda let her do it, I saw it in his eyes. He hated ya, and you were just a poor little baby then. He's a bad man, Farrah. Don't you ever go looking for him, 'less you wanna die."

"We hoped that she stayed clean, we thought maybe she'd just changed her mind. She never asked for more money or contacted us again. Back then, dads didn't have a whole lot of rights to their kids, so even if we would have found you, there was a good chance we wouldn't get you back. After a couple of years we stopped looking, hoping you were okay, that she'd proved us wrong and gotten her shit together."

She was looking at me, I could feel it, but I couldn't make

myself look back. My chest felt like someone was sitting on it, and my arms had gone completely numb from the elbows down by then. It took all I had just to keep standing.

"Please get the fuck out of my room," I choked out, my voice weak and shaky. "You're a liar and I don't want to hear any more."

"I named you Cecilia, for my mother. Your dad called you CeeCee his bumblebee—"

"Stop! Stop it, you cunt! You know what my name was? Kid or asshole or little shit or piece of shit or goddamn-it-Farrah or get-the-fuck-back-in-your-room." I heard her sob, just once. "She hit me and yelled and had junkies in and out of the house at all hours—and that was *before* I was twelve years old. I was yours? Fuck you. You didn't find me, you stopped looking. I was within miles of an Aces chapter. Fuck you and fuck your piece-of-shit husband."

She stood up from the bed and took a step toward me.

"Stop!" I wheezed. "Get out!"

I wasn't sure what finally made her listen, whether it was the way my body started to shake or the way I struggled for breath, but after a few seconds she raced out of the room. I took two shaky steps before falling heavily onto the bed, focusing on moving my hands so I could grasp my quilt. By the time I'd pulled it over my head, I was on the verge of passing out.

It wasn't bullshit. *Fuck*. It all made so much sense.

Oh God, she'd been telling the truth. They'd had me, they'd loved me, and when shit got hard, they'd given up on me. It was worse than believing that Slider just hadn't wanted kids. So much worse.

I was barely coherent when Cody found me.

Chapter 21

Casper

"Vera's in your room," Cameron told me quietly as I sat at the bar with a few of the boys. I looked at him in surprise for a moment. "With Farrah."

I was off the barstool and striding toward the door before he'd finished Farrah's name. *Son of a bitch.* Things had been going so well; at least, better than I'd expected. My girl had kept her cool. She hadn't brought out the don't-give-a-shit attitude or sarcastic comments, even though I knew she wanted to. The old ladies at the club weren't exactly welcoming, and she'd taken that shit and kept her head high without causing any drama.

I knew, I fucking *knew* it would be bad when I ran down the hallway, but I couldn't have imagined how bad it would be.

The room was silent as I walked inside, the door wide open. A quick sweep assured me that Vera was long gone, but I couldn't be relieved because a familiar quilt-covered lump was hanging halfway off my bed.

"Ladybug?" I called anxiously, moving toward the bed.

"What's she doin'?"

I hadn't realized that Cameron had followed me, but I was thankful as all hell that he had when no reply came from under the blanket. Fuck me. The top half of her body was limp on the bed, but the bottom half . . . God. She was on her knees. She was on her goddamn knees and the bare soles of her feet were peeking out of the quilt, one of them twisted slightly to the side.

"Farrah!" I shouted, wrapping my arms around the entire quilt to move her completely onto the bed. "Cam, run and get my gram. I think she's in the kitchen," I ordered frantically, pulling at the quilt.

I worked my arms under her, trying to find the quilt's edges, but she'd wrapped herself so tightly that it took me a few tries before I could start to unpeel it. I was scared as hell when she didn't fight me, her body staying limp and pliant as I moved her around on the bed. When I'd finally rolled her onto her back, I took one look at her face and swallowed back the bile rising in my throat.

Her lips were practically blue and her skin was paler than I'd ever seen it. She looked dead, but I could see the pulse in her throat beating frantically.

"Hey, Ladybug," I whispered.

She opened her eyes and gave me a slight smirk before her face crumpled.

"Think I might have passed out," she rasped, her brows drawn in confusion. "That was a doozy."

"Fuck, Ladybug." I groaned, pulling her into my arms. "I'm so sorry, baby. What happened?"

She pushed her face into my shoulder without replying, and as I slid my hand into the hair at the nape of her neck, Slider stomped into the doorway. Goddamn it, she'd rather die than let him see her like this. Her makeup was smeared across her fucking face.

"The fuck is your problem?" he bellowed, causing Farrah to flinch before growing unnaturally still. "What the fuck did you do to my wife?"

"Boss—"

"None a your business, boy!" he interrupted. "I want to fucking know what your bitch said to my wife that's got her fuckin' hysterical in my room! This is the thanks I get for taking your skanky ass into my club? You can't fuckin' stay away, have to start fuckin' one a my goddamn prospects, and now I've got a fuckin' second-generation club whore as an old lady to one of my men?"

Farrah started shaking, her tears wetting my neck, and I tightened the hand at her nape to keep her where she was. I wished I could cover her ears while I was at it. I wanted to stand and make the fucker leave, but Farrah was on my lap and there was no way I was putting her down.

"I fuckin' warned you to stay away from my wife!" Slider roared.

Farrah startled in my arms, making a keening noise that was so quiet I barely heard it.

Fuck it, I was done. I tightened my arms around Farrah and braced my legs to stand. That was when Gram walked in calmly, meeting my eyes before coming to a stop with her back to Farrah and me.

Slider's bafflement was almost funny as Gram straightened to her full height of barely five feet, her curved back no match for the way she squared her shoulders.

"I appreciate you taking us in these past few days, but I'll be taking my granddaughter out of here as soon as we can be packed."

Farrah's body relaxed into mine at Gram's words.

"Woman, I ain't got no fight with you."

"Wrong," Gram argued. "If you'll step outside, I'll get Farrah packed and out of your clubhouse."

"Yeah, take that trash with you," he blustered back.

"Be very, very careful with what you say next," Gram hissed back, her voice taking on a tone I'd never heard before. "Your daughter is shaking and upset on that bed, and what you say next could be the straw that breaks the camel's back. She has a family now, she no longer has to allow *trash* into her life."

"What fucking back? The little bitch has treated me like shit since the moment I met her and fixed her fuckin' problems for her. As far as I'm concerned, the fuckin' camel is dead."

"Well then, you won't mind *stepping outside* so we can get packed up. And Slider?" Gram's voice dropped to a whisper. "You leave her alone or I'll remember I've got *contacts* of my own."

"Fuck this shit. Get that little cunt outta my clubhouse." Slider sneered, spinning toward the door.

Farrah's head snapped up then and turned to face him as he hit the doorway. "CeeCee the bumblebee," she called out quietly.

She caught him midstep and he stumbled as he spun back toward us, his face a mask of horror as he met her eyes.

That was when Gram slammed the door in his face.

Chapter 22

Farrah

Gram had me packed in less than twenty minutes, but it took us close to an hour to figure out the logistics of leaving the club in broad daylight. After all, they were under lockdown for a reason.

I stayed on Cody's lap for most of that hour, but we barely spoke. What was there to say, really? Slider had given up on me as a child, and any uncomfortable wishes that I'd harbored about one day having a relationship with him disappeared in a puff of smoke when he made his feelings known. I was nothing to him. A club whore spawned from another club whore, a designation that I assumed came from my long-ago relationship with Echo.

Grease and Callie came in not long after the blowup to see what the hell had happened, and she automatically decided to pack Will up and leave with us. There were few times I'd ever seen Callie so livid, as if she would burst out of her skin like the Hulk if anyone looked at her sideways. She was fierce in her protection of me, and all her mother bear instincts had risen up when she'd caught a glimpse of my face. I must have looked like shit.

Callie and Grease got into a huge fight, arguing about her and Will leaving the grounds, but after a few minutes I'd put a stop to it. Whatever the threat was outside, it was very real, and for once I completely agreed with Grease. It wasn't safe for them to leave, no matter what Gram and I were doing. Frankly, it wasn't all that safe for us to leave either, or we wouldn't have been there in the first place.

Cameron wasn't happy to be left behind. His anxiety skyrocketed when we told him I was leaving, and I was afraid for a moment that he was going to punch Cody in the face for telling him he couldn't go with us.

It was harder leaving him behind than I imagined, but I knew that there was no way I could bring him along. His family had already been targeted, and even though we'd kept his survival pretty quiet, he was still in danger. I couldn't stand the thought of something happening him. I doubted his father would have let him leave anyway. Tommy seemed to fade in and out of the parenting role, but I knew he still worried.

Gram and I were headed to her sister Lily's house, on the outskirts of a little town called Sutherlin about an hour south of Eugene. It was so far off the beaten path that Gram was sure we'd be safe in the old farmhouse, but just to be careful we took two separate cars and two different routes to get there, with Grease and Gram in her car, and Cody driving me in mine.

The club didn't do a thing to help with our departure, no plans were made to make sure we weren't followed, and it was another nail in the father-of-the-year coffin. He didn't even care what happened to me. It was as simple as that.

We stayed quiet most of the ride; I was nervous and Cody was concentrating on our surroundings. But as we passed the

Sutherlin city limits sign, he finally spoke.

"You're gonna like my aunt Lily, Ladybug. She's a lot like Gram. Quieter, though." He reached over and laced his fingers through mine, finally relaxing a little.

"I just wish we weren't potentially bringing shit to her doorstep." I sighed. "The fucked-up part of this whole thing is I didn't even *do* anything. She fucking cornered me in your room. I didn't have a choice."

"You want to talk about it?" he asked. "I feel like I'm missing a big part of whatever the hell is going on."

I took a deep breath and gave him the CliffsNotes version of Vera's visit as we pulled onto a back road and started up a mile-long driveway, but I left out the memories of my mom. It was enough for him to know what Slider and Vera had done or hadn't done; the filth that my mom had filled my head with wasn't something I wanted to discuss. I wasn't sure that he would get it, how much worse it was for me that they'd taken care of me and then pretended I'd never existed, but he did.

"That's fucked up! They just gave up?" he asked with a scowl as we rolled to a stop.

"Apparently. I guess there's just something about me. I can't seem to keep a parent's interest for any length of time," I told him with a droll smile as I unbuckled my seat belt.

"That's bullshit, Farrah," he replied, gripping my leg when I turned to open my door. "There isn't one thing wrong with you, baby. That's their fuckup, you know that, right? It doesn't have a goddamn thing to do with you."

The intensity in his voice had my throat clogging with tears, and I reached up to gently lay my hand on his cheek. "I love you," I told him for the first time.

He swallowed hard and leaned toward me, but our little

moment was interrupted by the unmistakable sound of someone pumping a shotgun.

"State your business!" yelled a little old lady holding the gun just feet from the front of my car.

Cody rolled down his window, leaving his other hand clenching my thigh. "Aunt Lil, it's me, Cody!"

"Cody!" she cried in delight, letting the shotgun fall to rest against her side. "Well, what the hell are you doing sitting in the car? Come on in!"

His smile was huge as he opened his door and stepped into the overcast day, and I watched in astonishment as he wrapped his arms around the small woman's waist and spun her around. She was still holding the shotgun as they spun, and I ducked down behind the dash as their revolution pointed it toward me.

"What the fuck is this, the Wild West?" I grumbled, climbing out of the car when they were done spinning.

"Farrah!" Lily smiled as I made my way toward them. "My little sister has told me so much about you, darlin'! I didn't mean to scare ya, but Rose let me know what was going on and I couldn't see who was in the car. Come in! Come in! I've got dinner on the stove."

"How were you planning on shooting someone if you can't see them?" I asked conversationally as we walked up the porch steps.

"Oh, honey, you just need the general vicinity with a shotgun. Got some bird shot in this baby," she said as we stepped inside and she set the gun against the wall. "Get close enough and you can spray the shit outta someone." She winked and turned toward the kitchen, leaving me with my mouth hanging open.

"I thought you said she was the quiet one!" I grumbled to Cody as he came in the front door, carrying my things.

"Said my eyesight's bad, not my hearing!" Lily singsonged from the kitchen, making Cody burst into laughter as my face burned in mortification.

I clenched my jaw and straightened my shoulders as I followed Lily into the kitchen, ignoring Cody as he walked my suitcase down a hallway off the left side of the entryway. I was having a hell of a time keeping my guard up; there had been too many things happening in the last week. I was off-kilter. I needed to get my shit together, starting now.

"So, you're old," I called out to Lily, trying to rile her as I made my way to the island separating the kitchen from the dining room. "You have your medical marijuana card?"

"Hell, no. I'm not that decrepit," she replied, turning to face me.

"Bummer."

"Said I didn't have a card, didn't say I didn't have weed," she told me with a small smirk.

"Hell yeah, mama! Hook us up!"

"Are you trying to corrupt my auntie?" Cody asked, startling me as he stepped in against my back and leaned his hands on the countertop on each side of me.

"I think it may be the other way around."

"Yeah, that doesn't surprise me," he mumbled into my neck, giving me a soft kiss there.

"Lily? Farrah?" I heard Gram call from the front of the house.

"In here, Rose!"

God, those old ladies had a set of lungs on them.

"Everything go okay?" Gram asked breathlessly as she shuffled into the kitchen.

"Yep, no problems. What about you guys?" Cody replied as

Gram walked around the island to give Lily a hug.

"No problems," Grease answered, setting down Gram's bags in the kitchen doorway. "Didn't see shit."

"Asa, this is my sister Lily. Lily, this is Callie's man," Gram said by way of introduction.

"Damn, you sure ain't small," Lily blurted, looking Grease up and down . . . and then up again.

"No, ma'am, I'm not."

"Callie being so small, you're lucky your baby didn't rip her in two," Lily commented, making Grease's face pale.

"Shut your trap, Lily!" Gram admonished.

"Well, shit! Look at him! The man's huge!"

Gram ignored Lily and turned to Grease. "Get that look off your face. Callie did just fine having Will, and I'm pretty sure you've seen that he didn't rip her in two."

Grease's face turned red at Gram's words, and I had a hard time controlling my laughter. God, Gram was funny alone, but with those two old ladies together? I had a feeling I'd be peeing my pants in the near future.

"Can't stay long, little brother," Grease told Cody seriously, immediately ruining the good mood I'd finally found. They shared a look and a head nod before Cody turned toward me.

"Come on, Ladybug," he called quietly, wrapping his arms around my shoulders. "I'll show you where your room is."

When Lily called out not to dirty the sheets, I couldn't even laugh.

It was almost time for him to leave me and I wasn't ready. If it were up to us, he would have stayed, but we both knew he was needed at the club. If the families were ever going to be safe again, they had to take care of the threat against them.

Chapter 23

Farrah

"I'll be fine," I assured Cody, running my hands over his shaved head as I straddled him on the bed in Lily's guest room.

"I hate leaving you, especially after all that shit at the club."

My breath shuddered as I remembered Vera's story, but I shook my head as if it were nothing. "It doesn't matter. It wasn't news that Slider didn't want anything to do with me."

"I found you wrapped in your quilt, Ladybug. It wasn't nothing," he argued, pulling me closer.

"I'm fine now, see?" I told him, leaning back so he could see the wide smile on my face. "I've got Gram and Lily to keep me occupied, and Lily's shotgun to keep me safe. We're good, baby."

"It still worries me."

"Hey, maybe by the time you come back, this'll have grown out a little and I'll have something to grab hold of," I said, pinching my fingers together to try to pull his hair. "Why did you shave it?"

He chuckled nervously, and my curiosity grew. "You said I looked like a douche bag."

"What? No, I didn't."

"Yeah, you said only douche bags had my haircut." He laughed again. "When I left with Grease the first time to meet the guys, I shaved it all off. I didn't want to look like a pussy."

"Aw, shit." I groaned, but couldn't keep my lips from curving up.

"It was stupid."

"You should grow a real Mohawk this time," I said with a kiss. "Let it grow, and when I see you, I'll cut it for you."

"You're gonna cut my hair?" he asked into my mouth.

"If—when you come back, I will."

"I don't think it'll take long," he said, raising both hands to run his fingers through my hair. "A week, maybe two. Then I'll come get you."

"I'm trying really hard not to ask questions, because I know that's how you guys roll. But I need you to tell me that everything is going to be okay," I replied before leaning in to bite his chin gently.

"It'll be fine, I promise. Ladybug, if you keep doing that I'm going to . . . *fuck*." He hissed as I ran my mouth down his throat and sucked on his Adam's apple.

"You have to be quiet," he ordered, pulling me with him as he stood from the bed. He walked over and pulled my quilt from where it was lying on top of my suitcase, and spread it over the edge of the mattress.

"I can be quiet."

"No, you can't," he murmured, spinning me to face the bed. "I'm going to fuck you fast and hard, and you're gonna want to scream."

I felt myself growing slick as he unbuttoned my jeans and ripped them down my legs. My underwear went next, and as I stepped out of the clothes around my ankles, his fingers slid into me from behind.

"Already fucking wet for me, goddamn," he said quietly, reaching up with his other arm to push my torso down onto the bed. "Stay just like that. Fuck, you're beautiful."

His voice was hoarse and his hands sure as he pulled his fingers out of me to push my shirt up to rest above my breasts. When he stood up, I glanced his way and saw him pointing his phone in my direction.

"What are you doing?"

"Taking your picture," he answered with a wry smile as he put the phone on the nightstand and unbuttoned his jeans.

"Great," I mumbled, my face burning as I dropped my head to the bed.

I heard him pushing down his jeans and rolling on a condom as I waited, and every little noise ratcheted up my impatience. I knew we didn't have much time before Grease came looking for him, and I wanted to be able to touch him one last time before he left. A sense of foreboding had me instigating sex with him, even though I knew there were people just down the hall.

Simply put, I was afraid. I was afraid that whatever he was going to do would take much longer than a week. I was afraid that someone would find us out there in the boonies, and we'd be sitting ducks. I was afraid that he'd go back to the club, and Slider's problem with me would rub off.

I was afraid that for one reason or another, he wasn't going to come back for me.

My muscles tightened in anticipation as he came up behind me, his jeans rubbing against the back of my thighs before I felt his hands run from my shoulders to my hips. I relaxed into the bed, arching my back when his nails dug into the cheeks of my ass and scraped down the back of my thighs.

Cody groaned, pulling my cheeks apart as he bent his knees slightly and pushed inside me. "One day soon, I'm gonna have more pictures of you," he said. "Kneeling on the floor with my cock in your mouth, laying on the bed with your legs wide, wet and ready for me . . ."

He moved slowly, watching himself move in and out, and it drove me crazy. I wanted him to move. I wanted to feel his balls slapping against my clit and his hips pushing against my ass.

"You're not taking any more," I replied snottily, gritting my teeth as I turned my head to look at him. He was holding my hips still as I tried to push back against him, and it was driving me insane. "I'm not that kind of girl."

He laughed quietly at my squirming and jerked me back hard as he thrust forward. "What type of girl is that, Ladybug?" he asked with a smirk. "You fucking love it. You love that I wanna see your wet pussy even when you aren't around."

"Oh God." I moaned, unable to argue. He was right, I loved it, and the picture he'd painted had me growing even wetter.

"Quiet, Farrah," he ordered, picking up the pace until he was moving in a smooth, fast rhythm. "I'm going to fuck you hard, and you're going to be really, really quiet. Aren't you, beautiful?"

I nodded my head, dropping it to the bed again as my nipples rubbed against the stitching on my quilt. When one of his hands left my hips, I braced myself in anticipation, picturing what he was doing in my head. I knew what was coming, but I still yelped as I felt his saliva-covered thumb slip into my ass.

"You're going to be so fucking sore," he rasped, turning his hand so his thumb stayed planted but his fingers surrounded where his cock slid in and out, rubbing my lips where they were stretched wide around him. "You're going to be thinking about me for days after I leave. Every time you sit down, you're gonna feel me here."

I couldn't catch my breath as my orgasm built, and the hand on my hip slid forward between my pussy and the bed. I completely stopped breathing when his fingers hit my clit and the ones covering me from behind pinched my lips hard against his cock.

Dear God.

My eyesight grew fuzzy as my orgasm hit, the mixture of pleasure and pain making me writhe against him. I didn't know if I was trying to get away or move closer, but it didn't matter because Cody wasn't letting me move. He slammed inside me in unmeasured strokes, cursing and praising me as he warned me to be quiet.

By the time we were both spent and he'd pulled out of me, I wasn't sure how I'd ever move again. I could feel my pussy throbbing in aftershocks and my body breaking out in goose bumps as he cleaned me up with tissues off the nightstand, and I didn't even open my eyes to see where he stashed the used condom.

A knock on the bedroom door had my eyes flying open. "Time to go, little brother," Grease called through the door. "Tried to give you some time, but I just got a call from Slider."

"Be right out," Cody replied.

"Hand me my pants?" I asked quietly, sitting up. Our time was really over, no more procrastinating.

"Call me if you need anything, okay?" he said, holding my jeans and underwear out together so I could step inside them. "Even if you think it's nothing . . . call."

"I will," I answered as he buttoned my jeans and wrapped his hands around my waist. He leaned in to rub his nose up the side of mine, the same way I'd comforted him weeks ago, and the gesture almost broke me.

"I love you."

"Love you too, handsome."

I followed him into the entryway where the old ladies and Grease were waiting, but I didn't meet anyone's eyes when I got there. My mask was on, though I wasn't sure who I thought I was hiding from. Every person around me except Lily had seen me sans mask, but I didn't care. If I was going to say good-bye, knowing that bad shit was going to happen before anything was resolved, I needed my mask. I needed the comfort and poise it brought me when I was feeling anything but confident.

I was afraid if I didn't wear it, I'd beg him not to go or burst into tears, and neither of those behaviors were acceptable.

Instead, I'd wave good-bye as if I didn't want to chase after the car. Afterward I played cards with Gram and Lily as if my mind wasn't an hour north with a man who had the ability to shatter me, and later, after the house was quiet and I was wrapped up tight in my quilt, I cried myself to sleep.

Chapter 24

Casper

The ride to Eugene was silent. Sometimes I forgot how thoroughly entrenched Grease was in our family, until times like those when I knew his anxiety over leaving Gram and Farrah was as bad as mine. Neither of us liked the situation but there was nothing to say, no argument or excuse to make.

We left them based on the belief that no one would find them or connect them to the Aces . . . and that was a pretty fucking huge leap of faith.

When we got to the club, the sun had already set and things were quieting down. There were so many families inside, most of the brothers had taken to drinking outside at the picnic tables so they wouldn't get bitched at by their wives, and were keeping things pretty calm.

I dreaded seeing Slider, my blood boiling at the shit he'd put Farrah through, but I knew I couldn't put it off. My loyalty had never been an issue; the club had taken care of my family in the past, more than I could ever repay. But for the first time, I didn't want to be there. I was livid that I'd had to choose between the woman I loved and the club I'd thought would have my back. If anything happened to Farrah, I knew I'd burn the place to the ground and screw the consequences.

"Casper!" Poet called the minute we'd stepped out of the car. He started toward us, Dragon following close behind, and I wanted so badly to fucking ignore him. I didn't have time for his excuses and platitudes. His daughter wasn't outside club grounds when there were people specifically targeting Aces families.

"What's up?" I asked coolly.

Grease came up behind me and set his hand on my shoulder in warning, but I shrugged it off. I didn't need his fucking warnings.

"Talked to Vera," Poet said as he reached me. "Got the story from her."

He shook his head and ran his hand over his beard before continuing. "She wants you to know that she's working on Slider. Says in a coupla days she'll have talked him down enough for Farrah to come back."

I scoffed. "You think she'll ever fucking step foot on this property again? He called her a cunt. A club whore. He's her *father*."

"Boyo, you weren't there when Natasha took Farrah away. It was a fuckin' mess. Slider was tearing apart the clubhouse every fuckin' day, and Vera was locked up in her room, refusin' to see anyone." Poet sighed. "There ain't a whole lot that can get to Slider, man's as cool as they come, but the moment he knew where his daughter was, he was like a man possessed. Imagine not knowing where your child is for fuckin' years and then findin' her, but she ain't nothin' like you'd thought she'd be."

"She's nothing like he'd thought she'd be?" I yelled, the veins in my neck throbbing. "I wonder how the fuck that happened?"

"Calm down."

"This is—" I looked at the ground as I felt Grease's hand on the back of my neck. "He's her father and he *failed* her. Over and over again. He doesn't like her? Who the fuck cares? So stay the fuck away from her! But he forced her out of the only place in the goddamn country that she was safe, all because his wife fucking blindsided Farrah and then got her feelings hurt. I hope to fucking God I never understand that shit."

"Enough!"

I turned my head to find Slider, bleary-eyed and wrecked, standing just outside the doors of the club. "I need you, and that's the only reason you're still standing, you preachy little fuck. But one more word and I'll fucking drop you."

Grease's hand squeezed tighter on the back of my neck, keeping me silent, and I thought my head would explode as I tightened my jaw to keep my mouth closed.

"We got business to take care of." Slider cocked his head toward the back room and ordered, "Church," then spun back around and disappeared through the door.

We followed him in, anxious to hear the plans for fixing the fucking mess we were dealing with.

"He's a good man," Poet told me quietly as he passed me. "He ain't got no point of reference for this shit. Think about if it was your woman, crying like her life was ending."

I looked him straight in the eye and told him the only thing I could. "It *was* my woman, crying like her life was ending. But mine stopped breathing until she passed out because she *couldn't fucking deal*. So I've got no sympathy for his."

He moved ahead, his gaze on the floor, and as soon as I

knew we wouldn't be overheard, I looked at Grease.

"I'll see this through until I know the women are safe. But after that, I'm out."

Chapter 25

Farrah

The days flew by surprisingly fast. I talked to Cody daily, getting updates on what was happening with the club, and before I knew it two weeks had passed. The club still wasn't anywhere close to figuring their shit out, and I'd had to quit my job at the salon, which sucked. I really liked it there, but thankfully I wasn't spending any money at Lily's house, so I was okay financially at least until we got back to Eugene.

It was idyllic in that little valley, and for the first time in years I felt fully relaxed. We spent our time outside on the back porch, drinking sun tea and playing cards, or out in Lily's little garden that was surrounded by a fence to keep the local wildlife out.

Speaking of wildlife, she had *deer*. Like actual freaking deer that came onto her property to eat her grass and lie in the sun. My entire life had been spent in the suburbs, so the first time I'd seen a doe and her two little babies, I'd stood there with my mouth open for God only knew how long until the sound of Gram and Lily laughing at me had broken me out of my stupor.

I'd grown comfortable with Lily right away, which I really shouldn't have been surprised about. She was so much like Gram, taking me in as if I belonged to her. My little personally chosen family had grown yet again, and it felt good. Really good.

A few days into the second week, I'd hopped out of bed at the butt crack of dawn to try to catch sight of the deer family, and had spent the next few hours sitting on the back porch in my cutoff shorts and one of Lily's old T-shirts. It wasn't until I'd gone to the bathroom after lunch that I realized that I hadn't done anything with my makeup or hair all day.

It was the first time for as long as I could remember that my bare face and naturally loose hair in the mirror didn't make me want to turn away in revulsion. I'd tanned a bit after all the time spent outdoors, and my hair had lightened in the sun.

I looked healthy. Not impeccable and done up, but actually healthy, with rosy cheeks that had filled out from three solid meals of Lily and Gram's cooking every day, and clear eyes.

I didn't bother with makeup after that, or my own clothes for that matter. I went barefoot and lay around in Lily's old housedresses from the sixties. Gram and I never left the property anyway, leaving Lily to pick up groceries and other odds and ends we needed at the local grocery store, so it wasn't as if anyone saw me. Most of the time I just showered and threw my hair into a messy bun, anxious to get outside or up to Lily's attic to explore.

Lily's house was a freaking treasure trove of vintage goods. I swear to God, the old broad never threw anything out, which was fantastic as far as I was concerned. I wasn't sure if it was because Natasha hadn't kept anything for more than a few years or because I'd lost most of my things when I'd left my old life, but I loved anything that had a history. There were old quilts, toys, clothes, and furniture in Lily's attic, and I spent hours and hours going through her things while Gram and Lily ignored me as if I were out of my mind.

I was in the attic, going through an old trunk filled with clothes from the eighties, when Cody called. The first words out of his mouth sounded frustrated.

"Hey, Ladybug."

"Hey, handsome. What's up?"

"Not gonna be able to make it out this weekend." He sighed. "Grease and I talked it over, baby. After two weeks with nobody bothering you . . . just not sure that I should be drawing attention to where you are."

"Shit." I knew what he said made sense. We were in our own little bubble out there in the boonies, and if he came to see me, we took the risk of someone following him.

"Yeah. My thoughts exactly."

"Well, are they figuring out how to fix shit? Because seriously, babe, I can't stay here forever. I mean, it's great, but I have a life. I can't imagine the people at the club are too fired up to live there forever either."

"No shit. It's like *Wild Kingdom* up here. The kids are bouncing off the walls, the women are snapping at their men and each other, and the single guys are getting pissed that they can't have the club whores out. It's a fucking mess."

"Well, are you guys almost done . . . doing whatever you're doing?" I asked.

"Yeah, baby. Had to postpone some shit. Brenna had the baby, so Dragon's been up there for the past few days, plus the boys have been taking shifts at the hospital just to be safe. Leaves us with less men than we need to do anything about the threat."

"Fucking Brenna," I mumbled, making him laugh.

"Not a whole lot she could do about it, baby. The little dude had to come out," he replied. I could hear the smile in his voice.

"Everything go okay there?" I asked reluctantly.

"Yeah, went good as far as I know. They named him after me."

"No shit?" I asked after a few moments of silence.

"No shit. Leo Cody White."

"Well . . . that's pretty cool," I grumbled.

"Yeah, I was surprised, but Brenna was pretty firm on the name. She'll be coming home today, I think."

"I miss you," I blurted, done talking about Brenna and her perfect little family.

"I miss you too. Don't think it'll be much longer," he replied quietly. "I miss those ladybugs."

I giggled, then slapped my hand to my forehead in irritation. I was *not* a freaking giggler. "I miss your cock."

He sucked in a loud breath through his teeth. "So that's the game we're playing? Okay, I'm down. I miss those gorgeous tits that I can fit in my mouth."

"Not so sure you can do that anymore," I answered. "I miss those beautiful long fingers of yours."

"Wait, back to your tits," he said quickly. "What do you mean, I can't put them in my mouth anymore?"

"They're bigger—" He groaned. "Lily and your gram are fattening me up like a pig for the state fair."

"Good, you needed to gain some weight," he said.

"What?" No, seriously, what?

"Farrah, you're always beautiful, but sometimes you get so fucking small that if you turned sideways you'd disappear."

"Ouch." Really, ouch.

"Don't do that. Don't get defensive. All I'm saying is that I'm glad you're getting healthy, Ladybug. I worry, okay?" he said gently. "Now I wish I was there so I could show you all the places on your body I fucking love, skinny or fat or anywhere in between."

I couldn't help but be a little hurt at his comments, but I knew he wasn't trying to be an asshole. I also knew that sometimes I got too small. I tried not to, but it was a struggle for me. The first time Gator had made comments about how perky and full my tits were, I felt so disgusting that I'd immediately started dieting to get rid of some of my curves. I'd only been fourteen and poor, so the diet had mostly consisted of not eating. It wasn't healthy and it wasn't right, but it had started a pattern of eating habits that I'd had a hard time shaking. If I was stressed, I didn't eat. It wasn't a conscious thing; I just forgot or told myself I'd do it later, and then before I knew it I'd lost five or ten pounds that I couldn't afford to lose.

I'd gone to therapy when Callie did in Sacramento, so I knew my triggers, but sometimes I let myself slide. If Cody had noticed, that meant I hadn't been doing a very good job.

"I'll do better," I told him nervously, hating the fact that he'd noticed one of the things that made me so far from perfect.

"Baby, you're doing fine, okay? I love you and I fucking love your body. I just want you to be healthy."

"How did we even get on this subject?" I asked.

"I was talking about how I miss your tits."

"Ah, breasts," I sang, a relieved smile stretching across my face.

"Yeah, those. I can't fucking wait to get my mouth on them. I think next time I see you, I'm gonna fuck you bare and then come all over those beautiful pink nipples . . ."

We went back and forth, describing the parts of each other's bodies we missed the most, and by the time we were done, both of us were panting with frustration. We made plans and detailed exactly what we'd do first. It was one of the hottest conversations of my life.

We had no idea that it would be close to three months before I'd see him again.

Chapter 26

Casper

"Time to head out," Grease called from the doorway as I lay on my bed talking to Farrah.

Three months had passed since I'd dropped Farrah and Gram off at my aunt Lily's, and I was so fucking sick of waiting. Slider had brought in a couple of camping trailers so we could spread the families out a little, but it didn't help much. There were too many people in too little space, not to mention that people had lives outside the club that they'd had to completely put on hold. It was a mess.

We'd been making plans, going over shit with a fine-tooth comb, and for the first time I was right in the middle of shit. I'd gone up to Portland a few times, trying to get a feel for things on the street, but it hadn't done us much good.

I'd always been a huge history buff, not just of American history, but also world history. And one thing that all really successful leaders had in common was their ability to inspire loyalty in their followers. They instinctively knew what would endear them to the masses and they used it. A well-known cartel leader in South America funded hospitals and jobs, and Hitler exploited the economic weakness of Germany after WWI; the tactic was as common as the lies politicians in the US spouted during elections.

The McCafferty brothers in Portland had found their loyalty with meth distribution, a drug epidemic that was becoming common all over the US. They'd created perfect little minions, dependent on them for their supply and loyal to the death. It was irritating as fuck, but it did give us a bit of an edge. Our men weren't junkies, for the most part. There were a few who used on a recreational level, but the minute they got sloppy Slider took care of it, one way or another.

However, it did mean that no one was talking, not the men on the streets or the drunk shits in the bars. We hadn't heard any more news in all the months we'd been trying to ferret out information, which left us standing around holding our dicks while waiting for the other shoe to drop. They'd been quiet, too fucking quiet, which meant either the information I'd gathered had been false, or they had someone watching us.

The problem was that I didn't make shitty mistakes. I'd been studying the body language of the people around me since I was seven years old, at first in a desperate need to fit in, and later to become invisible. That meant that they had someone—or a network of people—who knew that we'd battened down the hatches, and they were just waiting for us to let our guard down.

I guessed that Slider was finally ready to make the first move, and hopefully the last.

"I gotta go, Ladybug," I told Farrah as I sat up in bed. "I love you. I'll call you soon."

"Wait, what's happening?" she asked, sounding scared that I'd cut her off midsentence.

"Nothing, baby. Grease needs help with something. I'll call you later."

She was quiet, then with a small sigh, she replied, "Okay. Love you too."

I hung up without saying anything else, my mind already focused on the task ahead. As we walked toward church, Grease updated me on what he knew.

"I think we're going in quiet. Chaps my ass, but I'm pretty sure we're leaving our bikes down here. We're too fuckin' close to Portland." He stopped mumbling as we walked into the small room, closing the door behind us.

As soon as my ass hit the chair that had become way too fucking familiar, Poet started to speak.

"Tonight's the night, boys." He looked around the table, meeting each man's eyes before continuing. "Be ready to leave at seven. Leaving the bikes home for this one—"

The guys grumbled until Slider raised his hand in warning, instantly shutting them up.

Poet paused and then continued. "We've got close to fifty women and children we're leaving behind with a skeleton crew to guard them. Any of you want to paint a giant fucking bull's-eye on my club by riding ten bikes up to Portland?" He looked around the room and nodded once as the words sank in.

"We're hitting them hard tonight, taking out as many as we can on their property in Southeast. Used to be an old drive-in, now it's a series of warehouses. Top of one a those warehouses is their living space," he said. "Not sure if they've got women there, but we're gonna assume they do. Not usually the way we do business, rubs all of us the wrong way. But they wrote the rules to this fuckin' war, and fuck if I'm gonna worry about their women when they were fuckin' targeting ours."

I took a deep breath and kept my eyes on Poet. I knew about the property; I'd been the one to find it and check it out, but it made my stomach turn that I hadn't been able to figure out if they'd kept women there. It was the one thing that worried me about the entire situation.

In a perfect world, the women would cower or hide and wouldn't be a problem. We didn't live in a perfect world. If there was anything I'd learned after living in the clubhouse with old ladies for the past three months, it was that most of them were as hard as their men. They had to be to survive. If the McCafferty women were anything like ours, they'd be in the middle of the fucking fight, and fuck me, but I didn't want to shoot a goddamn woman.

"Leave your cuts in your rooms and head into the armory to suit up. Not leaving anyone behind if shit goes south, but we sure as hell don't wanna leave any evidence either. Patches and leather tend to get left behind fighting hand-to-hand, and if it gets to that, we ain't searching for your shit before we leave," Slider informed us.

"Smokey and Doc," he went on, "you're backup. You'll stay close but out of things in case we need you. You're in the Jeep Cherokee in bay two. Grease and Poet, you're in the piece of shit Toyota Brenna used to drive. Grab Samson, Tweak, and Gump. Let them know we're going, but don't fill them in until we get there. Dragon and Casper, you're with me. Pack up the van parked out back and let Ramon and Goliath know they're riding up with us. Same goes for information. Confiscate all phones."

He looked around the room, his face emotionless. "Only the men in this room have open communication. You take those phones. You find a phone on any man—shoot him. We're flyin' fuckin' blind here, still don't know who's feeding these fuckers information. I don't care if the man was calling his mother. He has a phone, he's dead."

I swallowed hard and stood from the table as the men exited the room. I only had a couple of hours to prepare before we left, and I needed to get in the right headspace. It wasn't the first time I'd been part of a fight, but the entire dynamic was different from anything I'd ever experienced. It felt as if we weren't sure who was loyal and who wasn't. Add on to that the women we might have to deal with, and I was sweating.

Fuck.

"Casper," Slider called quietly.

"Yeah?"

Our relationship was cool, and he'd never invited Farrah back or made any mention of the way he'd fucked her over. I couldn't stand him.

"Sit," he ordered calmly and I immediately dropped back down. It didn't matter if I respected him as a man; I sure as hell respected his strength.

"Before we head out and I'm counting on you to have my back, I wanted to get a few things straight with you," he said. "Your loyalty's not in question, and the minute this shit is over, we'll be voting you in."

I let that sink in. It was the culmination of everything I'd been working for, but with one thought of Farrah, I no longer wanted it. So I said nothing.

"I know you're still hot about the shit that went down with my daughter."

My jaw clenched against the words bubbling in my throat. Fuck him for all of a sudden remembering he even had a daughter.

"I want to get one thing clear with you. I don't give a fuck about how you feel about me. You hate me? Fuck you. I'm twice your age and got more experience in this life than you'll ever have." His eyes never left mine. "I fucked up with Farrah and I knew it right away. I've known it since I stopped fucking searching for her twenty years ago. But three months ago when I made her leave with your grandmother, I knew what the fuck I was doing."

My heart started thumping in my chest, my hands in tight fists beneath the table.

"You're pissed I fuckin' kicked her out? You think she don't mean shit to me? Good." He gave a slow nod. "Everyone else got that same feeling. You get what I'm sayin' to you?"

What?

"She's safer where she's at than she'd be here. That girl's my fuckin' weakness. Anyone who knew me then, anyone that's seen me in the last coupla years knows that. I know Vera can take care of herself—don't have to worry about her much—she's got bigger balls than most a my boys. Farrah's different. Fuckin' softer. Too soft for this shit." He stood from the table. "She can fuckin' hate me. Long as she's breathing, long as she's safe, I don't give a fuck how she feels about me."

Slider walked toward the door and spoke quietly to my back as he reached it. "In all the time you been here, you ever known me to yell, boy?"

He left the room while I sat dumbfounded, staring at the scarred wooden table in front of me.

Holy fuck. The man had played us. He'd fucking played everyone.

Chapter 27

Farrah

I didn't move from the floor of the attic for a long time after Cody hung up on me. Something wasn't right; there was just a little something off, and his "I love you" was a little too adamant. I wasn't sure what was happening, but I instinctively knew that after months of waiting, it was all coming to a head. And that terrified me.

For the first time in months, I stood and walked downstairs to my room, intent on finding the perfect outfit. It was the only thing I could think of as I started to feel panicky, my emotions all over the place. I needed my things. I needed the comfort of preparing my hair and face, as if perfection on the outside would create calm on the inside.

The closet in my room had filled up as I found more and more clothes that Lily had stored for decades. She was shorter than me, and I think she'd had bigger boobs when she was young, but most of the clothes she gave me fit pretty well. I hadn't been wearing them, though, and I knew today wasn't the day to start. I needed my own clothes.

I pulled out a 1950s thin-strapped dress that flowed to my knees in little pleats, and brought it with me into the bathroom. It was a bit wrinkled from being stuffed behind Lily's old clothes in the closet, which made me a little twitchy, but I hoped the steam from my shower would take care of the issue. I tried to clear my mind as the shower poured over me, but I didn't succeed, and my hands were shaky as I applied thick black eyeliner above my lashes, forcing me to wipe it off and reapply it three times before I got it right.

To say that I was a mess by the time I pulled my dress on would be an understatement. I was on the verge of tears, a situation that was so far from common it made me even more upset, and as I tried and failed to pull up the zipper at my side, I let out a frustrated screech.

What the fuck was going on with me? The fucking zipper wouldn't move more than an inch up my side, no matter how much I sucked in my belly. Beneath my armpit the dress gaped a good three inches, assuring me that it wasn't going to close without cutting off my boobs.

I stormed out toward my room, yelling at Gram that I was fine as she stood at the end of the hallway looking at me in confusion. *Goddamn son of a bitch.* The dress was too small. Okay, so I'd try another, even if that meant that I'd have to redo my makeup to match something new.

The next dress I tried didn't have a zipper, but wouldn't pull down over my boobs or up over my hips. The one after that had buttons that wouldn't close. I finally decided on a small halter that was stretchy enough to fit over the girls, but the high-waist shorts that went with it wouldn't fucking button.

By the time I made it downstairs, my room a mess and my face sweaty, I was wearing a lime-green pair of leggings and a Wham! T-shirt that hung off one shoulder. I'd thrown my hair into a side pony, and added a little blue eye shadow to my eyes and called it good, my irritation too far gone to make any more changes.

"I'm having a fucking salad," I announced as I walked into the kitchen. Gram and Lily were setting biscuits and gravy on the table, and my mouth watered as I walked right past them toward the fridge.

"Why the hell would you do that?" Lily asked as she sat down.

"Because eating your food is making it so I don't fit into any of my freaking clothes," I griped, searching for any type of greens I could find. "Where the fuck is the lettuce?"

Gram huffed as she sat down and started serving up three plates. "Need to go grocery shopping. Unless you want to eat a cucumber I got from the garden this morning, you're outta luck. Sit down so we can eat."

I slammed the door shut, irritated as hell, and stomped over to the table. The food smelled really good and for the first time in my life, I couldn't pretend I wasn't hungry. "Nothing fits," I announced, pulling my plate across the table. "I need to start being more careful or I'm gonna start busting out of Lily's housedresses."

I shoved a bite of food into my mouth and watched as Lily and Gram's concerned eyes met. "What?" I asked, my mouth still full.

"Honey, if my food could make women grow breasts, I wouldn't still be living in a broken-down old farmhouse in the middle of nowhere. I'd be in a villa in Greece with a cabana boy feeding me grapes and fanning me with palm fronds," Lily said, laying a paper napkin on her lap.

I swallowed my food in embarrassment and drew my own napkin onto my lap. I was eating like the little piglet Cody had called me when we first got together. It took a few moments for her words to sink in and when they did, I was confused.

"Huh?"

"Darlin', it ain't the food that's making your boobs and your belly grow," Gram informed me, reaching out to grab the butter from the middle of the table.

They were speaking calmly as if about the weather, but there was some sort of undercurrent that I wasn't quite grasping. I looked from one to the other, trying to read their faces, but still couldn't figure it out.

And then I did, and I burst out laughing. "What?" I gasped. "I'm not pregnant!"

Gram scowled. "You sure as hell are."

"No, I'm really not. I haven't had a period in like three years. My shit doesn't work right. No period, no getting pregnant." I shrugged my shoulders.

"You been to the doctor?" Lily asked cautiously, glancing at Gram and then back to me.

"Well, not in a while, no. But when I went a couple years ago, he said I probably wasn't ovulating because I had so little body fat. He thought it would probably correct itself if I ever got bigger, but it never did." I looked between them, trying to make them understand. "I haven't had a period in three years. I'm not pregnant."

It was quiet at the table for a few moments, all of us looking at one another, before Gram spoke.

"Unless you got pregnant the first time you ovulated," she

told me seriously, making my stomach drop. "I know you, Farrah, and I know pregnancy. You're pregnant."

My chair screeched across the floor as I stood up, unable to remain sitting any longer. "I haven't seen Cody for *three months*! Who got me pregnant? Lily?"

Gram followed me from the table as Lily stayed in her seat, and I felt my skin grow hot and my fingers start to tingle as she began to speak. "You're further along than three months, darlin'. My guess is close to four. Not sure how you didn't seem to have any morning sickness, but we've been watching you, baby girl. You're getting thicker around the middle, not to mention your boobs."

"What?" I asked, my head feeling light. "How long have you been watching me? I don't understand."

"Since about two weeks after Cody left. Something seemed different, but I couldn't put my finger on it."

"Why haven't you said anything?" My breath grew frantic as tears built in my eyes. "You just talked about me behind my back instead?"

"You had to figure it out on your own, baby girl." She took a step toward me, but I backed away. "I wasn't sure at first, and then after you'd calmed down and seemed to be taking it easy here, I thought you'd figure it out."

"How the hell would I figure it out?" I yelled, wrapping my arms around my waist and digging my fingernails into my arms to anchor myself. "I haven't had a period in three fucking years! It's not like I could miss one and think, 'Oh shit, Cody knocked me up!'"

"You're twenty-one years old, Farrah. Forgive me for believing that you'd know your own body," she answered, turning back toward the table where Lily was wringing her hands.

I watched her sit back down at the table as if nothing had occurred, and my mind finally calmed. It wasn't her fault. Not at all. Did I wish she would have told me sooner? Of course. While I hadn't smoked with Lily or had anything to drink in over four months, I also hadn't been taking vitamins or any of that other shit that Callie had done when she was pregnant with Will. *Shit.* What foods were off-limits? Had I eaten anything I wasn't supposed to?

As if like magic, my breathing slowed down to normal. It was as if this new development had wiped out any other concerns I'd had because there wasn't room in my mind for them. If Gram was right and I was pregnant, I had things to do. I needed to prepare. Shit, I was almost halfway done being pregnant already. I needed to go to the doctor; could I go to the doctor while we were hiding out?

My mind whirled with plans and questions as I stood silently in the middle of the kitchen, and after a while Lily stood from the table and gently led me back to my chair.

"You just sit right down and finish your dinner," she ordered softly, kissing the side of my head as I sat.

I ate like a robot, silently and without any extra movements until I'd cleared my plate. It wasn't until I was finished that the most pressing issue made itself clear in my mind. I looked up and met Lily's kind eyes across the table, and had to clear my throat before speaking.

"Do you think you could go to the drugstore and get me a test? Just so we know for sure."

"We've got two in the bathroom cabinet," Gram answered for her, reaching out to pat my hand. "Let's have some ice cream first."

She wasn't in any hurry because she knew without a doubt that I was carrying her great-grandchild.

And had been for months.

Chapter 28

Farrah

After peeing on a pregnancy test to prove Gram and Lily right, we spent most of the night curled up on her couches talking. They assumed that I was keyed up because of the baby, and I guess it was partly true. But neither knew about my worry over Cody, or what I imagined happening while Gram knitted and Lily painstakingly sewed together small quilt pieces by hand. I'd been so immersed in my own little world while I was at Lily's that I hadn't noticed until that night that Lily's quilt pattern was tiny, and Gram's projects were being finished quickly.

They were making things for the baby. Things I'd seen Will use but had never connected to the old women sitting next to me. Tiny beanies and booties and quilted pieces done in soft colors . . . all for a tiny little baby who hadn't even made its arrival yet. It made me want to cry, or smile, or learn to do some of it myself. It made me ache that I'd never had things like that, precious little baby items that took hours to make and were given with love.

It was close to four a.m. before Lily and Gram headed off to bed, and I followed them and said good night from my doorway. But I didn't sleep. I crawled into bed and wrapped myself in my quilt, just lying there thinking until I saw the sun rise through my window. I was antsy with an emotion that I couldn't name, and after a couple of hours, I wasn't able to stay in bed any longer.

I dragged my quilt behind me as I walked quietly through the house, and ended up on the back porch in one of Lily's rockers. The rhythmic sound the curved rockers made against the wooden porch soothed me as I rocked back and forth, trying to imagine being a mother. My own mother had been so horrible that before I'd met Gram, I would have assumed that I'd screw it up somehow. I'd had no role model for good parenting, and the thought of doing some of the things my mother had done to me to my own child made me shudder.

Thankfully, as an adult I'd had a couple of really good role models. Both Callie and Gram had taught me a lot about being a parent, whether you gave birth to someone or not. Unfortunately, that train of thought brought me back to the anguish on Vera's face when she'd described losing me to Natasha. I couldn't imagine just giving up on my child, or even think about Will going missing. What was it that made a person just stop looking? I didn't understand it, not at all, but I think knowing that I was carrying my own child gave me a small glimpse into how I'd feel if it were suddenly gone.

It had been only hours since I'd found out that the little thing was in there, and I was already completely enamored with it. Instead of a hypothetical child that I enjoyed the idea of, I already felt as if I knew him or her, as if he or she were already an integral part of me. I wondered what it looked like, if it would be dark like Cody or light like me, and if he or she would have Cody's clear blue eyes or my darker cloudy ones.

My mind wandered through the different scenarios, boy or girl, dark or light, until I finally drifted off to sleep, my mind finally clear of my worry for Cody. He had to be okay; there was no other option because we were having a baby.

When I woke up from my nap, the sun was high in the sky and Gram was sitting next to me in the matching rocking chair. For once her hands weren't busy, and she sat still except for the movement of her feet that set the chair gently rocking.

"Didn't want you to fall out of that chair, so I figured I'd sit with you a while," she said as I turned my head to face her. "Couldn't sleep?"

"No, I guess there was just too much going on in my head."

"I can understand that," she said with a nod. "Big changes coming up for you. Cody too."

"Yeah, I'm not sure how he's going to react." I chuckled nervously, reaching down to rub what I'd thought was a result of Lily's cooking. "We've always been pretty careful, you know? Even though I didn't think I could get pregnant, we were still careful."

"All the precautions in the world ain't gonna matter if it's meant to be."

"Yeah, well, you might have to tell your grandson that after he passes out from shock," I said ruefully.

"Eh, I think my boy might surprise ya. Cody's never been one to place blame on anyone but himself. Gets that from his father. I think his reaction will mirror your own, truth be told." She leaned her head against the back of the rocker, and her voice dropped as we watched the mama deer and fawns come into the yard. "You tell him scared, like you're worried about his reaction? He'll worry right alongside you. You tell him with excitement—because that's what this is, it's exciting—well, I have a feeling that's the reaction you'll get out of him too. He takes his cues from you, darlin', always has."

"I hope you're right," I said, trying to imagine Cody's face when I told him the news. It *was* scary. It wasn't that I didn't think I could do the single parent thing. I could. And it wasn't because I thought it would ever come to that; Cody would never walk away from his child. It was the knowledge that Gram might be right, that he'd pretend to feel however I was feeling, even if it was the last thing he wanted. That thought *killed* me.

"Something feels off today, don't it?" Gram asked suddenly, her eyes coming to mine. "Can't put my finger on it. Just feels off."

"Yeah, I've been feeling the same way," I replied, unsure whether I should burden her with my concerns about what was happening with the Aces.

"Callie called me last night, said Grease was heading out with the boys. He told her to tell us so we'd be extra careful the next few days," she said knowingly. "You talk to Cody?"

"Yeah." I bit the inside of my cheek. "I figured it was something like that, but he hadn't told me."

"Probably didn't want to worry ya," she said.

"You're probably right," I said, but that didn't help the hurt feeling in my chest. "Wait, does Callie know I'm pregnant?" My raised voice carried over the field and the deer scampered off into the bushes.

"Hell no! That's your news to tell, darlin'."

"Oh, good." I sighed. "I just think Cody should know first."

"You tell people as you see fit. Ain't none of my business," she assured me with a nod, reaching her hand out as I stood so I could pull her from the chair.

"Do you think the baby's going to be messed up since I haven't taken any vitamins or anything?" I asked nervously as we walked into the house.

"Nah, we didn't take any of that crap and my boys were just fine. 'Course, back then we smoked too. No, she'll be fine." She patted me on the shoulder. "Lily'll get you some vitamins when she goes to the store."

"You think it's a girl?" I asked curiously.

"Yeah, I've got a feeling." She started taking things out for breakfast, slamming around the kitchen until Lily stumbled into the room.

"What's all that racket?" she yelled over the noise, her hair sticking up in fifty different directions.

"Time for your lazy ass to wake up," Gram informed her with a mischievous smile.

"Shit, a woman needs her beauty sleep!" she retorted before turning to me. "How you doing, sweet cheeks?"

"I'm okay. Wigging out a little, but okay."

"You should go on up and go through the green trunk in the attic while we make some brunch," she said, patting my belly as she passed. "Pretty sure that's the trunk with my old maternity clothes in it."

"No shit? Wait, you have kids?"

"Had two, a girl and a boy, both gone now," she answered stiffly. "You'll probably find something in there that you can use. Go to town."

"You sure?"

"When the hell am I going to wear it?"

By the tone of her voice, she was clearly done with the conversation, so I left her and Gram and raced into the attic. I was excited to see what she'd kept that I could wear; vintage maternity clothes weren't something I'd come across very often as I'd searched in old thrift stores. I spent close to an hour looking for the right trunk, and made three trips to my bedroom with my arms full of clothes to try on. It gave me something to keep my mind off Cody, and the fact that it was midafternoon and he still hadn't called.

Later as I washed and dried dresses, jumpers, and a pair of elastic-waisted bell-bottoms, I tried to ignore the fact that I still hadn't heard from him, and Callie hadn't heard from Grease either. It seemed everyone was in the dark as we waited.

I fell asleep that night worried out of my mind, but too exhausted to stay awake a minute longer.

We still hadn't heard from the men.

Chapter 29

Farrah

Morning found me quietly rocking myself in the same chair I'd been in the day before. I'd woken up early to check my phone, and hadn't been able to fall back asleep when I hadn't seen any missed calls or text messages. Waiting for Cody to make contact was brutal, and it reminded me of when he'd been shot and I'd hoped for any type of reassurance that he was okay.

I wrapped my quilt closer around me, waiting for the sun to finish rising over the hill. Gram and Lily were waking up, I could hear them moving around the house, but things were still pretty quiet as I soaked it all in. I was going to miss this place when it was time to leave. I'd grown used to waking up to birds outside my window and crickets chirping me a lullaby as I fell asleep, and I wasn't sure how I'd ever get accustomed to the sounds of the city again. I hadn't even heard the sound of a car in days. The quiet soothed me in a way nothing else ever had.

I'd also miss my little deer family. They were in the field

again, taking advantage of the apples Lily had left for them. She claimed that she couldn't stand the things because they got into her garden, and said she'd shoot them if her eyesight were better. But after dinner almost every night when she thought no one was looking, she'd bring a few apples out into the yard for them to find the next day. The old softie.

If I hadn't been watching them closely, if I hadn't been completely focused on the graceful line of their necks and the white-speckled coats on the babies, I would have missed the way the mama deer's head shot up and looked toward the side of the house before fleeing into the woods with her little ones trailing behind her.

My heart racing, I turned my head slowly toward whatever had spooked her.

Chapter 30

Casper

We staggered our departures, driving in and out of the club gates over and over using different cars and some of the women to cover our tracks, and it was dark by the time we reached Portland.

Poet knew the area pretty well, and had decided that we'd meet up outside a McDonald's that turned out to be less than a mile from the warehouses. Half the lights in the parking lot were burned out, and there was a row of overgrown trees at one edge of the lot that hid us in plain sight. It was insane how smart the guy was; I had no idea how he would have known in advance how deserted it would be that time of night. The guy's instincts were always spot-on, though, and while I didn't understand how he'd picked the perfect place to meet up, I also wasn't surprised.

So far we hadn't heard anything from the boys we'd left down south, which meant dick in the larger scheme of things, but still made us feel like we'd gotten away clean.

The boys hadn't had any problems giving up their phones,

but I'd stayed completely out of those conversations and kept mine hidden in my pocket. I was still a prospect, no matter how trusted I was, and I knew if I tried to tell the patched-in members what to do, they would have balked for that reason alone. I didn't want to be the cause of someone getting killed because they were too stubborn to listen to someone they didn't respect, or refused to give up theirs if I wasn't giving up mine. Didn't matter that I was supposed to have mine and they weren't; I was still just a prospect to them.

"Doc, you got everything you need if shit goes south?" Slider asked quietly as we walked up to the window of the Jeep he and Smokey were riding in.

"Fuck, Slider." Doc shook his head. "It's not like I'm driving a fuckin' ambulance here, but I can probably patch some shit up if I need to."

"All I can ask for," Slider assured him. "You and Smokey stay here and wait for my call."

We made our way around to all the vehicles, speaking quietly as Slider gave directions for the—what the hell was it? Assault? I guess that was as good a word as any. Fuck, I hoped that they didn't see us coming. I wasn't trained for this shit.

When we reached Poet and Grease, I left Slider by Poet's window and walked around to where Grease was smoking on the passenger side.

"You ready, little brother?" he asked.

"Guess so."

"You'll do all right," he told me with a nod. "Follow Slider and keep your eyes open."

"That's the plan."

"Usually have Tommy at my back, feels fuckin' weird that he ain't here." He took a deep inhale of the cigarette. "Know we couldn't bring him, the man's a loose fuckin' cannon, but shit if it don't feel off."

"Hopefully he's watching over the women and not drunk off his ass," I replied.

"No shit."

"If something happens—"

"Don't," he said, cutting me off. "You don't have to ask me that shit, and if you go into this with your head in Eugene, you're a fuckin' dead man."

"Fuck," I mumbled.

"Looks like Slider's loading up, better get to your rig. Feels fuckin' off not being on my bike. This whole fuckin' thing feels off."

I tapped the hood of the car as I started around it, but before I could climb back into the van, I heard Grease calling out behind me.

"Head down, little brother."

"You too," I called back.

The warehouses were less than a mile away from where we'd met up, and before I knew it we were parking in a shitty little strip mall only a block away from the front gates. The night had grown dark, and as we climbed out of our rigs, I couldn't shake the feeling of someone watching us.

Jesus Christ.

"You feel that?" Slider asked quietly.

"Yeah," I mumbled back.

If it hadn't been so dark, I doubt we would have seen anything. We would have walked into a goddamn trap.

"The fuck?" Slider hissed before moving quicker than any man I'd ever seen. His knife was out and sliding into Ramon's lower back before I could even process what was happening. As Ramon's phone dropped to the ground, the screen lit up his face, and I had to look away from the desperation there.

Fuck. *Fuck.*

"The fuck is wrong with you?" Slider asked, holding Ramon up by his hair as the rest of the men came running.

"Daughter's at the University of Portland," Ramon rasped. "Didn't have a choice."

"You had a choice, motherfucker," Slider growled back. "Casper, he get that text out?"

I grabbed the phone off the ground and scrolled through the still open screen to find that he'd only typed out a few words but hadn't sent it yet. I looked through his history, shaking my head in defeat.

"He's lucky Tommy didn't find this shit," I mumbled under my breath, then answered Slider. "Nah, nothing tonight. We're good."

"I'll take care of your family," Poet told Ramon quietly. "Though you sure as fuck don't deserve it."

Ramon gave a thankful nod, his entire body going slack in resignation. The lack of resistance or fight surprised the shit out of me. I doubted I'd be so fucking calm in his situation, but I also knew he must have balls of steel if he was willing to betray the club and then spend months acting as if he weren't.

Slider pulled the knife out of his back with a hard jerk, and I felt the urge to vomit and had to look away as he used it to cut Ramon's throat. His gaze never left Ramon's and though his face was emotionless, the betrayal and remorse in Slider's eyes was hard to miss. He didn't want to do it. He had to.

We stripped Ramon of weapons and ID, and then carried his body through the hole I'd cut in the fence over a week before, leaving him just inside. We'd grab him on our way out and take him back to Eugene with us if we could, but I knew we couldn't just leave him in the van for anyone to find. The entire situation had me in a cold sweat, and by the time we'd taken up position to take out the guards at the exits of the warehouses, I could feel it trickling down my back.

The first guards had to go down quietly so they wouldn't sound an alarm, so Poet, Grease, Dragon, Samson, and Slider took care of those on their own. I was okay with a gun, but I was glad as fuck that I wasn't expected to do those outside guards. Killing a man with a knife wasn't something I looked forward to.

As our group moved through the warehouse with the living quarters, I was surprised at how quiet it was. There were rows and rows of pallets wrapped in plastic filling the area, but no more guards or workers in sight. It was fucking eerie.

There was a TV on upstairs, and we heard it as we hit the first landing, walking as quietly as we could across the metal walkway. I had the unwelcome thought that I really hoped it wasn't one of those kid shows that Will watched. *Fuck.* There had been no indication whatsoever that the McCaffertys had kids. I didn't know why it was messing with my head so bad.

After all the preparation, stepping into the brothers' living room was pretty fucking anticlimactic. If the way they sat in their recliners in their underwear were any indication, we shouldn't have worried that they knew we were coming. They didn't even notice us at first, they were so fucking toasted from their own supply.

Slider and Dragon raised their guns and set them at the back of their necks at the same time.

"You don't fuck with family," Slider whispered, his voice making me shudder.

They startled and began to rise, but before they'd gotten more than an inch from their seats, the sounds of simultaneous gunshots had blasted through the room.

They hadn't given the brothers any time to plead their case or reach for the pieces I could see tucked down near the arms of their chairs. It was finally over. Thank Christ.

The other men were standing near the door watching Dragon and Slider, looking relieved that we'd finished what we came for, and none of the dumb assholes were watching the back hallway.

I saw her standing there in the dark an instant before Slider did and moved to call out, but before I could, her gun was in the air and pointed toward us. The sound of gunshots filled the room again and I couldn't even look at Slider as he was hit in the thigh and dropped beside me. My eyes were filled with the beautiful woman in front of me who'd dropped her gun and was using her hands to try to stem the blood running from the hole in her chest.

The hole I'd put there.

"Shit!" Dragon hissed, unbuckling his belt as he dropped down next to Slider.

I was frozen, staring at the woman as she dropped to her knees.

"Carmella?" Samson asked, his face drawn in confusion.

"Oh, fuck no." Slider groaned from the floor beside me. "What the fuck were you thinking, sweetheart?"

My mind raced with questions, but I couldn't make a sound as I watched her slump against the wall. What the hell had just happened? Who was she? Shit! Who the fuck had I just shot?

The rest of the men poured into the doorway, their relief palpable until they took in Slider and the woman on the floor. I stumbled to the side and braced my forearm against the wall, as looks of confusion and horror crossed the normally emotionless men's faces.

What the hell had I done?

Chapter 31

Farrah

I got to my feet shakily, keeping the quilt wrapped firmly around me as I faced the corner of the house. I couldn't see anything at first, but within seconds a familiar shape stepped into the light and I felt my shoulders slump. Cody, thank God.

"Hey, Ladybug," he called out. He looked exhausted as he walked toward me. "Time to go home."

My feet flew across the scarred wooden porch as his steps sped up, and within seconds his arms were tight around me, his face in my neck.

"I'm so glad you're here," I whispered, wrapping my arms around his head, holding him against me, and he shuddered.

"What's wrong, handsome?" I asked.

"Need to get you home, baby," he answered gently, rearing back against my arms so he could look me in the eye. He let go of my waist before I was ready, and his entire body was jittery as he ran his hands over his head.

I stumbled as he suddenly grabbed my hand and started towing me toward the back door, grabbing the quilt as we passed it. "What's going on? What's the hurry?"

"Slider's asking for you."

I dug my heels into the worn linoleum as we reached the kitchen, jerking my hand out of his.

"And?" I asked, crossing my arms as he turned to face me.

Gram and Lily stood from the table as we reached it, their eyes filled with a mixture of relief and concern as Cody and I stared at each other.

"Farrah." He paused, a large sigh lifting his chest. "Got shit taken care of, but we had some problems."

My heart started racing, but I tried to keep any trace of concern from my face. I didn't care what happened to Slider. I hated him—no, that wasn't right—I was indifferent. Yeah, that was better. He didn't matter to me at all. He was a sperm donor.

I couldn't help swallowing hard as they watched me.

"You're okay? Grease is okay?" I asked, lifting my chin.

"Yeah, Ladybug. We're good."

"Then I've got no reason to leave. I need to pack and spend some time with Lily before I can go anywhere."

Cody made a frustrated sound in his throat, almost a growl, and my chin lifted even further.

"I can get your things, Farrah," Gram said.

"I'll be up next week and we can have a nice visit," Lily said at the same time.

My head jerked toward them, betrayal washing through me. They might as well have just kicked me out, but both of their faces were wreathed in concern as they looked between Cody and me. Gram's hand had lifted to her mouth, rubbing at her bottom lip in a nervous gesture I was familiar with, and my stomach sank.

"What? Is Slider dying or something?" I asked flatly.

My words must have hit some trigger that I hadn't known existed, because Cody snapped.

"Get the fuck upstairs and get dressed!" he shouted, making me flinch as he leaned into my face. "You've got fifteen minutes, Farrah. Fifteen fucking minutes or I'm coming up there to get you."

I whimpered, my eyes wide as I took in his flexing muscles and red face. What had I done? I didn't understand what was happening. When his arm raised to the back of his neck, I flinched again and then turned and ran, silent sobs shaking my body with each step I took away from him. He was scary. For the first time since I'd met him, Cody had actually *scared* me.

I didn't know how to process it, and so, with my quilt downstairs in Cody's hand, my body did the processing for me. The panic attack hit me hard. I stumbled into the wall outside my room, falling to my hands and knees on the hardwood floor with a loud thud.

"Cody!" Gram called from the end of the hallway. "Get your ass over here! Son of a bitch!"

I felt her arms go around me as I struggled to breathe, completely forgetting the normal exercises I used to calm myself down. Slider was dying? I didn't care. I *didn't*. Shit, he couldn't die. I was having a baby. God, why did it hurt so bad? He was nothing. *He was nothing.* And why was Cody yelling at me? What did I do?

My mind whirled in confusion, my emotions all over the place until I finally reached the point where breathing was my only concern. I felt my quilt wrap around me, and my body was lifted and carried into my room.

"Breathe, Ladybug," Cody urged as Lily pressed a small

paper sack to my face. "You're okay, baby. You're okay."

Cody took over holding the bag, then the quilt was flipped over our heads, encasing us in a multicolored cocoon. The sun coming through my window streamed through the quilt, and I traced the stitching with my eyes. My entire body was stiff as I tried to ignore the way Cody was pressed up against me, holding the bag to my face.

He did this. He was the one who walked into my sanctuary and gave me the first panic attack I'd had in months. He was the one who'd screamed at me.

With the bag over my face, reminding me to take deep breaths, I was able to regulate my breathing faster than I'd ever done before, but it still took a while.

"I'm sorry. I love you. I'm sorry," Cody repeated into my hair, dropping the bag from my face to wrap both arms around me.

I was determined to ignore him, too mad and confused to give an inch. But then, quietly and without any warning, his breath hitched in his chest and he moaned quietly, pressing his forehead against my crown.

"Cody?" I whispered.

"I missed you," he said, his voice low. "Fuck, I missed you. I'm sorry, baby. I shouldn't have yelled at you."

I heard footsteps leave the room, and when the door closed quietly and I was sure we were alone, I gently pulled the quilt off our heads.

"Are you okay?" I asked, my breath still unsteady.

"Yeah, just tired. Fuck, I should be asking *you* that." He took a deep breath. "I know you don't wanna go, baby, but we need to head to Eugene. Slider needs surgery and he's fucking refusing to sign the paperwork before he talks to you."

"That's bullshit."

"I know it is—he's a fucking idiot. But you still have to go, Ladybug. A lot of people are depending on him, and the man's gonna lose his leg if he doesn't get that shit taken care of—"

"Okay, I'll go," I said, cutting him off. I didn't want to hear any more about Slider. I didn't know if I could handle it. "But I need to get ready first."

I climbed off his lap, my legs still a bit unsteady, and he reached out to grip my hips. Thank God for the sweatshirt I'd worn to bed last night, hiding the new bulges I was sporting. I hadn't thought about it when I'd first seen him, too intent on getting as close to him as I could, but as he watched me gathering my clothes to take with me to the bathroom, I prayed that he wouldn't notice the changes.

This was the absolute last way I wanted him to find out about our child.

"You look good," he commented, leaning his elbows on his thighs.

"Uh, thanks," I mumbled back, hurrying toward the door. "I'll be back in a couple minutes. I'll go grunge today, so I won't have to do my hair."

"Okay, Ladybug," he said tenderly, his small grin completely at odds with his slumped shoulders. "Go fix your war paint."

I gave him a small smile before hurrying out of the room.

As soon as I reached the bathroom, I closed the door behind me, locking it for the first time since I'd arrived at Lily's. I hadn't worried if one of the old ladies would walk in on me; we were all girls, after all. I wasn't even sure if the thing worked, but I was afraid if I tested it, I'd look like I had something to hide, so instead I just watched the door nervously the entire time I got ready. Thankfully, I'd packed a flannel shirt and some old baggy jeans in my suitcase, even though I hadn't planned on wearing them, and by the time I was dressed and ready, my weight gain was pretty well camouflaged. I was ready . . . even if I didn't *feel* ready.

Cody didn't say a word as I kissed Gram and Lily good-bye, and soon, my head was stuffed into a helmet and I was on the back of his bike, riding gingerly down Lily's bumpy driveway. I forced myself to keep my eyes straight ahead, afraid if I glanced back for even a second, I'd completely lose it.

Things were happening fast, and scenarios raced through my head the entire way home as I tried to keep my body from pressing into Cody's back. I did a pretty good job of keeping a little space between us, but as we climbed off the bike in the hospital parking lot, my muscles burned in protest. He looked at me oddly as I pulled off my helmet, but I didn't acknowledge it. I was already bracing myself for my meeting with my father, and I wasn't doing a very good job of controlling my breathing.

Shit, it wasn't like he could do anything worse to me, right? I mean, the blowup at the club had been pretty epic and I doubted he could top that, especially laid up in a hospital bed with a bullet in his thigh. As Cody grabbed my hand and led me into the elevator I took a deep breath, praying that I could continue to do so. I just needed to get in and get out, no drama and no panicking.

"You grabbed my quilt, right?" I asked nervously as the doors opened to a hallway full of bikers and their old ladies.

"It's in my saddlebag," Cody assured me, squeezing my hand.

My stomach started cramping, and I felt beads of sweat form on the back of my neck as the bikers parted like the Red Sea, forming a clear path to Slider's hospital room. I felt naked as they stared at me, and tried to pull out my trusty mask, but I couldn't do it. I couldn't find the calm facade I'd used as protection for years. What was wrong with me? *Oh my God.*

No. *No.* I refused to give them the satisfaction of seeing me break. I lifted my chin as we passed by them, never meeting anyone's eyes. I was just here to see the sperm donor. I didn't need their approval. I could do it. I knew I could do it.

In and out; no drama, no panicking. I silently repeated the mantra over and over again as Cody opened the door and guided me inside.

Chapter 32

Farrah

"You came," Slider rasped from the bed, his voice forcing my eyes from the gray-speckled floor tiles.

"I didn't realize I had a choice." I glanced at where Vera sat in a chair next to the bed. She looked haggard, her hair in a messy ponytail and a large black sweatshirt hanging off her skinny frame.

The room grew uncomfortably silent as we watched each other, and Cody's hand no longer felt comforting, but heavy on my back. I stepped to the side, moving away from him, but I couldn't go far. The room was so tiny that we couldn't even close the door, and the sounds from the group outside made me feel even more unhinged.

"Give us a minute," Slider ordered Vera and Cody, never looking away from my face.

"Baby—" Vera tried to argue.

"A minute, Vera," he stated firmly.

Cody reached out and squeezed my bicep before stepping

out, and I scooted even closer to the wall as Vera got to her feet and walked around me.

"Close the door."

"You're awfully good at giving orders when you can't even stand on your own two feet," I bitched, swinging the door shut. It was heavier than I'd imagined.

The room grew quiet again, and I forced myself not to fidget. It was the first time we'd ever been closed in somewhere alone, and I wasn't sure what to do with myself. I couldn't even look at him, instead keeping my eyes on the dry erase board on the wall.

YOUR NURSE TODAY IS **NATASHA**.

Ironic.

"I don't think you're a club whore," he suddenly blurted, startling me.

"Uh, okay." When he didn't say anything else, I turned my eyes toward him. "Is that all you needed?"

"No." His face was weary and his eyes unfocused as he rubbed a hand studded with an IV over his closely cropped beard. "Can you sit?"

"I'd rather not." That chair was way too close to him.

"Fuck."

Slider was as uncomfortable as I was, and it comforted me as much as it pissed me off. Why the hell had he summoned me if he didn't have anything to say?

We sat in silence for a moment, the second ticking by before he looked away and muttered, "I love ya."

"What?" I screeched. The door slammed into my back as someone tried to force their way in, and I stumbled before catching my footing.

"Get the fuck out!" Slider yelled, his face immediately contorting into a grimace.

The door behind me slammed shut again, and I turned my head to watch it wearily before stepping back against it.

"Jesus Christ!" he mumbled.

"Can you just say whatever the fuck you need to say? I'd like to go home to my apartment sometime this year. My houseplants are dying."

"If you had any houseplants, they're fucking dead as shit by now," he said flatly.

"Seriously, Slider. What do you want?"

I slid my hands into the back pockets of my jeans just to do something with my hands, then immediately pulled them out as I saw where his gaze had landed. I'd unconsciously emphasized the roundness of my belly.

"Casper's?" he asked quietly, glancing up at the door behind me.

I gave him a curt nod. "He doesn't know yet."

"Bet he'll be happy."

"Maybe."

"Gotta learn to trust him."

I laughed humorlessly.

"I love ya," he repeated, stronger this time. "I've always loved ya. No matter where you were, no matter what was happening. If I'd known—" He stopped to clear his throat. "I didn't know, Farrah. That's the fucking truth. Your mother, she came back with the cops, and I thought she'd changed her mind. Vera was goddamn inconsolable, and at first I was just waiting to hear from her. Natasha was clearing our fuckin' bank account left and right, up until she gave you to us. When she didn't come back around asking for money, I thought maybe she'd decided to keep ya. Wanted to be a mom or some shit."

"You didn't look for me," I reminded him.

"I did. I did fuckin' look for ya. I never stopped lookin'! She was a fuckin' ghost. She didn't hook up with Gator 'til you were what? Twelve? How the fuck would I think to look right under our noses? Who the fuck is stupid enough to start messin' with the same fuckin' club you were hidin' from?"

"Natasha," I answered. "Obviously."

"Sweetheart, the minute I knew where you were, I fuckin' came to you. You remember that?"

He was saying all the right words, pushing all the right buttons, and I was so fucking torn. My entire life I'd been told that my father hadn't wanted me. That he was dangerous. That he'd kill me. And now, here was this man, laying it all out for me—completely fucking sincere—and I didn't know what to do with that.

So I bluffed. "Three months ago—"

"No. No, fuck that." His hand formed a fist on the bed, and I couldn't look away from the veins bulging in his forearm. "I did what I had to do to keep you fuckin' safe. I'm not apologizing for that."

My gaze snapped to his. "What?" I asked in confusion.

"We had a fuckin' mole, Farrah. Fuckin' killed me to do it, but you weren't safe there."

"What?" I whispered again.

"Had to get you outta that clubhouse."

"No."

"Couldn't see who it was, didn't know where the threat was coming from."

"No."

"Had to make it look like I didn't give a shit."

"No."

"Stop saying no, goddamn it. I did what I had to do, and

you're fuckin' standin' here lookin' at me, which means it worked."

I stepped forward to grab the edge of the bed to steady myself, and watched in horror as Slider tried to climb from the bed, pulling at his IVs.

"Stop! What are you doing?" I hissed.

"Sit the fuck down before you fall down!" he ordered. He was scowling, but it didn't hide the fear in his eyes.

"Fine!" I snapped back, taking a deep breath as I rounded the bed and sat in the chair Vera had been sitting in.

"This is so fucking confusing," I mumbled, rubbing my forehead with the tips of my fingers. My head had begun to pound, and my stomach was getting more and more upset the longer I was in the room.

"It ain't confusin', baby girl," he told me quietly. "I've loved ya since before you were born, and I'll love ya after I'm six feet under. Only thing you gotta think about is what you wanna do with that."

"I don't ..." I shook my head, trying to untangle my thoughts. "I'm not calling you Dad."

Slider burst out laughing. "Don't expect ya to."

"I just—this is a lot to deal with. Okay? And shit, I mean, I know you're hurt and everything, and I know you're hoping for some father and daughter dance through the wildflowers." I met his eyes and put my hand on my rounded belly. "I've got a lot of my own shit I have to deal with. I don't have room for you."

His face fell, and I knew then that he'd been hoping for a different outcome. I just couldn't give it to him.

"Thank you for telling me ... all this," I said, standing from my chair. "Maybe I'll stop by after you've broken out of here."

"You'd be welcome," he replied gruffly.

I turned around and reached for the door, but I couldn't help but turn back one last time as I opened it. The look on his face killed me. He'd laid himself bare, something I instinctively knew he'd never done before, and I'd rejected him.

"Sign the papers and get your leg fixed, old man."

He nodded and looked away. That was my cue to leave.

"Take me home," I ordered Cody as I strode out of the room and straight for the elevators. Before I could reach them, wiry arms were wrapped around my waist, halting my progress.

"Farrah!"

I jerked to a halt and looked at Cameron in confusion, and then for the first time that day I felt a wide smile stretch my face. Man, he was a sight for sore eyes.

"Hey, dude! How've you been?"

He shrugged. "Bored as hell."

"Watch your mouth." There was no heat in my words. Shit, I'd missed that boy. We'd talked a few times while I was gone, but never for very long. There was something going on with him, something I couldn't pinpoint, and it had almost seemed like each time we'd spoke he was choosing his words very carefully to say what I wanted to hear.

"Are you going home? Can I come with you?" His arm tightened around my waist as the elevator doors opened, and I glanced at Cody to see his face completely emotionless.

My attention was brought back to Cameron when his arm bumped my belly deliberately, and as his brow creased in question, I shook my head once at him in warning. Shit, at this rate, everyone was going to know about the baby before Cody.

"I'll come get you tomorrow. Okay, bud? We'll hang out then."

Cody walked into the elevator and held the door as Cameron's face fell.

"Yeah, okay," he answered quietly.

"Tomorrow, bud. I promise," I whispered, giving him a squeeze. "I need to talk to Cody tonight."

I let go of Cameron and made my way into the elevator, but as we rode it to the first floor, Cody and I didn't say anything. We didn't speak the entire way home, and nervousness was like a pit of snakes in my belly, making me so nauseous that I'd broken out in a cold sweat by the time we walked into my apartment.

The place smelled musty, but someone must have come in and took out the garbage, because thankfully it didn't stink to high heaven. I dropped my purse on the kitchen table and turned to say something to Cody, but he'd set my quilt on the back of the couch and wasn't moving into the room.

"What's up?" I asked.

"Gonna run to the club for a bit."

"*Now?*"

"Yeah, baby. Got some shit to do."

My shoulders dropped, disappointment feeling like a heavy weight on my chest. I hadn't seen him in months. What the hell was he doing?

"Will you be back later?" I asked awkwardly, trying to think of some reason I could ask him to stay without blurting out the news of our upcoming delivery or vomiting on the floor. My stomach was seriously turning by that point, and I could feel my face beginning to sweat. Shit, this wasn't how our reunion was supposed to go.

"Yeah, Ladybug. I'll come back later tonight."

Cody didn't come to kiss me good-bye, but at that point I wouldn't have welcomed his face anywhere near mine. I was taking deep breaths, in through my nose and out through my mouth, trying to keep the bile in my throat from erupting.

He turned and walked out the door, and I could hear him locking it from the outside as I stood frozen in place. As soon as his footsteps faded away, I grabbed my purse and rushed into the bathroom.

After the first round of vomiting, I felt a little bit better, so I pulled my hair out of its bun and got to work. I had doubles of almost all of my toiletries—that was what happened when you could buy shit for super cheap at the beauty supply store and rarely got rid of anything—and I painstakingly ratted my hair and painted my face. It was slow going since I felt like shit, but eventually, I had a smooth bouffant and smoky eyes, making me feel a little more prepared for my upcoming conversation.

Gram still hadn't gotten back with my clothes by the time I was finished. She'd planned on being only a couple of hours behind me, but maybe she'd decided to visit Callie before she came home. I needed to call Callie, I thought, as I made my way to the couch. Maybe I'd do it in a little while after my stomach had settled.

I took my jeans and flannel shirt off, and wrapped myself in the comfort of my quilt, immediately sliding down so I was resting on my side. My mind wandered lazily through my conversation with Slider, and I tried to think logically about what it all meant, but I was freaking exhausted.

Barely sleeping the last two nights had depleted any reserves I'd built up, and I closed my burning eyes for a moment. I hadn't even realized that I'd fallen asleep until I woke up with a start and threw up my entire way to the bathroom, getting vomit everywhere.

As the sun lowered and the sky grew dark, I waited for Cody to show up, but he never did. Instead, I was alone in the quiet apartment, throwing up over and over until there was nothing left, and still the retching continued.

    What the hell was taking him so long?

After . . .

Chapter 33

Casper

Fuck, I'd fallen asleep at the club.

I rolled over to grab my ringing phone, not bothering to check who it was before answering.

"Yeah?"

"It's Gram. Hey, I can't get a hold of Farrah. Is she with you?"

My body jackknifed into a sitting position, the worry in Gram's voice like a bucket of ice water pouring over my head. "No, she's at home. I slept at the club last night."

"Why the hell would you do that?"

"I had some shit to do here."

"Bullshit," she said. "I knocked on Farrah's door but she's not answering. You still have your key?"

"Yeah, don't you have one?"

"Think I mighta left it at Lily's. I can't find the damn thing anywhere."

"Shit. Okay, I'll go over there now," I told her, pulling on my jeans.

"Hurry, son. Something's not right."

"I'll have her call you when I get there. I'm sure everything's fine," I reassured her before hanging up.

Why the hell wasn't Farrah answering her phone? This felt a whole hell of a lot like the shit we used to deal with when she went off the rails; I couldn't remember the number of times Gram had called me to see if I knew where Farrah was. I usually had, since I'd followed her ass around like a lost puppy.

I knew that Gram hadn't consciously appointed me Farrah's watchdog, but resentment still hit me out of nowhere when I thought about all the time I'd spent chasing after her. I didn't have time for her shit anymore; bigger things were going on than her finding out her daddy loved her. No, I was worried for no reason. My head was all over the place, but I knew she wouldn't fall back into her old habits. That wasn't her anymore.

It only took me about twenty minutes to get to Farrah's apartment, and as I opened up the front door, the first thing that hit me was the smell. Fucking disgusting.

Fucking disgusting, but familiar.

Goddamn it.

She'd thrown up all down the hallway, and I had to breathe through my mouth and step around spots of it on the carpet as I made my way to her bedroom. My emotions were swinging between overwhelming fear that she'd killed herself, and fury that she'd done this again. So when I saw her kneeling in front of the toilet, safe and looking like shit, fury won out.

I laid into her, pissed as hell and completely unfiltered. What the fuck was she doing to herself? She'd promised that she was done with the drugs and booze, yet here she was, too fucking wasted to even make it to the bathroom before losing her shit. I vaguely wondered who she'd been partying with, but had to focus on anything else when the thought of her being trashed with some other guy made me see red. What the fuck was I doing?

She wasn't answering me, too drunk or high or whatever the fuck she was to give me a coherent answer, and I'd had enough.

Why the hell was I even still standing in her apartment? With absolute certainty, I knew that I'd never again be the guy that watched her get so wasted that she couldn't hold up her own head. I couldn't do it. My head was fucked up enough; my dreams the night before filled with the woman I'd killed. I couldn't be Farrah's fucking savior again.

Frankly, I just didn't have it in me, and I hated myself for it.

I turned and walked out the door, ignoring her as she tried to call me back. We'd been down that road before, her begging me in her drunken stupor to take care of her, to love her, to make everything better. Hadn't she figured it out yet? I didn't make shit better. I could barely take care of my fucking self; taking care of someone else was completely beyond my capability.

I hated to do it, but I decided I'd call Gram. She could take care of it so I could stay far, far away from it.

I left the door unlocked as I left her apartment, but I couldn't make myself leave once I'd climbed on my bike. My hands were shaking so badly, it looked like I was having a seizure. I needed to go back up there. I did. She needed me, and I'd left her. Could I really make myself leave when she was in that shape? God, it had been worse than I'd ever seen her.

I loved her so much, and my determination to let her figure her own shit out was faltering. Maybe it was just a small setback. Maybe I'd misunderstood. No, no, I couldn't think like that. I knew what I'd seen. But if I took care of her this time—from the very beginning, instead of cleaning up after her—maybe I could stop it before it got bad.

I shouldn't have left her the day before. I'd been selfish, needing a little time to myself, and I'd spent the day on my bike instead of making sure she was okay. I'd known that whatever went on with Slider would mess with her head, but I'd been too stuck on my own shit that I hadn't given it a second thought when I'd left her standing in the middle of her kitchen.

Had I done this? Had she needed me and I hadn't seen it? She'd seemed okay when she'd left Slider's room the day before, but I knew, I *fucking knew* how well Farrah hid her emotions. I should have taken better care of her. I should have looked below the surface.

Goddamn it.

I climbed back off my bike and froze as I watched Gram leave her apartment and run toward Farrah's, her cell phone pressed to her ear.

Jesus Christ.

I started running.

Gram left the door wide open behind her, and I raced through the apartment, ignoring the mess as I made it back to Farrah's bedroom.

She was on the floor and she wasn't moving.

"Where the fuck were you?" Gram yelled, brushing Farrah's tangled hair away from her face. "I asked you to check on her!"

"I did." My mind spun as I tried to process what I was seeing. Farrah was on her side, breathing slowly, her skin clammy and pale, but that wasn't what had caught my attention.

Her belly was rounded, thicker, and her tits were too.

No.

I dropped to my knees.

No!

"You left her like this? What the hell is the matter with you?"

"I didn't—" I felt my chest heaving, unable to catch my breath. "I thought—"

"Goddamn it, Cody," Gram said tersely as the sounds of an ambulance grew closer. "I warned you! I specifically warned you about taking off when she needed you." Her voice rose with every word. "You can't keep running off when shit gets hard!"

I made a noise in my throat, somewhere between a moan and a sob, and moved closer to Farrah. "You're okay, Ladybug," I whispered, ignoring Gram as I lifted Farrah from the floor, making her whimper. "You're okay. I've got you, baby."

We'd just climbed to our feet, Farrah in my arms, when the paramedics came through the front door. It felt like it took them hours to place her on the stretcher and strap her down, and she moaned deeply as they forced her body to flatten out. She'd been curled around our baby in the fetal position, and even though she wasn't conscious, she was somehow aware that whatever protection she'd been providing to our child was being taken away.

"One person can ride with her," the lady paramedic informed us.

Gram spoke up immediately. "I'll go. Cody, your sister's next door with Will. Go get her and follow us there."

I wanted to be the one with Farrah, but I think I was still too shell-shocked to argue as they left the apartment—taking the love of my life with them.

Chapter 34

Farrah

I woke up slowly, memories of fading in and out of consciousness after Cody left me filtering into my mind.

Shit.

I barely remembered being in an ambulance with Gram, and then the bright lights and water-stained ceiling of the hospital before everything went blank. My hand automatically went to my waist, the IVs in my arm pulling at my skin as I reached it.

Thank God. My belly was still tight. That meant she was still in there, right? I would have felt it if she were gone.

My eyes opened slowly, and I took in the room around me. It looked a lot like Slider's had, and I had the fleeting thought that we were in the same hospital, before movement from the side of my bed caught my attention.

"Hey, Ladybug." Cody's voice was quiet, and I squeezed my eyes shut at the pain in his voice. "I'm so glad you're awake."

"What happened?" My voice was scratchy as I tried to form

the words, and my mouth was dry as hell.

"I'm going to tell the nurses you're awake," he said, unfolding himself from the chair.

"No. Just—the baby?" I asked, reaching out to grab his arm.

His face fell, his eyebrows drawing together over bloodshot eyes.

Oh God.

"The baby's fine, Ladybug," he finally rasped. "Let me go get the nurse."

My breath left me in a huge whoosh, making pain radiate from my torso, and I froze as I tried to ride it out. Fuck, that had hurt. I was too afraid to lift the plain white blanket covering me to see what had caused the ridiculous amount of pain, so instead I just relaxed into the bed and waited for the door to open again.

"Dude, you could have just told me you needed some attention," Callie called out as she walked in a few minutes later, a nurse and doctor following her into the room. "You didn't need to be so dramatic."

I gave her a small smile as they surrounded the bed, and her returning smile couldn't hide her worry as she grasped my hand.

"What's up, Doc?" I asked dryly, causing Callie to snicker next to me.

"Looks like you're feeling better," the doctor answered with a smile.

"Define better." I wrinkled my nose. "I feel like I got hit by a truck."

He sat down gingerly at the edge of my bed as the nurse adjusted the tubes hooked up to me. "So, I'm not sure how much you remember, but when you got here you were in pretty bad shape."

"Yeah, I kinda figured that with all the passing out and

stuff," I quipped, going silent as Callie's hand gave mine a warning squeeze. Shit, I hated doctors, and even though I knew he was trying to help, my natural inclination to be a smartass was rearing its ugly head.

"Your grandmother thought at first that you were having a miscarriage, but thankfully that wasn't the case," he went on as if I hadn't said anything. "You actually had a pretty bad case of appendicitis, and we had to take you into surgery to remove your appendix. We went in laparoscopically, and everything went beautifully."

"The baby's okay?" I asked, letting it sink in that I hadn't been losing her like I'd thought.

"Baby is just fine," he assured me, resting his hand on my ankle comfortingly. "Appendectomies are actually one of the most common reasons for surgery in pregnant women. It happens, and you aren't the first one, or even the fifteenth one I've done."

"Oh, okay, good," I mumbled. "Are you sure everything's okay, though? Because I haven't been to the doctor yet, and I didn't know I was pregnant for like, a long time, and I haven't taken any vitamins and—"

He squeezed my ankle gently, making me pause in my rambling.

"Hey, Sam?" he called out to the nurse. "Why don't you go grab the ultrasound machine in room four and bring it in here. I think Mama's gonna feel a whole lot better if she can see her baby safe and sound."

With a nod and a smile, Nurse Sam left the room, passing by Cody and Gram as they filed in the door. Gram had a huge relieved smile on her face as she came closer to kiss me, but Cody's face was tight, his eyes focused on the way the doctor's hand still wrapped around my ankle.

"Hey, good timing," I rasped, bringing Cody's attention to my face. "The nurse just left to get the ultrasound machine so we can see the baby."

His face lost a little of the harshness, and his lips lifted up in a small smile as he moved toward me. Gram and Callie took a step back as he reached the bed, and after Cody gave the doctor a pointed look, he stood up and moved back too.

"Hi," Cody whispered, leaning in to kiss my lips gently. "Sorry I freaked when you woke up."

"That's okay," I whispered back.

"I know I fucked up, Ladybug."

He sighed as he rested his forehead against mine, and the entire room faded away as I reached up and gently cupped the side of his head.

"Shhh, let's just see our baby, right now. Okay? We'll deal with all of that later."

"I fuckin' left—"

"No. We're not doing this right now, okay, handsome? Right now, we're going to see our baby."

His breath shuddered out against my mouth, and I couldn't help myself as I reached up to give him another soft, closed-mouth kiss.

"Here we go!" Nurse Sam called out as she pushed the machine into the room.

"Will you be able to tell if it's a boy or a girl?" Callie asked excitedly, her hand on her own belly in a gesture I was becoming very familiar with.

"Callie?" I asked, raising my eyebrows.

"Yeah, we just found out a few days ago," she answered with a dreamy smile.

"You bitch! You stole my thunder!" I teased, making

everyone in the room burst out laughing.

"You're gonna beat me, though, obviously," she replied as the nurse pulled my gown up and the blankets down, baring my belly and the small incisions there.

"Not unless I'm having twins. You've already got Will," I grumbled as the nurse squirted lube on my belly. Nasty.

"Nope, just one in there," the doctor informed me, rubbing the little ultrasound wand over my belly gently. Suddenly, a rhythmic *whoosh whoosh whoosh* filled the room, making Cody go still beside me.

"That's your baby's heartbeat. Nice and strong," the doctor said.

Cody leaned in and rested half of his ass on the bed beside me, as Gram and Callie huddled in close so we could all see the monitor. Slowly, the unmistakable shape of a baby formed on the screen, and tears filled my eyes.

"The baby's measuring about fifteen weeks. That sound about right?" the doctor asked, moving the wand a little more so we could see the profile of its tiny little face.

"What? Oh yeah. Maybe," I answered, too enthralled with the picture on the screen to care what he was talking about.

"It's a little early still, but if we can get a good look, would you like to know what you're having? Baby seems pretty active, we might get a peek."

"Yes!" Cody and I both answered, causing the doctor and nurse to laugh.

"Okay, so the heart is the little thing that sort of looks like it's blinking," the doctor explained. "Baby's looking really good. Oh, look, he's saying hi."

The baby's hand was waving around near its face, and I watched in awe as the hand moved toward its mouth. Whoa.

Apparently babies sucked on their fingers in the womb.

"It's a boy?" Cody asked, his fingers lacing with mine.

"Oh no, that was a slipup. It's hard calling babies 'it' when you've been doing this as long as I have. I'm normally not the one who does these ultrasounds, and I guess I'm not very good at watching my words," he told us ruefully. "Okay, let's see if we can figure out the gender."

The wand moved across my belly and I tensed in pain, but I didn't stop him. I was on pins and needles, waiting to hear if we were having a girl or a boy. When the doctor finally paused, he clicked a couple things on the little keyboard in front of him, typing out a little message across the top of the screen.

"You see those three little lines?" he asked, a smile in his voice as the words on the screen finally formed a sentence.

I'M A GIRL!

Holy shit. We were having a girl. My face felt like it was going to split in two as I turned my head to Cody.

His gaze was frozen on the screen.

"We're having a girl," I told him, squeezing his hand in mine. He took a deep breath, and his eyes moved to mine for just a second before he bent almost completely in half so he could push his face into the side of my neck.

"Hey? Hey, baby, we're fine," I whispered, my eyes glancing to the people surrounding us.

They must have read the message in my gaze, because the nurse wiped my belly quickly and pulled up my blankets before they all left the room in a rush. When it was just us, I gingerly scooted my body away from Cody to give him more room on the bed.

"Come on, lay down with me," I ordered, using the hand not trapped between us to rub over his head.

"You could have died," he said softly, aligning his body with mine as he lay down beside me. "I left you there and you both could have died."

"We didn't," I whispered back.

"I left you." He leaned up until we were nose to nose, still whispering.

"You came back."

"I didn't make it farther than the parking lot."

"Of course you didn't."

"I'm so sorry."

"*I* knew you were sorry before *you* did."

He dropped his head and ran his nose up the side of mine, and I couldn't stop the sob that rose in my throat.

"I love you so much, Ladybug." He still whispered, but his voice seemed stronger somehow. "I can't believe we made a baby."

"Me either. I was freaking clueless for months."

"No shit? I thought you just waited to tell me." He chuckled softly.

"Yeah, I just thought I was getting fat."

"You're not fat."

"Well, I know that *now*."

We smiled at each other for a moment, reveling in our news and the fact that we were finally lying in a bed together—even if it was a hospital bed—before his face fell again.

"I'll make it up to you," he told me earnestly. "I promise. I won't ever leave you again."

"Okay." I took a deep breath of relief as he leaned down to rest his head next to mine on the pillow.

Did I forgive him? How could I not? I knew what it had looked like, what he'd walked in on. The truth was that sometimes in life, there was just too much history to get past. He'd seen too much and been through too much with me to ever fully trust me again, and I completely understood it.

I knew he loved me as much as I loved him. But that didn't mean that someday, something like this wouldn't happen again.

I'd forgive him then too.

I'd never hold it against him, because I knew without a doubt that at some point in our future, he was going to run again. It was what he did when things got to be too much for him.

So I couldn't fault him for not trusting me, because I didn't trust him either.

Chapter 35

Farrah

My phone blew up the next day as I was leaving the hospital.

    CAM: Hey u ok?

    CAM: Farrah?

    CAM: Its me Cam

    CAM: Are u there?

    CAM: Hello?

    FARRAH: Hey dude, what's up?

    CAM: R u ok?

    FARRAH: Yeah. Small problem with the appendix so they took the sucker out. No worries.

    CAM: Dad wuldnt let me go 2 hospital last night with grease. Srry

FARRAH: Grease was here? I didn't even see him. No worries, bud.

CAM: Ya. Vera called grease cuz slider was freaking out

FARRAH: Crotchety old man. Why was he freaking out?

CAM: Because you were in the hospital. Duh

CAM: What does crotchty mean?

FARRAH: Grumpy.

CAM: O ya. That fits lol

FARRAH: Did Grease take care of it?

CAM: Think so. Didn't here anything else

FARRAH: Good. How have you been? Sorry, dude, you were supposed to come over yesterday.

CAM: Ha. Im fine. Maybe dad will let me come over in a couple days. Prob not tho

FARRAH: Everything okay?

CAM: Ya. Hes a dick

FARRAH: Careful, bud. Don't get in trouble

CAM: Ill erase my texts

FARRAH: Not what I meant—but that's probably a good idea

CAM: Wish I didn't have to listen to him

FARRAH: He'll come around. You guys are dealing with a lot.

CAM: I wish he would have died not my mom

FARRAH: Don't say that, dude.

CAM: K

CAM: I gotta go help brenna talk 2 u l8r

FARRAH: Okay. Stay out of trouble so you can come hang out.

CAM: Ill try

My stomach was in knots when he stopped texting. Cameron was usually pretty easygoing, and he'd never complained to me before. I wondered if it was the anonymity of texting that had him so chatty, or if things were getting worse for him.

My house had become his safe haven before I'd left for Lily's, and the thought of him having nowhere to go for the past few months made me sick. I'd been selfish, I should have called him more, I should have checked in more often. Who was taking care of him? I knew Tommy wasn't any better from the way Callie had described things.

The dude had seriously fallen off the deep end when his wife and kids were killed, and I couldn't fault him for that. But I did fault him for ignoring his remaining child. Tommy just seemed to ignore the fact that Cameron needed him, preferring to drown his sorrows in alcohol and disappear for days at a time, even during the lockdown. It was fucking frustrating.

I wished I could just take Cam home with me and be the parent I knew he needed.

Chapter 36

Farrah

"I need to get out of this motherfucking cock-sucking bed!" I yelled to the ceiling in annoyance.

Cody had just left for the morning, and I could hear Gram making breakfast in my tiny kitchen.

"Then get your ass out of bed!" Gram yelled back.

"I've got a fucking cramp!" I moaned, rubbing my calf gingerly as I tried to flex my foot.

Shit, when the doctor had told me when I left the hospital that my recovery time would be minimal, I'd figured that it would be smooth sailing from then on. I'd been up and around the house after a few days, and within a couple of weeks I'd been off shopping with Gram, hanging with Lily when she'd come up to visit as promised, watching movies with Cameron and driving over to see Callie and Will. I'd felt fantastic.

But as time went on, I felt less and less fantastic due to a number of different factors. My back hurt. My ribs hurt. I got excruciating cramps everywhere from my ass cheeks to my feet, no matter how many bananas I ate. Yeah, bananas were supposed to help with muscle cramps—who knew? On top of all that, my eyes became super sensitive to sunlight for some ungodly reason, and I had to wear the blackest shades I could find, even when the weather was overcast.

I was so done being pregnant, and I was only thirty-four weeks. God, the next six weeks were going to blow big, hairy donkey dick.

Oh yeah, and I'd started cursing like a goddamn sailor because my mood swings were so extreme it was either do that or scream at the top of my lungs, and I'd already had the neighbors complaining to the landlord. Twice.

I'd seen Slider and Vera a few times in the last few months, and I couldn't say that our relationship had progressed, but it had gotten easier to be around them. We weren't quite friends, but maybe in the future when I wasn't dealing with Cody's spawn turning me into a maniac, I'd be able to make the first move. Maybe. I had to admit they were being cool, though, in a way that I knew they were letting me set the pace.

The biggest problem weighing me down, other than the thirty pounds of extra weight I was lugging around, was Cody. He'd been nothing but helpful since the moment I'd left the hospital, but that was it. He was helpful, but he wasn't anything else that I'd come to expect from him.

He barely touched me, and we hadn't had sex in so freaking long that if a hymen grew back from lack of penetration, the doctors would be encountering a virgin birth in six weeks. It was frustrating as hell and I didn't understand it, but I knew with complete certainty that it didn't have anything to do with me. There was something weighing on him, and after hearing about the member and his daughter who'd betrayed the Aces, I wondered if that had anything to do with it.

The playful, sexy Cody I'd fallen for was gone, and left behind was a man who rarely showed any emotion at all. He was good to me, and I really had no room to complain, but I missed him.

I missed him kissing me like he couldn't get enough of me, and copping a feel as I walked by. I missed the way he would waggle his eyebrows at me like a complete idiot when he was teasing me, or kiss a scowl off my face when he'd done something especially irritating. I missed the way he would piss me off and then fuck me into forgetting what I was mad about, like he'd done that one day . . .

• • •

I had been listening to the Beatles while standing at the sink in the kitchen, completely irritated that Cody couldn't remember to rinse a single dish. I'd been trying to peel dried chili off the bottom of a bowl, when he walked up behind me.

His hands grasped my hips through the long summer dress I was wearing, and before I could spin around, he pressed against me, guiding our hips so they were slowly swaying from side to side with the beat of the music.

My breath caught in my throat as I felt him grow hard against my ass.

Then he began to sing, and while his voice usually sounded like a dying hyena anytime he sang along with music on the radio, this time it was so low that he was practically whispering as he used his chin to pull my hair away from my neck.

"Come together, right now, over me," he sang.

How he made the song sexy, I will never understand. But as

he began to pull my dress up and over my hips, I dropped the bowl into the sink with a loud crash, completely absorbed in the way he moved against me, and the feel of his breath against my throat.

Within minutes I had been sitting on the kitchen counter—my irritation completely forgotten—and he had been inside me, chuckling at the way I'd come unglued.

• • •

I shook my head at the memory, a small smile on my face as the cramp finally abated. God, those things freaking hurt.

Gram and I were headed over to Callie's in less than an hour so we could take Will off her hands for the day. Where I'd barely felt any different during the first few months of pregnancy, Callie had had the absolute worst first few months, and things didn't seem to be getting any better. She was into her second trimester, the time period that every pregnant woman looked forward to as the end of her morning sickness, but Callie's wasn't going away. She was still sick all day long, and you could see the weariness on her face no matter what time of day it was, or even if she'd just woken up. She'd pretty much gotten screwed both literally and figuratively this time around. She just lay around the house most of the time, so on top of feeling like she was going to constantly vomit, she also had to deal with the guilt of foisting Will off on family members.

Bottom line: Pregnancy sucked. I was glad mine was almost over.

"Whatcha making?" I asked Gram as I waddled my ass into the kitchen. Shit, my hips hurt today.

"Bacon and eggs," she replied. "You want toast, you make it."

"Wow, someone woke up on the wrong side of the bed this—" My words were cut off by someone knocking on the door. "I'll get it," I grumbled, grabbing my sunglasses from the table and sliding them on.

I couldn't have been more surprised by the visitor than if the pope himself had decided to grace me with his presence.

"Uh, hey?"

"Hi, sorry. I don't have your number or I would have called. Can I come in?" Brenna asked, shifting her baby higher on her hip.

"Yeah, sure," I replied, stepping back from the doorway so she could scoot past me. "You can sit down if you want." She was carrying not only the baby, but a huge bag of crap, and she looked like she was about to fall over.

"Oh, thanks," she said, falling onto the couch with a huff. "God, I don't remember carrying this much crap with Trix."

"Hi, Brenna!" Gram called from the kitchen.

"Hi, Rose!"

"You want something to eat?"

"Oh no, thank you, I'm only staying for a minute."

What the fuck was going on? What, they were buddies all of a sudden? I tossed my shades onto the coffee table, then stood there with a confused look on my face as Gram shuffled around and eventually walked toward the front door.

"Farrah, I'm just gonna go grab Will and bring him back here so you two can visit," she informed me as she picked up her keys. "Look away from the door, you don't have your sunglasses on."

I turned my head away just in time to escape the sunshine pouring into the apartment, before the door was closed again.

"So, I messed shit up with us," Brenna began, speaking so fast that her words tumbled over each other. "I don't have any excuse, except for the fact that I was pregnant and irrational, and worried about Cody. It was stupid. I was an idiot, but I'm hoping we can start over because you seem really cool and Callie seems really cool, and the Aces are a family and I don't want things to be weird forever—"

"Jesus, do you ever take a breath?" I asked in awe.

"Occasionally."

"Okay, well, we're fine. So don't worry about it."

"Oh," she said with a frown. "Well, that was easier than I thought."

"If you would have shown up a few months ago, you'd be leaving here bald after I'd snatched all of that pretty red hair right off your head. But now, eh," I told her seriously, walking to the other end of the couch to sit down. "I've got bigger fish to fry, dude. I'm over it."

"Are you sure? Because I was a total bitch."

"Yeah, you were," I replied with a grin. "It's water under the bridge. Back then, Cody and I had just gotten together, and shit was weird and I was freaking out. Now? I know the dude's not going anywhere. So, we're good."

The lie about knowing Cody wasn't leaving rolled smoothly off my tongue. I'd had years of practice.

"I'm glad," she said with a warm smile. "So, when are you due?"

"Six more weeks," I said with a whine, leaning back into the couch cushions. "It's going to be the longest six weeks of my life."

"Nah, it'll fly by," she assured me, pulling out a little toy for her boy to stick in his mouth.

"He's cute."

"Thanks! He looks just like his dad." She rolled her eyes. "It seems that dominant genes will forever make sure that my children look nothing like me."

We talked for close to an hour before she had to leave, and

by the time she'd left, I was ready for a nap. I was just dropping off when the front door opened again and Cody strode inside.

"Hey, Ladybug. What are you doing sleeping on the couch?" he asked as he made his way toward me, then leaned down to lift me into his arms. "We've got a perfectly good bed in the other room."

"I hate sleeping in there without you," I mumbled, laying my head on his shoulder. "God, I'm so *done* being pregnant."

"Only a few more weeks, beautiful," he reminded me, laying me gently in the bed.

"Will you lay with me for a while?" I asked sleepily.

I could see the indecision in his gaze, his wish to be somewhere else, but I didn't take back my question. If he wanted to be somewhere else, he had to say it; I wasn't going to give him an out.

"Okay, baby," he whispered, his face softening as he slid his cut from his shoulders.

The Aces had patched him in not long after Slider had gotten out of the hospital, but I hadn't gone to the party. I'd still been recovering from surgery at that point, and thinking back, he hadn't invited me anyway. I didn't complain, though, because he hadn't stayed out late that night, and when he'd gotten home, I'd been the one to cover his new tattoos with ointment.

Yeah, tattoos. More than one. He'd gotten the big tattoo that all the guys had on his back that day, but the day before, he'd done something else ...

• • •

"**W**hat is that?" I'd called blearily from the bed as Cody had pulled his shirt off and I caught a glimpse of some sort of bandaging on his chest.

"Lay back down and I'll show you," he'd ordered, unbuttoning his jeans and shoving them down his legs.

I didn't know how he expected me to lie back down when he was giving me a personal strip show. He walked around the far edge of the bed and crawled in beside me, leaning up on one elbow until he was hovering over me, the bandage on his chest right in front of my face.

"Take it off, baby."

"God, I've been waiting to hear those words for freaking months," I teased, watching his mouth pull up on one side in a small grin.

I reached up, feeling proud of myself that I'd made him smile, and gently pulled the tape that held the bright white bandage to his skin. When the tattoo came into focus, at first it looked like scribbly lines. I must have looked confused as hell, because he began to explain.

"The top tattoo is your heartbeat," he said quietly, making my breath hitch in my throat. "I marked the little paper they had hooked to your monitor when you were out, so I knew what part I wanted to use. I didn't really need it, though, your heart sped up whenever I started talking to you, so even if I wouldn't have marked it, I still would have known what piece I wanted."

I reached up to ghost my finger over the tattoo, careful not to touch it. My heartbeat.

"The one on the bottom is our baby girl's from when we had the ultrasound."

My finger ghosted over that one too, but I still couldn't find anything to say.

"They're patching me in tomorrow, and I'll be on the chair for fucking hours getting my back tat, but I wanted yours to be there first."

He had leaned down to kiss my lips, sliding his tongue into my mouth before pulling back again. "You come first, Ladybug, you and our children. Always."

• • •

I smiled at that memory as I snuggled in as close as I could. Cody lay down on his back next to me, pulling the covers over us both.

"Don't leave without waking me up, okay?" I whispered, wrapping my arm around his waist. "I don't like waking up with you gone."

He tightened his arm, understanding the meaning beneath my words. "I'm not going anywhere, baby," he promised.

I fell asleep knowing that I'd wake up with him beside me, but I was under no illusion that he'd always be there.

Chapter 37

Farrah

The last week had been brutal. I was ornery, pissed off, and had a six-pound baby pushing on my bladder about ninety percent of the time, which meant most of my days and nights were spent on the toilet. I was done, done, done with being pregnant.

Don't get me wrong, I was happy as hell that the little nugget was sticking in there, waiting until she was fully ready before she made her appearance ... but *come on*. It was time for her to vacate the premises. Like, yesterday. My due date was only three days away, and I was doing anything and everything I could to get her out.

I dragged Cameron with me all over the neighborhood, walking for hours until I felt like I couldn't take one more step. I ate the spiciest food I could stomach, which did nothing but give me righteous heartburn that kept me awake all night. I'd even tried using castor oil to get things started. After sitting on the toilet for hours, I wouldn't recommend that to anyone.

I was finally at the end of my rope, and I was taking it out on Cody. He had something I wanted.

"Fuck me," I demanded the minute he walked through the door that night.

"What?"

"Fuck me. Get undressed and meet me in the bedroom." I pulled at the elastic top of my strapless sundress and dropped it to the floor, leaving me in nothing but a pair of panties that had covered a whole lot more of my ass a few months ago.

He stared at me, dumbfounded, as his gaze roamed over my body, and he was silent and immobile for so long that I began to get really irritated.

"Strip!" I snapped.

"What the fuck are you doing?"

"Are you joking?" I asked in annoyance. "Hello? I'm practically naked, let's go!"

When he still didn't move, I strode toward him, my huge belly bouncing with each step. "Okay, I guess you can stay mostly dressed," I conceded. "We just need to unbutton your—"

He grabbed my hands in a tight grip as I reached for his jeans, and the pressure on my fingers had my head snapping up in surprise.

"Stop, Farrah! Fuck!"

"What is wrong with you?" I screeched, yanking my hands out of his. "You haven't touched me in months! Is it because of this?" I gestured to my belly. "Because seriously, dude. You put that in there, so you can just deal with it for a couple more weeks!"

"You're beautiful, Ladybug," he answered calmly. "More beautiful than ever."

My breath caught in my throat, and I could have screamed in frustration when I felt tears start falling down my cheeks. "Then what's wrong?"

"Nothing, nothing's wrong."

"Then touch me. Please. I've tried everything. Nothing is getting her out of there!" I started sniffling, my words coming out garbled. "The doctor said sex might work. Please, Cody."

I'd been reduced to begging the man I was living with to have sex with me.

"You want me to fuck you so you'll go into labor?" he asked incredulously, reaching for the button on his jeans. "Well, shit, I'll just drop my pants and you can go to fucking town then!"

That was it. I was toast.

I dropped my face, hiding it behind my hands, and sobbed.

"Ladybug," Cody said with an exasperated sigh, wrapping his arms around my shoulders. "She'll come when she's ready."

"I know!" I wailed, still hiding my face. "I just miss you. It's been so freaking long, and I need you."

"Okay, baby," he replied, rubbing my back gently. "Okay, come on. *Shit.* It's all right. Don't cry."

He leaned down and slid his arm under my legs, lifting me up to carry me like a baby. And even though I was a snotty, crying mess, it felt so good that I couldn't be sorry for it. He smelled like home to me, his familiar cologne and the leather of his cut that I'd grown accustomed to over the past couple of months.

When he laid me on the bed, I refused to let go of his neck, whimpering deep in my throat and pulling him with me until he was kneeling over my body.

"Shhh," he said, shrugging his cut off his shoulders. "I've got you, Ladybug."

He leaned down and kissed my face, running his lips over my cheeks and forehead before meeting my lips and pulling the bottom one with his teeth. "You gotta let go so I can get my shirt off," he whispered.

I immediately let go of his neck, my hands going to the bottom of his shirt as he grasped it behind his neck and pulled it off. When he leaned back down, I could have cried again at the feel of his bare chest against mine. It had been so long since we were that close, and I'd almost forgotten the sensation of the hair that grew in a small diamond on his chest rubbing against my skin.

I raised my head to kiss him again, and before I could do anything, his hands were all over me and he had parted his lips, pushing his tongue against mine. His hands glided down my sides, then back up over my belly, stopping to rub where my belly button had popped out from the pressure on my skin.

"You're so gorgeous, Ladybug," he said on a breath into my mouth as his hands slid up to cup my breasts. My nipples were sensitive as hell, and he used it to his advantage as he ran his fingers over them in feather-light touches, teasing me until my back was arching off the bed.

"God, what is *wrong* with me?" he mumbled to himself, watching his hands on my chest. "I'm an idiot."

I was frantic, wrapping my legs around the back of his thighs and squirming, trying to get his hips closer to mine as he dropped his mouth to my breasts. He used his tongue to flick at my nipples, then closed his mouth around each one, sucking them hard in turn as I writhed and moaned.

When he leaned up and pulled my underwear down my thighs, I sighed in relief. Finally. It was finally happening after months of waiting and trying to be patient, doing everything I could not to take whatever was bothering him personally.

"I like this." He groaned, running his fingers through the closely cropped hair at the apex of my thighs. "It's different."

"I didn't want to wax while I was pregnant. I didn't trust

them not to fuck it up," I explained, my voice hitching as two of his fingers slid inside me.

"Yeah? How do you keep it short? Can you even see down here?" He moved down the bed and lay on his belly between my legs, looking at me as if fascinated.

"I use your beard trimmer," I answered as his tongue took one long swipe at me. "And a mirror."

His head popped up, and his eyes were so dark I could barely see the blue irises in them anymore. "Yeah?"

"It's not easy," I replied jokingly.

"Why do it?"

"I kept hoping—" My voice trailed off, my face growing hot.

"I'm an asshole," he said flatly.

"You're here now."

"Baby, you gotta stop cutting me so much slack. *Fuck*." He dropped his head until it rested at the base of my belly. "You remember when I asked you to fight?"

"Yeah, I remember."

"I need you to do it. My head's so fucked up, Ladybug. I keep messing this up."

"You're not messing it up," I argued.

"You're not getting what you need from me. I'm messing it up." He lifted his head and shook it slowly.

"So, fix it," I whispered, pushing my hand into his hair and gripping it tightly. When I pulled his head to my hips, he growled, and within seconds his tongue was everywhere. He licked and sucked and bit me tenderly, his hands holding my thighs open as he loved on me.

When my orgasm finally rushed over me, I called his name, making noises I didn't even know I was capable of.

"Fuck, you're so goddamn sexy." He groaned, climbing from

the bed so he could take off his boots and drop his jeans and boxers to the floor. "I missed the way you taste."

I smiled blearily at him as he climbed up between my thighs, still feeling hazy from my orgasm. I just wanted to cuddle at that point, my body so boneless I felt like I could slither right off the bed.

"No, you don't, beautiful," he said teasingly as my eyelids started drooping. "Up on your knees."

"Why?" I whined as he used my arms to pull me up.

"You've been on your back too long already, Ladybug," he said, chiding me.

"Have you been reading my pregnancy books?"

"Shut up and get on your knees."

He positioned me so I was sitting on my heels, my hands holding on to the headboard. When I didn't feel him move up behind me, I turned my head, flicking my hair over my shoulder so I could see him.

"Well?" I asked.

"Let me look for a second."

"No. I've been waiting long enough. Get up here," I ordered, making him smile.

I loved the way the skin around his eyes crinkled when he smiled; it was like he didn't just smile with his lips, but his entire face. Gorgeous.

He moved in behind me, and I leaned forward so he could scoot his knees under me and between mine. He ran his hands down my back from neck to tailbone, and tears hit my eyes at the familiar gesture.

"You ready?" he rasped, reaching down to position himself as one of his hands gripped my hip.

"For fucking months now," I smarted back, the words

turning into a yell when he got sick of my smart mouth and jerked my hips down until I was full of him.

"You okay?"

"Stop asking!" I griped, moving my hips against his hands.

"There's my girl," he replied. "Take it, Ladybug."

He let go of my hips, reaching around to hold my breasts and tweak my nipples as I rode him.

Both of us were breathing heavily, and my head fell heavy against his shoulder when his hand slid down my belly in a soft caress and didn't stop until he'd reached where our bodies connected.

"You wanna come again, beautiful?" he asked.

"Yes, please."

"So polite. Where's the filthy-mouthed woman I've been living with for the past three months? Hmm?"

His fingers twisted, and his breath shuddered against my skin before he bit down on the back of my neck, pushing me over the edge.

Holy hell, I'd missed that.

"I love you," I said with a sigh as he held me close and lowered me to the bed.

"I love you too, Ladybug," he whispered into my neck.

Chapter 38

Casper

Farrah was passed out across the bed. She'd moved around so much trying to get comfortable that she'd ended up completely sideways, with her head resting on my lower stomach and her hands in one of my armpits. The way her body was positioned looked ridiculous ... and beautiful. I propped a pillow underneath my head so I could stare.

Her body had grown curvier and curvier as her pregnancy progressed, and it wasn't just her belly. Her ass, legs, arms, and tits had grown too. Even her face had changed, her cheeks rounding out and her lips swollen into a pout that was as sexy as hell. It was like looking at a completely different woman, still just as beautiful, but in a different way.

She looked like some sort of fertility goddess.

I ran my fingers through her hair as she slept, and hated myself.

God, I'd been such an idiot. I hadn't touched her in so long that I'd felt like my dick was going to fall off, but I thought that was what she wanted. After her surgery, she'd been out of commission for about six weeks, and we'd gotten into a pattern by then that I hadn't been able to shake.

Farrah had never been shy about sex. We'd tried everything, and more often than not she'd initiated it. So when she wasn't pushing me or asking for it, I'd assumed that she just wasn't feeling it. And you know what they say about people who assume.

Christ.

I should have known. I really should have. Because here was the thing about Farrah—if she was sure about someone, she was an open book, but if she wasn't sure, she closed up tighter than a bank vault. I *knew* that. But after her discussion with Slider and my complete fuckup, she hadn't been sure about me anymore and I'd missed it. She'd needed the reassurance that I still wanted her in order to get to the place where she'd ask me for what she deserved from me. And I hadn't given her that reassurance.

Instead, I'd walked around on fucking eggshells, trying to show her how much I loved her without stepping on her toes.

My head was still so fucked up from that shit in Portland, I couldn't tell which way was up.

The whole time I was trying to give her fucking space, she'd been waiting for me to make the first move. Me—the guy who had left her on the fucking bathroom floor while her appendix was close to bursting because he thought she'd been out partying. The guy who could have killed her because his head was so far up his ass he couldn't even see what was happening right in front of him. She'd waited for me to figure my shit out and take charge like I had before, but somewhere along the way I'd lost my balls and hadn't done it.

What a goddamn mess.

The woman I'd killed in Portland had been Ramon's daughter, and that shit was messing with my head. I wasn't sure if it would have been easier if she'd just been some McCafferty whore, but I thought it probably would have been. Then I wouldn't have had to deal with the fallout.

Ramon's wife and teenage daughter had been in the club when we'd gotten back, and I'll never forget the sobbing I'd heard when she realized that he hadn't come back with us. We'd ended up leaving his body with his daughter's for the police to find, hoping that they'd assume all the players had been killed for the same reason. Drugs. We'd left him like the traitor he was, and I knew none of the boys felt comfortable with it, including Poet, who'd made the call.

After Poet had ushered Ramon's wife, Roberta, into one of the back rooms, her screams had echoed through the clubhouse.

I'd never forget the sound of that as long as I lived.

I knew logically that I hadn't had a choice. Carmella had shot Slider and wouldn't have hesitated to keep shooting if I hadn't dropped her, but that didn't make it any easier. I'd been raised to protect women, to coddle them and make sure they were safe. It was one of the things that my dad had been absolutely relentless about, teaching me from the time I was old enough to understand that women were made to be protected, that it was my job to look after my sister and any other women in my life.

I'd failed more times than I could count.

I was still failing, and for some reason I couldn't name, it felt like something was coming and I had no clue how to prepare for it.

I turned my head to the side to check the clock, surprised to find it was already close to ten. Farrah had been sleeping for almost three hours already. Apparently the sex hadn't worked to get her labor started. Poor thing, she was miserable. My little princess needed to get a move on before Farrah completely lost it.

I was debating whether I should get up and make her something to eat, or let her sleep, when she began to stir.

"Hey, handsome," she called sleepily, moving her hands out of my armpit. "Did you get any sleep?"

I shook my head, and couldn't help but smile as she crinkled her nose at me. Why was that so fucking cute?

"You've just been watching me sleep like a creeper?"

"Pretty much."

She thought about it for a minute, then smiled and nodded. "I'm okay with that."

"You hungry, Ladybug?" I asked, running one finger down her cheek and into her mouth. God, her lips had been killing me since they'd started to swell up a couple weeks before. I wanted them around my cock.

She sucked my finger into her mouth, smiling around it.

Game on.

"Hands and knees, baby," I ordered, then waited for her to comply before climbing to my knees.

Her eyes were sleepy, looking half-drunk and mysterious, and I wondered if I'd ever completely know the woman in front of me.

I pulled her hair gently from her face as I knelt in front of her, gathering it into a ponytail and wrapping my fingers around it. When she licked her lips, I shuddered.

"Keep your hands on the bed, Ladybug," I warned her. "I don't want you to fall."

I slid one hand over her shoulder, making my way to where my cock rested against my belly, but before I could push it level with her mouth, she'd leaned forward, pulling against the grip I had on her hair to suck one of my balls into her mouth.

"Motherfucker!" I hissed, making her laugh. The vibration of it was like a jolt to my already sensitive cock and it flexed, bobbing against my stomach. "Holy hell, baby," I said with a groan.

She switched to the other side, humming quietly, and my head snapped back. God, that felt incredible.

When she pulled back, it took me a second to get with the program. She tilted her head back as far as it would go to meet my eyes, and the smile on her face made me want to cry like a bitch. She was happy, and it was the first time I'd seen that look on her face in a long fucking time.

"You set the pace," I said, pushing my cock down to her lips. "Don't want you to choke."

She pulled me into her mouth, using her tongue to rub over the sensitive spot right under the head, and I huffed out a shaky breath. She knew exactly what I liked, and there was something to be said about learning a person for months. The sex—any type or variation—just got better and better.

I cupped her face gently, rubbing my thumb over her lips where they were stretched around me.

"Sexy as fuck," I said.

Swaying her hips, she bobbed back and forth, pulling back until she could lick the tip and then sliding forward until I was as far back into her throat as she could stand. She could go deeper, she'd done it before, but I didn't care. It was her show, and while I loved the silky feeling at the back of her throat, I had absolutely no complaints.

My balls drew up tight, and I relished the feeling for a moment before pulling out of her mouth, gripping her hair tightly as she tried to follow.

"No more, Ladybug." I gasped, trying to catch my breath. "Lay down."

She pouted as she followed my direction and lay down on her side, and if my jaw hadn't been clenched tight enough to crack a tooth, I would have smiled.

I leaned down to kiss her, and my cock jumped when she sucked my tongue into her mouth. Reaching behind her, I drew one of her legs up so I could run my fingers over her pussy. Wet. Fuck me.

"You like sucking my cock?" I asked, raising one eyebrow.

"I've missed him," she answered with a shrug.

I laughed. I couldn't help myself. How had we gone so long without this?

"Lift your arm up," I whispered, running my lips up her side. Once her top arm was lying relaxed over her head, I leaned back to take her in.

She was on her left side, her belly resting against the bed, one leg slightly bent, and the other pulled up until her thigh touched her belly. One of her arms was curled under her, pillowing her head, and the other was lifted high, showing off her fucking fantastic tits.

They'd grown a lot. More than I could have ever imagined. They were so big that they sloped toward the bed, resting against each other, something they wouldn't have done before she was pregnant. Her nipples and areolas were darker too, and they'd grown right along with the rest of her tits.

I decided right then that as soon as she had the baby and I didn't have to worry about her on her back for too long, I was going to fuck those tits.

"You want me here?" I asked, running my fingers over her clit and pinching it hard. "Or here?" I slid two fingers inside her. "Or here?" I pulled my fingers back, running them lightly over the small pucker of her ass.

She moaned long and deep, arched her back, and groaned. "Fuck me."

"You didn't answer my question."

"Vagina," she said with a growl as I continued to play.

"Are you a doctor?"

"I'm going to kill you." She moaned in frustration. "Quit fucking around."

"That's my girl. Use your words, Farrah."

She screeched in frustration as I pulled my fingers away, and the hand resting above her head gripped the sheets. "My cunt!"

"God, that dirty mouth is sexy," I said, scooting up her body until I was braced above her and pushing inside.

Then I saw her face more clearly. "Aw, don't cry, baby. What's wrong?"

Tears were running over the bridge of her nose and dripping onto the sheet under her.

"I'm frustrated," she said, then sniffled, arching into me. "Stupid fucking hormones!"

"I was just teasing, Ladybug," I murmured, leaning down to run my lips over the eyelid I could reach as I started to thrust.

"I know. Ah, harder," she demanded.

Leaning back up so I had some leverage, I slammed in harder, trying not to worry that I'd hurt her. She'd tell me if something hurt, right? Yeah, she'd tell me. And, fuck, I didn't want to stop, she felt so good.

As I watched, her face flushed and her eyes closed. She was concentrating hard, trying to get there, but I knew she wouldn't. She needed my hand for that, and I wasn't ready to let her come yet. I started thrusting in short jabs, my eyes locked on the way her tits bounced up and down, and almost paused as her pussy started tightening around my cock in pulsing waves.

Holy shit.

Her moan was high pitched and sounded almost painful as she came around me.

I couldn't stop my orgasm. The surprise of hers and the way her muscles gripped me pulled me right over the edge.

Well, shit. That had never happened before.

"Good Lord." She groaned as I panted above her, not ready to pull out quite yet. "I take it back, these pregnancy hormones are the shit."

"You think you're in labor yet?" I asked, leaning down to rest on my forearms above her so I could reach her lips.

"Nope," she answered against my mouth.

"We'll just have to try again."

"Damn right," she said with a tired smile.

Chapter 39

Farrah

After two days of reconnecting with Cody, I went into labor.

I don't think the sex worked, but the relaxed state of my body probably helped.

It took ten hours from start to finish, and most of those hours were spent walking the maternity floor. So. Very. Boring. Then after getting an epidural—I was no masochist—just fifteen minutes of pushing like my life depended on it and she was there.

My room was full of people, including two nurses, the doctor, Gram, Cody, and Callie. But when they placed my baby on my chest for the first time, everyone else faded away.

She was bald as a cue ball, covered in nasty white gunk, her skin all red and wrinkled. Perfection.

"You did good, Ladybug," Cody murmured, covering my hand on her back with his own.

"I pretty much rocked it." I nodded, sniffling.

The entire room burst into laughter, and I closed my eyes to take it in. I was done. After months of waiting and impatience, she was finally there.

"You're not done yet, Mama," the doctor reminded me, pulling me out of my bliss. Crap.

Cody cut the cord connecting us, and he didn't leave her side as they took her to the side of the room as I finished pushing out all traces of my pregnancy. It was seriously unpleasant.

"Six pounds, eight ounces!" Cody called excitedly.

"We're gonna go outside and give you guys a little time," Gram said, leaning down to kiss my forehead. "You did real good. Way better than Callie."

"Hey! Extenuating circumstances! My guy wasn't there!" Callie argued with a smile, bumping her hip against Gram as she leaned down to give me a hug. "She's gorgeous," she whispered in my ear. "Nice work."

When it was just me and Cody, I scooted gingerly to the side of the bed so he could sit with me. They'd piled shit under me while I was laboring, and like magic, had whisked it all away when I was done, leaving me on clean sheets. Those nurses knew what they were doing.

"She looks like you," I murmured as he handed her to me.

"Yeah." His voice was barely audible as he watched her. "She's got your eyebrows, though."

I searched her face, almost completely devoid of any eyebrows. "How do you know? You can barely see them."

"God wouldn't saddle a girl with these things," he replied seriously, making me smile.

"I can't believe she's finally here."

"Me either. We should probably name her," he reminded me.

We hadn't talked about it, even though people had been asking us her name for months. I didn't know why he'd never brought it up, but I'd been too nervous. It had felt like I'd be jinxing her or something if I named her before she was born. Like tempting fate.

"I want to name her after Gram," I said.

"Yeah?"

There was a knock on the door, and both of us looked toward it as it opened a few inches.

"Can I come in?" Slider called quietly.

He'd been cool, showing up at the hospital after news had spread around the club. He hadn't bothered me, or got in my face, but he'd spent the entire ten hours in the waiting room with Vera and other club members.

My little circle had grown once again over the last few months, the members and their wives slowly but surely connecting with me like they should have in the beginning. It was odd, and I wasn't completely comfortable with it, but I kind of liked it too. It was like a big family, a completely dysfunctional and awkward one.

"Sure," I replied to Slider, glancing up to Cody for affirmation.

"Yeah, man, come on in."

"How you feelin'?" Slider asked as he made his way farther into the room.

"Okay. Tired."

"I bet." He limped nervously toward the bed, trying to hide his unease. The man everyone else feared was uncomfortable around me, and it was just the slightest bit endearing.

"Damn, she doesn't look nothin' like you," he said honestly, immediately snapping his mouth closed in embarrassment.

Cody laughed.

"Nope. Thanks for pointing that out," I answered dryly.

"Fuck." He hissed through his teeth, rubbing a hand over his beard.

"It's fine," I reassured him. "Want to hold her?"

"Uh, no. I better not." He raised his hands out as if holding me off. "You hold her."

"Aw, come on. You're her grandpa," I said in a wheedling tone.

I don't know if it was the drugs they'd given me or the endorphins still flowing through me, but suddenly and without any warning, I realized that I loved Slider. Maybe not the way I'd love a parent—not the way I loved Gram—but maybe like I'd love a distant uncle. One that I knew loved me, but I didn't feel quite comfortable with.

"Her grandpa?" he questioned, his body freezing.

"Uh . . ." I looked to Cody, who was watching me with an amused smile. "Well, yeah. Aren't you? I mean—"

"I can be her grandpa," Slider assured me quickly. "Sure. Yeah."

We watched each other in uncomfortable silence until Cody lifted the baby gently from my arms and climbed off the bed. He walked around to Slider, and without any warning laid her against Slider's chest, forcing him to wrap his hands around her little body.

"Whoa," Slider mumbled, looking into her face in awe. "She's small. Really small. They check her out and everything?"

"You wouldn't think she was small if you'd just pushed her out." I'd been joking, then realized he was deadly serious. "No, yeah, she's fine," I assured him. "They said everything looked good. She's not even that small for a newborn."

"Good," he replied with a nod. "You were bald too. Natasha tell you that?"

"No." I cleared my throat as an emotion I couldn't name hit me. "No, she didn't talk to me about stuff like that."

"Ah, well, she didn't really see you much when you were this little." His comment did nothing to help the knot in my throat. I gripped Cody's hand as he sat back down beside me, and he leaned over to kiss the side of my still sweaty head.

"You were bald," Slider told me again. "And you were tiny. Too tiny. But it didn't take you long to catch up where you were supposed to be. Probably because you never fuckin' slept, always eatin'."

He glanced up to gauge my reaction, and whatever he saw on my face made him continue. "You were a pain in the ass," he told me with a smile. "Always wantin' to be held, refused to sleep, hated havin' your diaper changed. Always needin' somethin', swear to Christ, I didn't fuck Vera for months." His cheeks turned ruddy as he realized what he'd just said.

"Great." Cody huffed, and I elbowed him in the side as Slider scowled.

"You were lighter than this," Slider continued, ignoring Cody. "Your skin was so pale, I could see all the tiny little veins in your head. Freaked me out, but Vera said it was normal."

"Is she here?" I asked.

"Yeah, she's been waitin', pacin' the floors," he answered with a smile. "I know you don't know her, don't feel like she's your parent, and that's fine. We understand it. But Vera, well, she's always considered you hers."

I took a minute to digest his words, running over in my mind the months that I'd barely seen her, the times when I'd needed her but wouldn't have let her near me if she'd tried. I wondered how that felt—knowing that the child you'd loved all their life didn't want you anywhere near them—and I came to a decision.

"You can go get her if you want," I said quietly, the words tasting weird on my tongue. "Wait, you can't take the baby out with you!"

"Oh shit, right," he answered, walking back to hand her to me. "I'll be right back, she'll be pleased as fuck. I'll be right back." His words were rambling and fast, and I felt my stomach jump as he leaned down and kissed my forehead before leaving the room.

I'd felt that stomach jolt only once before, when Slider had kissed the back of my head after slaying my demons a few years ago. I hadn't liked the feeling then. My skin had felt too small for my body, crawling and itching until he'd walked away. But the sensation felt different sitting in that hospital with my daughter snuggled up close to my body. It felt . . . almost comforting.

"How about Cecilia?" I asked Cody abruptly.

"What?" he asked, distracted by running his fingers over our daughter's hands.

"Do you like Cecilia?"

"Isn't that the—"

"Yeah, that was my name. Before."

"You sure, baby? Can't exactly take it back once you decide," he warned, making me second-guess myself.

"I guess not," I said. Damn, it had seemed like a good idea. But maybe he was right, and I'd hate it once my mushy gushy feelings were gone again.

"I like it, Ladybug," he replied, leaning down to kiss me softly on the lips. "I think it's beautiful. I like that it gives her some of your history, that it's something you can pass on to her. Plus, it's the girliest name I've ever fucking heard, and my girl's a princess. She needs a girly princess name."

"Are you sure?" I asked, worried. God, who knew picking a name would be so completely nerve racking? How did people have the balls to name their kids weird shit? Weren't they afraid they'd hate it later when they had to yell for Rufus or Tomahawk to come in for dinner every night?

"Yeah, Cecilia Rose Butler. Got a nice ring to it, right?"

"It kind of does," I said, my mouth starting to curve up at the edges.

"Then that's her name." He leaned down again to take my mouth in a deep kiss. "God, I fucking love you."

"Back atcha, handsome."

"Hey," Vera's scratchy voice called from the doorway. "You want us to come back later?" She looked nervous, pulling on the bottom of her sweatshirt with fidgety hands.

"Come in!" I called cheerfully, trying to put her at ease.

Exhaustion was starting to set in, my movements growing sluggish as I leaned my head back against the pillows, but I refused to fall asleep yet. Having Vera in my hospital room seemed important somehow, and at first I couldn't figure out why. But as she came toward the bed and leaned down to take a look at Cecilia, I understood.

I wanted to show off. Like a kid who brings an art project home from school, dying to show it to their parent for validation. I wanted her to be proud of me, as weird as that was. I wanted to show her that I could do something incredible. And a small part of me wanted her to know that so she'd know that I did just fine without her.

I'd never been completely rational . . . or nice.

"Oh, look at her," she cooed, leaning over us but keeping her distance. "She looks just like you."

I looked up in surprise, confused after the conversation we'd just had with Slider, and saw that she was completely sincere. She wasn't trying to get on my good side, or blow smoke up my ass; in her mind Cecilia looked just like me, no matter the evidence to the contrary. I knew then that she was seeing what she wanted to see—a miniature version of her child.

That's when I began to love Vera.

"Want to hold her?" I asked groggily, nodding my head at her.

As soon as she'd picked Cecilia up, I turned my face into Cody's chest. "Tired," I mumbled, my eyes already closed. "Sorry."

"It's all right, Ladybug," he replied, running his hand through my hair before cupping the back of my head. "I'll take care of Cecilia. Get some sleep."

I heard Vera inhale sharply but ignored it, falling asleep within seconds.

Later, I'd look through the photos that Callie took and see that Dragon and Brenna had brought Cameron to the hospital to visit us. The poor kid looked haggard as he'd held Cecilia in his arms, but strangely proud too—his chest puffed out in all the photos. I'd see photos of Grease helping Will hold the baby, the disgusted look on Will's face changing the scene from something tender to something hilarious. Photos of the man they called Doc, unwrapping Cecilia and counting her fingers and toes. There were pictures of Slider and Vera, Grease and Callie, Dragon and Brenna, and Gram and Lily. But my favorite—the one I'd blow up and frame for Cecilia's bedroom wall—was a picture of Cody sleeping on the bed next to me, his head resting against the top of mine, with Cecilia sleeping against his chest.

I'd slept through all of their visits. Giving birth was exhausting.

Chapter 40

Farrah

"Why the fuck are we doing this, again?" Cody complained, hanging cloth diapers on a little wooden rack I'd found at the dollar store.

"Because your daughter has sensitive fucking skin, and we can't use any of the disposable brands," I snapped back.

We were . . . struggling. A little. Okay, a lot.

Things hadn't been easy since we'd come home from the hospital, and we were both feeling the lack of sleep. Gram had helped out, and for the first couple of weeks the women of the club had taken shifts, bringing dinner and staying to hold the baby so we could shower and nap. But the help had gradually tapered off, and now that Cecilia was almost three months old, we were pretty much on our own.

"I can't believe she's still sleeping," he said with a sigh. "This must be a record . . . and it's the middle of the day."

"I know." I sat down hard on the couch as he hung up the

last diaper. "God, I don't know if I want you to bend me over the kitchen table and fuck me, or take a freaking nap."

"I vote kitchen table," he mumbled before looking at me, then changed his mind. "Ah, a nap would probably be better."

"I hate this." I sniffled. "I just want a little time and energy to have sex."

"She'll figure it out, baby," he reassured me. "She's only two and a half months old."

"She's three months!"

"Right. Practically an old lady."

"Shut up. I'm going to take a shower. Want to share?" I asked, dragging myself off the couch.

"Sure." He followed me to the hallway, but paused when someone knocked on the front door. "I'll be right there, Ladybug. Start the shower."

I gave him a kiss and dragged myself to the bathroom. I didn't care who was at the door; I just hoped he could get rid of them fast. We'd barely had any time alone since Cecilia was born, and we needed it. I was tired as hell, but even if we didn't have sex, I'd be just as happy to touch his skin and feel him against me.

I was completely naked and waiting for the water to heat up when Cecilia started to cry. *Shit.* My boobs started leaking all over the place, and I scrambled to grab a towel off the rack so I didn't drip all over the floor.

Fantastic.

I wrapped the towel around myself and headed toward where she was screaming in the living room. Why hadn't Cody picked her up?

When I got to the end of the hallway, I slammed to a stop, taking in the scene in front of me.

Cody was frozen, staring at the woman whose husband had

been killed as a traitor. Roberta. She was speaking, but I couldn't hear her over Cecilia's cries, so I hustled into the living room to calm the baby down. It only took me a second to get her latched on and a receiving blanket tossed over my shoulder. I was getting pretty damn good at the whole breast-feeding thing.

"I want to know why you killed her," Roberta pleaded with Cody, her hands raised in supplication. "I know it was you, I hear the talk. I just don't understand why she was there. Please, make me understand why my baby was in that place."

"Go home, Roberta," Cody said flatly, his tone making my stomach drop. "You know all there is to know."

He started to close the door in her face, and she braced her hands against it. "Please, what if it was your baby? You'd want to know, right? Please! Please tell me what happened."

Cody's entire body flinched at her words, before tensing again. "Get the fuck outta my house," he growled, slamming the door in her face as she cried.

"The fuck was that?" I whispered, tightening my hold on Cecilia.

"Not now, Farrah." He brushed past me, walking toward the bedroom, and I spun to follow him.

"What the hell?"

"I gotta run in to the club for a little while," he said as he sat down on the edge of the bed to pull on his boots. "I'll be back in a couple of hours."

"Are you serious right now? I'm standing here practically naked with a baby attached to my boob and you're leaving?"

"You got it under control, Ladybug," he murmured, kissing my slack mouth. "Not like I can help ya anyway."

"Uh, yeah, I guess," I mumbled as he stepped away and started putting his keys and wallet into his pockets. "Why was

Roberta here?"

"Nothing for you to worry about, baby," he answered dismissively.

Things had been good between us for the last few months, great even. We'd been stressed, sure, but who wouldn't be with a newborn baby? Underneath that stress had been something solid and sure. A safe place to land, a security net that I'd been so sure would hold.

As I watched him move around the room, I felt that security net start to fray.

I was losing him. Something was happening that I didn't understand, but I could feel it, like the way the hair on my arms prickled during a lightning storm. He was going to run, and I had no choice but to stand there in a towel, feeding our daughter, and let him do it.

As he walked out the door, the security net snapped.

Chapter 41

Casper

What the fuck was Roberta thinking, coming to my apartment like that? I was so pissed I was shaking as I climbed on my bike. I'd wanted to hit something, to tear apart the house with my bare hands, and that was when I knew I had to get out of there.

Roberta was asking questions none of us had the answer to, and it brought up the questions that I hadn't let myself think of in weeks. What had Carmella been doing there? How the fuck had she hooked up with the McCaffertys? Why the hell had she shot at us? It was a never-ending list of questions that we'd never have the answer to.

Farrah didn't deserve to be fucked over by my mess, and I tried to shield her and Cecilia the best way I knew how—keep her entirely in the dark. I knew she worried. She'd looked at me more times than I could count with questions in her eyes, but I'd ignored it.

What would she think of me if she knew what I'd done? It

didn't matter that it was something I'd had to do. It didn't matter that I'd probably saved her dad's life. I'd shot a woman and killed her, no excuses erased that fact. Shame burned like fire in my gut. Women were supposed to be protected.

I'd been doing okay, trying to put that shit behind me and moving on with our life, but the fucking moment I'd dropped my guard down, it came back to haunt me.

Fucking Roberta. The club had given her more than enough money to live on—more than her traitorous old man had deserved—to keep her mouth shut and go away. It wasn't that they didn't care about her and her daughter; they did. They just knew that nothing good could come from her hanging around the club after her man had been branded a traitor.

I shot out of the parking lot and made my way to the club. I needed a fight and a drink, not necessarily in that order. Shit, I wondered if I should call Gram when I got there to let her know that Farrah was home with the baby alone. She'd been fine on her own while I'd worked before, but the look on her face as I'd left made me question what was going on in her head.

She wanted answers that I wouldn't give her.

"Hey, little brother!" Grease called out from one of the bays as I parked my bike in the forecourt. What had him so fucking chipper?

"Fuck off!" I called back, turning away from him to start for the main doors. I didn't want to deal with his happy ass, or anyone else's for that matter. I just wanted a fucking drink. I wanted to forget Roberta asking me how I would feel if it were Cecilia in Carmella's shoes. It had sounded like a threat, even though I knew she hadn't meant it that way.

"Whiskey," I told the prospect standing behind the bar, shaking my head as he pulled out a glass. "Bottle."

Then I sat down on one of the couches facing the pool table, and proceeded to drink myself into oblivion.

Chapter 42

Farrah

I was going to kill Cody.

He'd been gone all day, with no word to let me know when he'd be home or if he'd be home. By eight o'clock that night, I was practically climbing the walls.

He always did that shit, completely shutting down whenever something happened, leaving me standing there with a stupid look on my face and wondering what the fuck was going on. I was over it.

I glanced over at Cecilia, sleeping strapped into her car seat, and picked up my phone.

"Hello, best friend," Callie said when she answered after the first ring.

"Are you at the club?"

"Yeah, the boys are having some pool tournament or something, so we're here for the night. What's up?"

"Is Cody there?"

"Uh, yeah."

"What's 'uh'? What's going on?"

"My brother, your baby daddy, is falling-down drunk, or would be if he ever moved from the couch he's been sitting on for the last few hours."

"That piece of shit!" I whispered.

"What's going on, Farrah?" she asked seriously, her voice dropping.

"Nothing," I mumbled, walking toward the bathroom. "I'm on my way. Can you keep CeeCee when we get there?"

"Sure ...?" The word was drawn out, turning it into a question.

"Okay, give me half an hour." I hit END on my phone as I stared at myself in the mirror. For the first time since Cecilia had been born, I'd gotten myself dolled up.

I was wearing the shortest pair of shorts I owned, with a high waist and frayed legs, and a crocheted halter top that left little to the imagination due to the fact that my boobs were still huge from breast-feeding. I'd feathered my hair away from my face, leaving it in long curls down my back, and completed the look with a headband across my forehead, ten bangles, and a toe ring that you could see through my sandals.

Yep, that should work.

Cecilia slept the entire way to the club, and didn't stir as we entered the noisy main room. I felt a little conspicuous as I walked in carrying the baby and all of her stuff, but the smiles I saw as I walked farther into the room put me at ease. It was a long way from the reception I'd gotten the first time I'd walked through those doors.

"I'll take her," Cameron called, rushing to my side to grab Cecilia's carrier. "Where do you want me to bring her?"

I searched the room, looking for Callie, but I couldn't see her. "Can you take her to Grease's room? I think that's where Callie and Will are."

"Yeah, Will started whining so they just went back there. Want me to take her bag?"

"Sure, bud. Thank you," I answered, handing him the diaper bag. "Have you seen Slider?"

"Yeah, he's over by the pool tables," he called back over his shoulder as he made his way through the crowd.

I watched him go until he hit the back hallway, and then turned toward the tables. There were a group of guys over there that I didn't know well, but sitting with them were Dragon with Brenna on his lap, Poet, Tommy, and Slider. Shit, I really didn't want to have to deal with Tommy's drunk ass. As I got closer to the tables, I saw the back of Cody's head resting against the couch, his Mohawk flat against his scalp.

I clenched my jaw in annoyance. "Hey, remember me?" I asked as I rounded the couch.

"The fuck are you doing here, Farrah?" he asked emotionlessly.

"Heard there was a party," I snapped back.

"Go home. Where's our kid?"

"Our kid has a name, dick."

"Whatever. Go home."

I stood motionless as he looked away. What the hell was his deal?

"Come home with me," I said quietly, trying a different tactic. "We can leave your bike here for the night. Come on, handsome."

His gaze moved slowly back to where I was standing, his face never losing its composure. "Go home, Farrah. I'll be home in the morning."

Just like that he dismissed me, and my blood boiled. Fuck him.

He wanted to ignore me? Well, he could sure as hell try.

I walked over and gave Slider and Brenna a hug hello while Cody kept his face turned away from me, making my irritation grow even stronger. Then I searched the room for Vera. Perfect. She was standing right next to the sound system.

"You might want to go to your room for a while," I warned Slider, nudging him with my elbow.

"Why would I wanna do that?"

"'Cause I doubt you wanna watch your daughter shaking it on top of the pool table," I said dryly, making his jaw drop before snapping shut again. I turned my head to Brenna. "Clear the table, would you?"

Her lips pulled up into a devilish grin while Dragon chuckled, but I ignored them both as I started toward Vera.

"Hey, girl," she called out as I got close.

"Hey, Vera." She leaned in to give me a hug, and I squeezed her back. It was kind of amazing how far we'd come since the baby was born.

"Hey, listen. Can you put something on I can dance to?" I asked quietly.

"Dance?"

"Yeah."

"Not sure we have a whole lotta shit like that, but I'll see what I can do." She looked around the room. "There a reason for this?"

"Yep."

"You gonna tell me what that is?"

"You'll see."

"Oh shit."

Oh shit was right.

She started fiddling with the stereo as I walked away, and by the time I'd made my way to the now empty table, Awolnation's "Sail" was blaring over the surround sound.

"Oh, this is a good one," Brenna said as I passed her, making Dragon growl against her neck.

I pulled myself on top of the pool table, and flicked a glance toward Slider as the men in the clubhouse started to cheer. He was very deliberately looking down at the table in front of him.

Ha.

I took a deep breath, and with a glance at Cody, whose eyes were closed, I began to sway my hips. I hadn't danced for a crowd in a long-ass time, years even, but as the beat of the song rumbled in my chest, it all came back to me. It was like falling into a familiar place, somewhere that you'd gone so many times that nothing surprised you anymore.

I knew how to catch the attention of a room, and I was fucking good at it.

The guys watched as I lifted my hands and used my fingers to hold my hair at the top of my head, bending my knees so I was crouched ass to the table. They quieted as I paused there, then roared again as I kept my torso down and straightened my legs, giving them a glimpse of the little half moons of ass peeking out of my shorts.

Their yelling and high-pitched whistles must have finally caught Cody's attention, because as soon as I'd lifted back up, he was at the edge of the table, fury darkening his eyes.

"Get the fuck down." He growled, his face pulled into a grimace.

I ignored him as I dropped my hair to fan around my chest

and circled my hips, making the men howl once again.

I was feeling pretty damn sure of myself, working the crowd and throwing smiles toward Vera as she stood across the room, looking worried. Then I looked toward where Cody had been standing to raise my eyebrow at him, as if to say, "Put that in your pipe and smoke it," but he wasn't there.

While I'd been playing the crowd, he'd circled around the edge of the table, and before I could prepare myself, he'd grabbed my wrist and yanked me down—directly over his shoulder.

I slapped my arm across my chest to keep from flashing my boobs as the crowd laughed.

He stalked toward the back hallway, and I was surprised he was so steady on his feet.

"Put me down," I ordered as we hit the dark hallway, headed toward his room.

His hand landed on my bare thigh with a sharp and painful slap, but he gave no other indication he'd heard me.

"Ow, asshole!"

He slammed open his room's door and dropped me on his bed. I immediately rolled to my knees as he silently paced back and forth across the room.

"Well?" I asked, throwing my arms in the air.

"Well, what, Farrah?"

"Are you going to tell me what the fuck is going on?" My voice was rising as I realized that my little stunt hadn't done shit. He was still locked away, refusing to give me a fucking inch.

"I wanted a night without a freaking screaming baby and you harping on me. That okay with you, *Farrah*?" He practically spat my name, and that pissed me off.

I didn't harp on him. Shit, that was part of our problem! Until that night I hadn't pushed him at all, and the longer it went on, the more and more he hid from me.

"You haven't even seen harping yet," I said through clenched teeth, my hands fisting on my thighs.

"What the fuck do you want from me?" he yelled, his eyes blurry from the whiskey he'd been drinking and his hands clenched in his hair.

"I want you to fucking talk to me! I want to know what's bothering you, for Christ's sake!" I raised my hands in front of me, palms up in supplication. "Why do you keep doing this?"

"Oh, is life so fucking hard for you, Farrah? I don't give you what you need? I've been home with you for months and you fucking follow me the one night I go out? You wanna put my nuts in your purse too?" He reached down and grabbed his crotch as if to prove his point.

"Fuck you!" I yelled back. "You know that's not what this is about! You freaked out when Rob—"

He stepped forward, startling me by grabbing my face. "Shut your mouth."

"What is *wrong* with you?"

He pushed me back on the bed and crawled on top of me, looking like I'd slapped him across the face.

"What's wrong with me?" he yelled, inches from me.

I whimpered in response as his whiskey-tinged breath hit my face.

"I joined this fucking club to keep my family *safe*! Do you know what that was like for me? Do you?" His fist hit the bed near my shoulder and I flinched, but still raised my hand to cup his cheek. I knew he wouldn't hurt me, no matter how drunk or upset he was.

"My parents were killed, those fucking drug dealers were gunning for my sister, and I couldn't do anything!" he yelled again.

"I had to stand there and watch some fucker I didn't know drive off with my sister because I *couldn't fucking protect her!*"

"Okay, baby." I whispered, regretting ever pushing him to that point.

"I had to do *something*! I had to make sure that I could protect Gram and Callie if I needed to." He was still yelling as I ran my hand over the side of his head.

"Okay, baby," I whispered again.

"I had to protect you! And now it's all fucked up!" He raised his arm and slapped himself in the side of the head, the movement making me burst into hiccupping sobs.

"I had to kill that girl, Farrah! I had to kill her!" He pressed his fists into the bed, making my shoulders shake. "How the fuck could I do that? I came here so I could protect my women! How the fuck could I kill one?"

As he yelled, I heard Cecilia start to cry in Grease's room next door, and my breasts immediately started to leak, soaking the front of my halter. Seconds later, someone started yelling and pounding on the door to his room, jiggling the locked handle.

"It's okay, baby," I said in a soothing tone, reaching up to try to pull his head down to mine. "It's okay."

"You're sleeping with a fucking murderer, Farrah!" he bellowed, yanking his head out of my hands.

He reared back so he was sitting on my hips, and as he did, the door to his room was kicked open, and Slider, Dragon, and Grease came barreling through the doorway.

Chapter 43

Farrah

"**D**on't!" I cried as Grease wrapped his arms around Cody, wrenching him from the bed.

"You okay?" Slider asked, deliberately avoiding looking at where I'd leaked through my white halter, making it practically transparent.

"I'm fine, we were just talking!" I yelled as Cody went limp against Grease, his eyes on mine. "We're fine, baby. Right? We were just talking," I called to him softly.

The look on his face made my stomach clench in fear.

"Why don't you sleep in another room tonight, yeah?" Dragon said quietly to Cody. "Have a cooler head in the morning."

I didn't know why they were so worried, and it annoyed the hell out of me that they'd barged in when they had. Other couples in the club had knock-down, drag-out fights and they didn't step in, so why the hell were they bothering us? Cody would rather cut off his own arm than take his anger out on a woman; it was the very reason we were yelling in the first place.

"No, I want you to stay with me!" I cried out, wrapping one arm around my chest as I knelt on the bed, reaching out for him.

"I'll see you in the morning, Ladybug," he told me gently, shrugging off Grease's arm to come toward me. "You sleep in here with CeeCee. Okay, baby?"

"I want you to sleep with me," I whispered back, wrapping my arms around his waist and digging my nails into his cut.

He shook his head. "Let's talk again in the morning."

"Why won't you stay with me?" I whimpered, scared as hell for him to leave me with that look on his face. "We'll just go to sleep, we don't have to talk."

The other men in the room were watching us closely, and I hated that they saw me like that. My mask was gone, it had shattered completely the day I'd given birth to Cecilia, leaving the emotions that I'd always kept hidden were out there for the world to see.

"I love you. Feed our daughter and get some sleep," he ordered, leaning down to kiss me softly.

"I love you too. Please stay."

He reached back to pull my hands from his cut and stepped back before turning to walk silently out of the room with Dragon and Grease, leaving Slider and me alone.

"You sure you're okay?" he asked, sitting on the bed as Callie walked in with a pissed-off Cecilia in her arms.

"I told you I was fine," I replied dully, taking the baby and throwing a receiving blanket over my shoulder before settling her at my breast. "We were just talking."

"Yeah, well, it didn't sound like talking," he commented as Callie walked silently back out of the room.

"He was yelling, yes. But Cody would never hurt me."

"I know that, baby girl." Slider reached out to pat my knee. "But we heard enough of it. Boy's got some messed-up shit in his head right now."

"He's—" My voice broke as I rubbed Cecilia's tiny back. "He's having a hard time with the stuff that happened in Portland."

"Yeah, I figured as much, but tonight proved it." He shook his head. "Me and the boys'll have a word with him tonight, see if we can't knock some sense into him."

"You better not touch him or I'll feed you your balls," I said, completely serious.

"Shit, Farrah, I'm not gonna hurt the kid. Just need to get some shit straight with him. That clusterfuck in Portland was not his fault. Not in any way. Ramon's daughter was a crazy bitch who shot me and would have killed me if she'd had the chance."

"Do you think he'll be okay?" I asked tearfully, wishing that Cody weren't somewhere else in the club dealing with that shit by himself.

"He'll be fine, darlin'. Probably in your bed before morning." He leaned forward to kiss my head before standing from the bed. "Gonna sleep here at the club for the night if you need me or Vera."

"Okay," I answered as he left the room, pulling the broken door mostly shut behind him.

I unlatched a sleepy Cecilia, making her cry as I pulled back the blankets and sheets on the bed so I could cover us up. As soon as I'd turned off the light and was comfortable on my side, I cuddled her up next to me and gave her the opposite breast, rubbing her head softly as she latched back on.

My head throbbed as I worried about Cody and thought about how all the puzzle pieces fit together.

My man was a protector; there was no doubt about that. I

thought about how hard it would have been for him when his parents were killed, knowing that the sister he had been taught to protect was in danger and there wasn't anything he could do about it. The men they'd been up against would have swatted fifteen-year-old Cody away like a pesky fly, and I gave a quick thank-you to God that he'd been too smart to go against them alone. It must have galled him to leave the protection to Grease while he was away at school, and been scary as hell for him knowing that Gram was still in San Diego where the murderers lived.

I wondered vaguely if he'd started protecting me during my downward spiral because he knew it was something he could do. *Protect Farrah from herself—piece of cake.* Only, I hadn't made it easy for him. I'd fought him and snuck around and generally made his job infinitely harder whenever I could, determined to prove that I could take care of myself.

As my mind wandered through the different threads of Cody's words, I suddenly realized that my best friend, Callie, wasn't the only one in that family dealing with survivor's guilt. Cody was obviously feeling it too, but not only for his parents.

The situation Callie had gone through, my idiocy that he'd witnessed and tried to stop, and not being able to do anything during the attack on Brenna had built up the idea in his head that he wasn't doing enough. That he was failing somehow at protecting his family.

Killing Carmella had just been the icing on a shit cake that had been baking for years. No wonder he'd finally lost it.

I hoped that Slider and the rest of the guys would be able to help him out. They had a ton of experience with problems like that—the ones that kept them up at night because of the things they done and hadn't done.

"Your daddy is having a hard time," I whispered to sleeping

Cecilia, pulling my nipple out of her mouth so I could smooth down my halter. "You're just gonna have to give him lots of love tomorrow, okay? Mama will too."

I fell asleep hoping that at some point in the night he'd crawl into bed with me.

But he didn't.

Chapter 44

Farrah

Cody's bike was gone the next day when Cecilia and I woke up.

Slider told me that they'd had a good talk and he thought they'd gotten shit straightened out, but I didn't buy it. If Cody had his shit straightened out, he would have come to me. He wouldn't have left the club without a word at the ass crack of dawn.

I felt... defeated. I wasn't sure what I was supposed to do to help Cody deal with the shit in his head. If the men who knew the life best hadn't been able to get through to him, I didn't think anything would.

"Hey, Farrah!" a voice called behind me as I latched Cecilia's car seat into the base in the backseat of my car. "You mind giving me and Cameron a ride to our apartment?"

I turned away from the car to find Tommy striding toward me, his hand on Cameron's shoulder, almost dragging the poor kid with him.

"Sure," I replied dully, my gaze shooting to Cameron as he

made a weird noise in his throat. "Hop in."

Cameron was trying to tell me something—his eyes were huge—but I couldn't tell if he was just pissed at his dad, which was a normal occurrence, or something was actually wrong. I watched them round the hood of my car, Tommy speaking quietly to Cameron until they reached the passenger side doors. Then he gave Cam a little shove, as if reminding him to climb in the car.

Weird.

"So, where are we going?" I asked calmly, my eyes moving from the road in front of me to my rearview mirror, where I could see Cameron shaking in the backseat. We'd just passed through the gates when I felt something hard press into my side.

"You're going to keep driving and go north on I-5. Once you're doing that, we'll talk again," Tommy answered in a cold voice, making my head snap sideways.

"What are you doing?" I gasped in surprise.

"Makin' sure you don't do anything stupid."

"I never do anything stupid. It doesn't take a gun in my side for me to make that choice," I said, my mind racing. What the hell was Tommy thinking? Cody was going to kill him.

"Shut the fuck up," he shot back, jabbing me in the side. "Don't wanna hear your smart mouth."

I closed my mouth quickly, my eyes meeting Cameron's in the rearview mirror. I finally understood the wide eyes. It was fear.

"Where do you want me to go?" I asked quietly as I heard Cecilia start making noise in her car seat. "North or south?"

"North," he ordered.

"Okay, do you know where we're going?" I was trying to keep my voice calm as Cecilia started whimpering in the backseat. I should have fed her before we left, but the drive between the club and my apartment wasn't long, and I'd thought I would have time to get her home before she started to fuss.

"I know where we're going," he replied. "Cameron, keep her quiet!"

I glanced back to see Cameron leaning toward Cecilia, doing something to quiet her down, but jerked my eyes toward the road again when I felt the gun push into my side.

"Why are you doing this?" I asked quietly, noting the familiar sensation of a panic attack beginning at my fingertips.

I'm okay. I'm okay. No, no, I'm not. But I can breathe. My thoughts spun as I struggled not to hyperventilate. *I can breathe. This is just my body playing tricks on me. I can breathe.*

"Well, Farrah, I'll tell you why," Tommy said seriously as he leaned against the passenger door. "Cody killed my woman and my kid, so I'm gonna take his. And then we'll be even."

More than one of Tommy's kids had been killed, and his words didn't make any sense.

"What do you mean, Tommy?" I asked meekly. "Casper didn't have anything to do with the fire."

"No, no, not the fire. That was Carmella," he informed me sadly, his chin dropping to his chest. "She got greedy."

"What?" I was so confused, I looked back again to make eye contact with Cameron, and saw the tears rolling down his face.

"Carmella?"

"Yeah, been seeing her on the side for a while, ya know?"

No, no, I hadn't known. I don't think anyone had.

"Visited her when I was up in Portland. Hot-as-fuck college girl—who could resist?"

Holy shit.

"Knocked her up," he announced in the silent car. "Told her we could still be together, knew Trish'd look the other way."

"So she lit your house on fire?" I asked for verification, bile rising in my throat.

"Didn't do it herself, I know that. I was with her that night."

Oh God. I looked to Cameron again, and he'd curled into himself on the seat, silently rocking back and forth.

"Why didn't you say anything?" I whispered, almost to myself.

"What was there to say? Carmella had my loyalty, just like Trish. Wasn't going to pull the club into our business." He reached up to scratch his head, and for just a moment, I considered running us off the road. If the kids hadn't been in the backseat, I would have.

"I thought you loved Trisha?"

"I did love Trisha!" he yelled suddenly, digging the gun into my side again. "Loved her since the moment I laid eyes on her at fifteen years old!"

I said nothing as I continued to drive. Who knew what would set him off, and I was afraid with one wrong word he'd shoot me and we'd all be dead. He made me take an exit off the freeway an hour later, and continued to give directions as we drove over back road after back road.

Finally we stopped in the middle of a clearing at the end of a long gravel logging road.

"Bought this property a while back," he commented, unbuckling his seat belt and rolling down his window. "Figure I'll get some camping gear and we can camp out until the house gets built."

"Camp out?" I asked, horror making my throat tight.

"Yeah." He nodded as Cecilia woke back up with a scream.

"You need to feed her?" Tommy asked calmly, his eyes watching me intently.

"That's probably what she wants," I replied.

"Then feed the poor girl."

Oh my God. His moods were giving me whiplash. I couldn't figure out if he was crazy or way smarter than everyone thought.

I unbuckled my seat belt and was reaching for the door handle when he set the gun on the dash and gripped my thigh. "Cameron, hand Cecilia up here to Farrah so she don't have to get outta the car," he ordered.

His eyes never left mine as Cameron started fiddling with Cecilia's buckles, finally handing her to me through the space between the two front seats. She stopped screaming as I took her in my arms, and immediately started rooting around at my halter top. Why hadn't I brought a change of clothes to the clubhouse the night before?

"Cam, can you hand me the little pink blanket with the yellow stars, please?" I asked quietly, trying to hold my top in place as Cecilia's little fingers grasped at it.

"No blanket," Tommy ordered, watching Cecilia. "In fact, take that top off. It's in her way."

My hand shook as I started to raise one side of my halter.

"You not hear what I said to you?" he asked conversationally. "Take the whole thing off. Ain't no one here to see you but me and Cam. Boy's gotta learn sometime."

I turned my head to meet Cameron's eyes, and his face flushed in embarrassment and shame as he broke eye contact and looked at his feet. The halter tied behind my neck and back, and I used one hand to slowly reach around and pull the strings. It fell off, covering Cecilia's face for a moment before I whisked it off of her, giving her access to the nipple near her face.

My stomach turned as I tried to wrap my arms more closely around her to hide my other breast, but it was no use. They were too big to hide with my arms, and the nipple she wasn't connected to started to leak, dripping breast milk onto my arm.

My eyes closed in mortification as my breathing started to falter. *You can breathe. Your body is playing tricks on you. You can breathe.*

"That's right," Tommy whispered gently, making me flinch as he reached out to touch the back of Cecilia's head gently. "Tastes good, doesn't it, sweetheart?"

My stomach clenched in revulsion.

"I loved when Trish nursed our babies," Tommy told me as he moved his hand to wipe the milk off my arm with one finger, then brought it to his mouth to suck it off. "Breast milk's so fuckin' sweet. Like candy." He reached forward again, and I held myself still by sheer force of will as he pressed down gently and slid his hand down my breast, making it leak even more.

"Trish never had much to spare, only got my taste after the kids were done. Looks like you got plenty to share, though," he commented with a tender smile, making my stomach roll as he ran his finger over and around my nipple.

"Look at those pretty nipples, Cam," Tommy called into the backseat, never taking his eyes off me. "Perfect for feeding babies and men."

Oh God. Oh God.

Cecilia's mouth went slack on my nipple, and I knew what that meant, so I leaned her up on my chest and started to pat her back gently. She let out a large belch and immediately started rooting around again as Tommy laughed like a hyena.

As I moved her face toward my still leaking nipple, Tommy stopped laughing and his eyes zeroed in on my newly freed breast, red and wet from her mouth.

"Lean up here, Cam," he called, waving his hand lazily.

I saw Cameron move out of the corner of my eye, but I

couldn't take my eyes from Tommy. I wasn't sure what he was going to do, but I ached for the poor boy who was moving as slowly as he could toward the front of the car. At least Cecilia had no idea what was going on; Cameron was living it all in vivid Technicolor.

"You see that?" Tommy told Cameron, using his hand to press Cameron's face toward me. He met my eyes before dropping them to glance at my breast, and then immediately raising them to me in mortified apology. That was when my eyes filled with tears for the first time since the whole thing began.

It's okay, Cam, I tried to tell him silently. Everything's going to be okay.

"Beautiful, huh?" Tommy said teasingly, pushing Cameron back into the backseat. "Looks like she's done."

I glanced down to find the baby asleep at my breast, and my heart thumped. Shit, now what?

Then it dawned on me.

Chapter 45

Casper

I paced the apartment that I'd covered hours before in wildflowers, waiting for Farrah. I'd been a dick last night—shit, I'd been a dick for months.

I'd had a long talk with Slider the night before, and he'd made me really think about the things I'd done over the past seven years. We'd talked about everything, even the shit that I hadn't wanted to discuss. It had felt like some sort of biker version of Dr. Phil, but I couldn't pretend that it hadn't helped.

He'd been right when he told me that I'd done everything I could. I had. I'd always done everything I could to make sure that my family was safe, even if had never been enough. That was the part I had to come to terms with, and I think I was figuring it out, at least a little.

I couldn't control everything that happened. It was fucking impossible. What I needed to do was control what I could and learn to let the other shit go, but that was easier said than done.

Dragon and Grease had come in at some point and added their stories to the mix, things that they'd done to protect their families and brothers, and times that they'd fucked up big and had to move past. All of us talked about shit that we would have never spoken of otherwise, and I couldn't help but be thankful that the guys who'd just seen me acting like a pussy and yelling at my woman seemed to know exactly where I was coming from.

We'd eventually moved to the stuff that went down in Portland, and all the guys had given me shit for my guilt over Carmella. They'd yelled and cussed and slammed their hands down on the table as we'd debated, but at the end of the conversation one truth remained.

If I hadn't shot her, she would have pulled the trigger again and one of us would have died.

I might have never met my daughter. Slider might not have ever fixed his relationship with Farrah. Dragon might not have gone home to his daughter and newborn son. The effects of that night if I hadn't made the split-second decision to pull the trigger were endless and far reaching.

I knew that the decision I made was the right one, and now I just had to find a way to forgive myself for it. The first step in my plan was to tell Farrah everything without freaking out on her like I'd done the night before. I'd been such an asshole, and I needed to come clean if I ever wanted to make things right with her.

Slider had told me one last thing as he'd left early that morning.

"You can't control everything," he'd said, "and you can't live this life keepin' shit separate. That ain't never gonna work. You wanna build somethin' with Farrah, you have to be willing to let her take some of the shit ridin' on your shoulders. She's your soft place, son. A man needs a soft place to land when life gets fucked."

I thought more about what he'd said as I paced, and fuck it, but the man made sense. Running a hand over my head, I glanced at the time on my phone.

It was already noon, where the fuck was Farrah?

I dialed Slider, growing more freaked out as time went by.

"Slider," he answered.

"Hey, has Farrah left yet?" I asked, walking to the front door to look out at the parking lot.

"What?" he asked quietly, his tone making my stomach drop.

"Has Farrah left the club yet?" I asked again slowly as I deliberately picked my keys off the back of the couch.

"Son, she left hours ago."

"What the fuck?" I slammed the door shut behind me as I moved toward my bike. Farrah never went anywhere for "hours" anymore. With Cecilia in cloth diapers and peeing every five seconds, Farrah would have run out of diapers early this morning if she was lucky.

"Come on in, I'll round up the boys and meet you here. It's probably nothin'," he told me, sounding like he was trying to convince himself.

"On my way," I barked, hanging up and trying to call Farrah before I started up my bike. Shit, I wished Gram wasn't down at Aunt Lily's for the weekend. Aunt Lily's—why hadn't I thought of that? My heart began to slow. Of course that was where she would have went. It made sense that she'd go to Gram after the blowup the night before.

I hung up when I got Farrah's voice mail, then immediately dialed Gram as I sat there on my bike. She answered right away.

"Hey, Gram. Is Farrah with you?"

"No . . ." The word was drawn out in question. "Should she be?"

"She left the club this morning and never showed up at home. I thought maybe she would have come to you." My voice wavered as panic hit once again, making my chest feel like it was going to cave in.

"What's going on, Cody?"

"I'm not sure. We got in a fight last night, and I came home before her this morning to surprise her with flowers, but she never showed." I tried not to let Gram hear the worry in my voice, but I'd never been able to fool her.

"I'll head home," she replied. "You let me know when you find her."

"I will."

I ended the call and slipped my phone in my pocket, then fired up my bike.

She hadn't said *if*. She'd said *when*. I hoped to God she wasn't wrong.

By the time I got to the club, the gates were open and waiting for me, so I didn't even slow as I passed the prospect standing guard. I'd traced her entire route between home and the club, and hadn't seen her car anywhere. No signs of a recent wreck either. My stomach was in knots.

Slider, Poet, Doc, Goliath, Grease, and Dragon were waiting for me in the forecourt as I pulled up.

"Hear anything?" I asked, climbing off my bike.

"Haven't heard from Farrah, but got some info from Goliath."

"What's up, man?" I asked the big guy with huge fists.

"Saw your woman leavin' this morning," he informed me. "As she was puttin' your baby in, Tommy and Cam walked up to the car and took off with her."

"Took off with her?"

"Looked like they were asking her for a ride or somethin'," he answered with a nod.

"What the hell?" I mumbled, pulling out my phone again.

I called Cam, but he didn't answer. What the fuck was going on?

"What do you wanna do, brother?" Grease asked, pulling his hair back into a knot on the back of his head. "Wanna ride out and start lookin'?"

Just then, my phone beeped in my pocket. "It's Cam."

CAM: Cant talk

My hands fumbled on the keypad as I texted him back.

CASPER: Where are you?

CAM: In the woods. Dad freked out. Has gun

CASPER: Gotta give me more, little man.

CAM: Drove N up I-5 took exit but not sure which 1. Dad says he bought prprty here

CASPER: You guys okay?

CAM: OK F feeding C. Dad scary.

CAM: Cant talk nemore

CASPER: What's going on, Cam?

CASPER: Cam?

CASPER: You there, bud?

"Shit, he's not answering anymore!" I slid the phone back into my pocket before I crushed it in my hand. "Fuck! What the *fuck* is going on?"

"Doc, call our contact at the police department. Find out what properties Tommy owns," Slider barked, his eyes dead in his face. Then he looked around the group. "The fuck is going on around here?"

"Has anyone noticed anything weird about Tommy lately?" Dragon asked the group.

"You're fucking joking, right?" Grease answered, throwing his hands in the air. "The man went off the fucking rails when Trish and the kids died."

"Been six months, brother," Dragon replied quietly.

"Doesn't matter. Six months or six years, that's gonna fuck a man up."

"Not sayin' that it wouldn't, just wonderin' if anyone's seen anything different lately," Dragon said.

"Nothing."

"Not more than usual."

"Nope."

We stood there looking at one another in confusion, and I knew we were missing something. There was some piece of the puzzle that we weren't seeing.

Goddamn it, why would Tommy take *Farrah*, of all people?

And where the fuck were they?

Chapter 46

Farrah

"**Y**ou know, I think this worked out good," Tommy told me as I held Cecilia close to my chest. "Carmella was a little bit loco, ya know? Don't think she woulda been a good mama to my boy. Too worried about making me president of the Aces." He snorted. "Me, president."

"You didn't want to be president?" I asked quietly, shifting my gaze to Cameron and then back to Tommy.

"Hell, no. What a fuckin' headache. Didn't mind where I was at, but I did want Carmella to be happy," he answered with a shrug of his shoulders. "Why don't ya put the baby down? She's sleepin'."

My heart started to thump hard in my chest as I reached down to check Cecilia's diaper. "She's wet. I need to change her first or these cloth diapers give her a rash," I told him calmly, welcoming the way my old mask slid into place.

"Well, change her then," he snapped, irritated.

"Hey, Cam? Can you hand me a diaper? The ones at the bottom that you need pins for," I told him, meeting his eyes for the first time since his dad had forced him to look at me. "Don't forget the pins."

He nodded slowly and reached down to grab the diaper bag off the floorboard, then I turned away from him and focused on Tommy.

"Did Trish ever use cloth diapers?" I asked conversationally, rubbing Cecilia's back lightly.

"Nah, she used the disposable ones. Less mess that way," he answered, eyeballing Cecilia's cloth-covered bottom. "You make those?"

"No, you can buy them in the store," I replied, staying focused on him as Cam moved around in the backseat.

Tommy leaned forward to grab the gun from the dashboard, and my stomach lurched into my throat. "You have to wash them and shit? Seems like that'd be pretty—"

His words stopped short as a loud bang filled the car, the scent of cordite and blood filling the air as I watched blood explode from Tommy's throat and splatter all over Cecilia and my naked chest. His eyes met mine and went blank a second later.

My head swung to Cameron as Cecilia let out a bloodcurdling cry. He was sitting in the backseat, his face filled with horror, and my .45 lying limply in his hand.

"Out!" I shouted, my breath wheezing in and out of my chest. "Out of the car!"

I fumbled with the door handle, finally grasping it and practically spilling out of the car as the door opened. Black spots danced in my vision.

You can breathe. Your body is just playing tricks on you. You can breathe.

I wheezed, falling to my knees as I held Cecilia close to my chest. *Holy fuck. Oh God.* Cameron.

When I'd directed him to grab the diapers, I'd prayed that he'd find my handgun hidden at the bottom of the diaper bag. As I'd held Tommy's attention, I'd waited for Cam to hand me the thick flat diaper, hoping the gun would be hidden in the folds.

Christ. I'd never expected him to shoot his dad. God, I would have never asked that of him.

"Farrah!" Cameron yelled, racing around the car to me. "Are you okay?"

Tears rolled down his face and his hands were shaking as he set the gun down next to me. "I-I'm sorry!" he said and sobbed. "I didn't know he was gonna do that, I swear!"

"Oh, buddy, no," I said, wheezing as I reached out to grab his hand while Cecilia wailed between us. "This was not your fault. Are you okay?"

I searched his face and arms for signs of any damage, then caught him as he wrapped his arms around me and the baby.

"I didn't know what to do!" he wailed into my shoulder, snot and tears running down my back. "I didn't know what to do!"

"You did exactly right, bud. You did exactly what you had to do." I spoke softly, reassuring him as Cecilia found my nipple and eventually quieted. "But we need to get out of here, Cam. We can't stay here."

"Oh!" He leaned back and gasped. Then his face turned as red as a tomato, and he whipped his head to look in the opposite direction. I guess he realized I still didn't have a shirt on.

"Here, take this," he called over his shoulder, ripping his plain black T-shirt over his head.

I caught it as he flung it at me, then glanced around, trying to find a place where I could put the baby. "You're gonna have to hold CeeCee," I said, tapping him on the back as I used the shirt to cover my breasts. "Here, I'm covered and she's sleeping."

He turned back toward me, avoiding my eyes as he gently took Cecilia into his arms, then immediately turned away again. "Your panic attack stopped."

"Huh," I said, pulling the sweaty T-shirt over my head. "Well, don't bring it up again or it'll sure as shit come back. Okay,

I'm covered."

He turned to me and we stared at each other silently, kneeling in the middle of the gravel-covered clearing. "You have your phone?" I asked.

"Yeah! Yeah, it's in my pocket. Casper called and I texted him back," he replied, handing me his phone.

"You did? What did he say?" I opened up the phone to three new texts from Cody, and tears filled my eyes. Thank God.

"He wanted to know where we were and if we were okay."

I nodded and pulled up Cameron's recent call list, hitting the contact for Casper before bringing the phone to my ear.

"Hey, baby," I whispered. "It's me."

Then I burst into loud, gut-wrenching sobs.

Chapter 47

Casper

"**W**here the fuck are they?" I roared, throwing my chair across the room after Doc left.

We'd been waiting on word for an hour, practically climbing the fucking walls. When Doc had finally heard back from his contact, we found out it was a dead end.

No properties were registered to Tommy. None. Even the house he'd been living in before the fire had been rented. Motherfucker.

Brenna had been the first old lady to show up, but Callie and Vera had been right behind her, followed by more women that I barely knew but belonged to brothers in the club. Eventually Gram and Lily had come racing in too, their faces anxious.

The entire club was waiting on news, and we still hadn't heard anything.

"You need to calm down, boyo," Poet called from across the room. "You start losin' your head, and we're gonna get nowhere."

"How the fuck am I supposed to—"

My phone rang in my pocket, and I fumbled to fish it out. Cameron. *Thank fuck.*

"Cameron?" I answered, catching the attention of the brothers waiting throughout the room.

"Hey, baby," Farrah whispered back. "It's me."

My knees hit the floor as she started sobbing, and my head grew light from both relief and worry.

"Are you okay? Are Cam and Cecilia okay?"

"Yeah," she choked out. "We're fine."

I nodded to the room, and heard Gram start crying in relief.

"Where are you, baby?" She sobbed harder into the phone and I couldn't understand what she was saying. "Ladybug, I need you to calm down. I can't understand you, baby."

My fingers went to my eyes and dug in, fighting back the moisture there. Thank God. *Thank God.*

"I don't know where we are." She hiccupped. "We're in the middle of fucking nowhere."

"Okay, okay." I motioned to Slider and he came jogging across the room, his keys jingling where they were connected to his belt.

"Where's Tommy?" I asked Farrah as Slider reached me.

"He's dead," she whispered back, and the relief made me dizzy.

"We need the cops in on this," I told Slider, covering up the phone with my hand. "Tommy's dead and Farrah has no fucking clue where they are. We could search for days on our own and never find them."

"She have the car?" he asked.

"Can you drive out of there, baby? Maybe find the highway?" I asked, uncovering the phone.

"I—I can't. He's in there." She hiccupped again.

"Okay, baby. That's fine."

"No car," I mouthed to Slider. He gave me a nod and pulled out his phone.

"We're gonna call the police, Ladybug. Okay? They should be able to figure out where you're at with cell phone signals, but it's gonna take a while." Frustrated, I ran a hand through my hair. I wanted her home with me *now*.

"We don't have coats, Cody," she told me quietly. "It's going to cool off before too long."

"Fuck, baby."

"I'm going to get Cam and start walking," she informed me, her voice growing stronger. "I think I remember where to go. I'll get as close to the highway as I can. Maybe we'll see someone."

"Ladybug, I don't know if you should be moving around," I warned her, the panicky feeling invading my gut again. "You could get lost worse, or hurt."

She was silent for a few moments, and I held my breath waiting for her reply.

"I've got two kids out here, handsome. I don't have the luxury of waiting for the cavalry."

Fuck.

"I hear you," I replied quietly, climbing to my feet. "How much battery's left on Cam's phone? Where's yours?"

"Cam's phone has like fifty percent left, and I've got no clue where mine is. I think it may be in the front seat of my car."

I didn't ask why she couldn't look for it.

"I'm going to hang up for now," she said, sniffling again. "I need to get us ready to go. I'll call you again when we hit the next road, okay?"

It killed me to do it. I fucking hated that she'd be out there alone and I'd have no idea what was happening or where she was, but I knew we had to conserve the phone battery.

"Okay, Ladybug. Give CeeCee a kiss for me and let me know when you're on your way. Okay?"

"All right. Love you."

"Love you too, so much."

I held the phone against my ear for a full minute after she hung up, refusing to let go of the connection between us.

"Cops are on their way!" Slider yelled on his way out the front door. "Casper, Grease, and Goliath, let's go meet them at the front gates!"

With no other choice, I was forced to drop the phone from my face and follow after him.

Chapter 48

Farrah

"Okay, dude, I've got a plan!" I called out to Cameron, who was still sitting on the ground with a sleeping Cecilia in his arms. "We're going to start walking."

"We're going to walk home?" he asked incredulously, wiping tears from his face as I got closer.

"Hell no," I replied, holding my hand out to him and pulling him to his feet. "We're gonna walk until we find a main road, or find something so we have a point of reference for the guys to come get us."

"Oh."

"Yeah, but first, I need to get some shit from the car."

His eyes gaze from me to the car and back again, and his face turned pale. "Do you want me to do it?" he whispered.

"No." I shook my head. "I'm just going to grab CeeCee's sling and her diaper bag, and then we'll be out of here. You don't go near the fucking car."

He was nodding before I'd ever finished speaking.

"Okay." I nodded back. "Go wait for me on the road. I'll be right there."

I moved toward the car, my stomach churning with dread. *Don't look, Farrah.* I kept my head down as I opened the back door, swallowing hard as the smell of Tommy's body filled my nose. *Fuck.* I reached through the door to Cam's side, the car closing in on me as I grabbed the diaper bag off his seat and the sling off the floorboard.

I pulled myself out and took a deep breath, catching sight of my purse strap hanging through the space between the front door and the driver's seat. *Shit.* I needed my fucking purse.

Decision made, I slammed the back door shut and moved toward the front, taking a deep breath before opening my door and reaching for my purse.

"What are you doing?" Cameron called anxiously, causing my head to jerk up until I was facing Tommy's dead body. His eyes were still open.

I pulled the purse out and slammed the door, vomiting on the ground beneath my feet. Fucking gross.

"Let's go!" I told Cameron as I reached him, slipping the sling over my head and then reaching for Cecilia. "You get the gun?"

He nodded, watching as I got Cecilia settled. "Okay, make sure the safety's on—"

"It's on," he replied without hesitation.

"Then put it in the diaper bag. Can you carry it?"

He nodded again, slinging the bag over his shoulder as we started down the road.

"I'm sorry, bud," I said quietly after we'd been walking for a while. "You didn't deserve this shit."

"How can you say that?" he replied, his angry eyes turning toward me. "I went with him. I got in the car with you knowing that something was wrong and I didn't say anything!"

"Cameron, you're twelve years old and your dad outweighs you by like a hundred and fifty pounds. What in the fuck do you think you could have done?"

"I could have told you that someone needed you inside the club! I could have said I had a stomachache so Dad had to take me back inside! I could have tripped and hit my head on your car so I was bleeding and you would have had to take me back inside!"

"You've been thinking on this a while, huh?" I asked, stepping around a pothole in the road.

"Since we pulled through the gates," he mumbled quietly.

"Dude, if you would have stopped him today, your dad would have just waited for another chance," I argued. "Maybe without you there to have my back."

He went silent.

We walked for hours, stopping only to change Cecilia—I was down to one last diaper—and so Cameron could pee. When we finally came to a road, I called Cody.

"Hey, baby. We just hit a road, but I have no idea what it's called."

"Okay, Ladybug. Cops are on their way. They figured out where you were at before, so they should be showing up pretty damn soon. You okay?"

"Yeah, we're tired and Cecilia's on her last diaper, but we're good."

"Slider's grabbing a van and we're headed to you. I'll see you soon, okay?"

"Can't wait. Love you."

"Me either. Love you too."

I stuffed the phone back in my pocket and turned toward Cameron.

"Cops are on their way," I told him, watching his face sag in relief.

We'd only walked maybe a mile more when I saw police cars in the distance, and we stopped on the side of the road.

"Careful what you say, Cam," I warned him as the cars got closer. "Your dad kidnapped us and held us at gunpoint. We don't know why. Right?"

"Right," he answered, taking a step closer to me as the cars rolled to a stop fifty feet from us.

"Farrah Miller?" the cop who was driving called out as he climbed out of his car and stood behind the door.

"Yeah, that's me." I took a step forward, and Cameron moved with me when all of a sudden we had four guns trained on us.

No, they were trained on Cameron.

"Hands where I can see them!" the same cop yelled, startling both Cameron and me into movement.

"Now, step away from the woman," he ordered.

"What the fuck are you doing?" I screamed back, moving with Cameron as he tried to step away.

"Ma'am, we need you to stop what you're doing so we can do our job!"

"Fuck you!" I screamed, then wrapped one arm around Cecilia at my chest and flung the other in front of Cameron. "Get your guns off my boy!"

Cameron's head whipped toward me as I moved closer to him.

"Excuse me, ma'am?" The cops looked confused, but they didn't drop their weapons.

"Get your guns off my son, or I swear to God I'll cause such a fucking stink not one of you will be able to flip burgers at McDonald's when I'm done," I growled, finally coming to a stop with Cameron directly behind my right shoulder.

"Your son?" the cop repeated, lowering his weapon to our feet.

"That's what I said," I yelled back, my heart racing in my chest as Cameron laid his hand against my back.

"Lower your weapons," the cop ordered, looking around to his men. "Ma'am, we were led to believe that you'd been kidnapped?"

My body sagged in relief.

It was over.

Chapter 49

Farrah

By the time we got back to Cody that night, Cecilia was getting a rash from the drugstore disposable diapers the police had provided, Tommy's body was being located and the scene examined, and someone had given Cameron a shirt to wear.

I'd cried when Cody finally showed up with my dad, and though he'd never admit it, I think he did too.

The cops were still calling Cameron my son, and neither Cody nor Slider corrected them as we left the station. It didn't matter, anyway. The case was pretty cut-and-dried kidnapping and self-defense, and even if they'd tried to do anything with Cameron they would have failed. Grease was Cameron's godparent—Trisha had left a will.

The men had brought a minivan to come pick us up, and as I cuddled next to Cody in the backseat on our way back to Eugene that night, I filled them in on all the things we'd learned from Tommy. They were in complete shock, but as I told them more, they seemed to start putting it all together. Later, Cody would tell me it was like the missing puzzle piece that answered a bunch of questions they'd had about the Portland deal. I didn't ask what the questions had been. Frankly, I just wanted to put it all behind me.

It took hours to say hellos and good-byes at the club, everyone wanting to hug us and make sure we were okay, and by the time we were driving home in Gram's car, I was ready to drop.

"I'll get some pillows and blankets for the couch," I told Cameron quietly, looking over Cecilia's new car seat that was buckled in between us. "We'll find a new place soon so you can have your own room."

"I don't mind the couch," he answered anxiously.

"Dude. You're not going anywhere," I told him firmly. "You belong with us, okay?"

"Yeah." His voice was almost inaudible.

"You sure you want to stay with us?" I asked. "Because seriously, dude. If you're staying, you're staying. You can't go crying to Grease if I yell at you for leaving the toilet seat up."

A small smile lifted the corner of his mouth. "I'm sure," he replied.

And that was that.

We hadn't really talked about where he would live or what would happen after we'd left the police station, but as we'd stood up to leave the club, he'd walked silently over to my side carrying a small duffel bag of clothes. I guess when I'd told him all those months ago that he was welcome at my house anytime, he'd taken that literally.

Of course, calling him my son in front of four armed police officers probably sealed the deal.

"I'm making breakfast whenever you wake up in the morning," Gram informed me as we climbed out of the car to find

Cody waiting next to his bike.

"I'm making coffee!" Lily called out, blowing me a kiss as she headed toward Gram's apartment.

"Let's go inside, Ladybug," Cody whispered softly, kissing my lips before moving me out of the way so he could get Cecilia out of the car.

My little family made our way over to my apartment door, and I paused outside it, searching for my keys before realizing I'd left them in the ignition in my car. I shuddered at the memory.

"I've got it, baby," Cody said, handing his keys to me so we could unlock the door.

As I walked in the room, my eyes widened at the sight of flowers covering every available surface.

"Holy hell!" Cameron gasped.

"Watch your mouth," I replied automatically, my gaze roaming the room.

"Uh, I was apologizing this morning," Cody grumbled as he set down Cecilia's car seat on the kitchen table on top of what looked like daisies.

"It's gorgeous," I called back. "I'm going to get Cam a blanket."

I hurried down the hallway to grab a blanket off the end of my bed, only to change my mind at the last minute and pull my quilt from the bed instead. Then I made my way back into the living room and sat next to Cameron on the couch.

"I'm gonna lay Cecilia down," Cody informed me, looking between me and Cameron. "'Night, Cam."

"'Night, Casper."

As soon as we were alone, I reached out and grabbed Cameron's hand.

"Sometimes shit happens that totally sucks," I started,

pausing when Cameron snorted. "Shut up. Sometimes things happen that totally fucking suck, and even though we think we're fine with it, eventually we're not so fine with it."

I met Cameron's eyes, giving him a sad smile. "This is my quilt. You probably saw it when we were staying at the club." I paused as he nodded. "I'm giving it to you."

I stood up and waited for him to lie back on the couch before flipping the quilt out so it floated over his body, covering him from neck to toes. Then I sat down again at his hip.

"Bad shit happened to me too, you know? If you ever want to talk to me, you can. If you don't, that's cool too. But this quilt right here? This was made with love, and it was given to you with love, so if you ever find yourself not okay with the bad shit that happened and you don't feel like talking to me or Cody about it, well, wrap yourself in this. Okay?"

My throat clogged with tears as he sniffled once, and I stood from the couch. "We're right down the hall. Yell if you need anything."

I made it to the entrance of the hallway before I heard his voice, sounding so young it was like a punch to my chest. "I love you, Farrah."

"Love you too, dude," I choked out. "Get some rest."

I shuffled quietly down the hallway, tears falling down my face until I was caught up in strong arms and carried into the bathroom.

"You okay, Ladybug?" Cody asked gently, wiping my cheeks with his thumbs.

"Yeah, just—Cam. Oh my God."

"He's gonna have a hard time," he said with a nod. "But tonight he's safe and loved, and he's got Aunt Lily's quilt wrapped around him, which we both know can heal a whole lot of shit."

"Noticed that, did you?"

He wrapped his arms around my shoulders. "Ladybug, I haven't taken my eyes off you all night," he replied, leaning down to rest his forehead against mine. "Don't know if I'll ever let you and the kids outta my sight again."

"We're okay."

"Thank Christ."

"Thank Cameron too."

"No shit," he murmured, reaching down to grab the bottom of Cameron's T-shirt that I was still wearing. "I don't wanna have sex, Ladybug. But I need to check you out, okay?"

"Okay," I whispered back, raising my arms above my head so he could pull the shirt off.

"He didn't hurt you?" he asked again for the twentieth time since he'd reached me.

"No, handsome. He didn't hurt me, I promise."

He nodded his head, then knelt down to pull off my shorts and underwear, pausing to run his fingers over the gauze on my knees. I hadn't realized at the time, but I'd cut the hell out of them when I'd fallen out of the car and into the gravel.

Cody leaned his head against my belly and took a deep breath, while I ran my fingers gently through his hair.

"He touched your tits," he spoke quietly, his voice barely noticeable over the sound of our heater blowing through the vents.

"Barely," I answered. "It was disgusting, but it's over."

"He touched you."

"Look at me," I ordered, pulling his head back so I could meet his eyes. "It's over. The man is dead and I'm right here with you. Safe and whole. Cecilia and Cam are in the next room, safe and whole. We've got a lot to be thankful for, handsome. Don't waste time worrying about shit that doesn't matter."

"You gut me," he whispered, reminding me of a time when he'd said those same words to me long ago.

"Why? Because I pretend to forget what's happened to me?" I asked quietly.

"No, because you protected our children and then walked eight miles carrying a twelve-pound baby to get them to safety. You are by far the strongest woman I've ever met, and I am the luckiest man on the planet."

I gave him a small smile as tears rolled down my face, then nodded once and replied dryly, "You really are."

Epilogue

Farrah

Seventeen years later

"You get on the back of that bike and I will beat that little fucker to death," Cameron growled as he and Cecilia walked through the front door. "End of."

"You're being stupid!" she screeched back. "We've known them forever!"

"I don't give a fuck. You know how many club whores that boy has hit already?" He shook his head as he walked into the kitchen, where I was standing at the stove. "Hey, Ma."

"You get the chips and beer I needed?" I asked as he came over and kissed my cheek.

"Yeah, the store was a fuckin' madhouse. Everybody and their bitch mother were shoppin' today. Where's Casper and Lily?"

"Mom, tell Cam he's being an idiot!" Cecilia whined, making my teeth grind.

"He probably knows more than I do," I grumbled back, making Cameron smile.

"Errgh!"

"Go make sure the barbeque is on, would you?" I asked her, trying to defuse the fight before turning back to Cam.

"Cody took Lil for a ride. He better hurry up, people are going to start getting here soon."

"Don't count on it. Daddy's little girl is gonna keep him out there for hours," he said with a smile, helping me put groceries away.

"Not so little anymore, she'll be twelve next week. You got her a present, right?"

"Of course," he said offhandedly, making me smile.

"Can you go wake Gram up while I start this corn? She said she was laying down for a while before the craziness started."

I paused in my corn shucking to watch him go, pride infusing my body. He'd grown up to be such a good man, and I liked to think that Cody and I had a little to do with that. When Cecilia was almost a year old and Cameron had started calling us Ma and Dad in an attempt to teach Cecilia the words, my heart had ached. When he'd continued calling us that long after she'd started talking, I'd felt complete. He was ours, no matter how we'd gotten him. Like I'd told the policemen seventeen years ago, Cameron was my son. He belonged to Cody and me.

A few years after Cecilia was born, Cody had bought us a house out in the country for the five of us—Cody, Cameron, Cecilia, Gram, and me. We'd known that Gram wouldn't be able to get around on her own for much longer, and we'd both agreed that we wanted her with us. The house wasn't huge or anything, but when we'd looked around, it had been the only one we'd agreed on. It was built in the 1920s and had a huge wraparound porch that I'd immediately filled with a porch swing and rockers. Three acres surrounded it, that Cody was able to build a big shop on.

Money had been tight for a few years, but we'd made it work and eventually grew comfortable on Cody's income. I never got a job at a salon again. We wanted me to be able to stay at home with Cecilia, and by the time she'd been ready for kindergarten I'd been pregnant with little Lily, so the whole thing had started all over again.

Callie and Grease had ended up buying the house they'd rented when we first moved to Oregon, and then they'd filled it up with kids. Two more boys, Thomas and Michael, had followed Will, and then a few years after that they'd had a little girl they named Rose. I think Callie would have kept on popping them out, but Grease put his foot down after they'd finally gotten the little girl they were hoping for. She never had an easy pregnancy after Will, and I knew Grease hated it when she was sick. Frankly, I'd been surprised that he'd gotten her pregnant again after Michael, though maybe I shouldn't have been. Grease had always given Callie anything she'd wanted.

I sat down at the kitchen table and lifted my feet to the seat across from me. I was tired as hell. We were having a barbeque for Gram's birthday, and the preparation for feeding so many people was insane. I knew Vera, Brenna, and Callie would be bringing food with them, which helped, but I still had a ton of shit to get done, and just the thought of it made me want a nap.

I was seriously debating lying down on the couch for a power nap when Cody and our twelve-year-old daughter came into the house laughing, their cheeks ruddy.

"Go on up and get changed," Cody said to Lily, meeting my eyes as he leaned down to kiss the top of her head.

"Hi, Ma! Bye, Ma!" Lily called as she raced up the stairs,

making me giggle.

"You guys have fun?" I asked as Cody strode toward me.

"Always have fun with our kids, Ladybug," he answered with a smile. "Unless one of them is being a pain in the ass."

"Speaking of, I think you need to talk to Cecilia or Cameron, or both, about Leo."

"What'd the little fucker do now?" he asked, lifting me from the chair.

"Well, nothing—yet." I sighed and leaned my head against his shoulder as he carried me up the stairs.

The way he took care of me and always wanted me with him, that never got old. And even though I was quite a bit bigger than when we'd first gotten together, he continued to carry me all over the place as if I still weighed a hundred pounds soaking wet. There were a million things I needed to get done in the kitchen, but I didn't say a word as he carried me into the bedroom with him. I'd learned along the way to never take for granted the time I spent with Cody or the kids. The food could wait.

"I think he wants Cecilia," I informed him, bracing for the blowup.

He didn't disappoint. "Oh, hell no."

"Yeah, that's what Cam said too," I said as he set me on my feet and started to undress me. "They were fighting about it when they got home from the store."

"He actually took her with him to the store?" he grumbled. "Brave man."

"Be nice."

"I got nothing but love for all of my brothers' offspring. You know that. But Leo isn't getting within spitting distance of either of my daughters."

"Maybe talk to Dragon about it?"

"Fuck that. Leo's a man. I'll talk to him."

"Cody," I said with a frown. "He's only eighteen."

"Don't remind me." He shuddered, then reached behind his neck to pull his T-shirt off. He looked stiff, and I made a mental note to give him a massage later. His old bullet wound had begun causing some muscle issues a few years before.

"Is there a reason I'm standing here naked?" I asked as he moved toward the dresser and started emptying his pockets.

"Yeah, I'm gonna fuck you and then we're taking a shower."

I made a fist and brought it toward my face before jerking my entire arm down sharply. "Yes!"

He looked at me oddly for a moment, and then started laughing hysterically at my move. "You remember when Cam did that for a whole year? God, I thought he'd never stop with that shit and he'd be a virgin forever."

"Are you kidding me? I encouraged it for the same reason," I said dryly as he started laughing again.

"Come here, Ladybug," he called gently, sitting on the edge of the bed. As I moved between his spread knees, all laughter between us stopped. "You got something you want to tell me?"

"How the fuck did you know?"

"Baby, I've been staring at your body for almost twenty years. Not a whole lot I don't notice." He reached up to pull the ponytail out of my hair, smoothing it to cover my sensitive breasts.

"I can't believe it happened again."

"Doctors told us it could."

"Yeah, but then it didn't for so long," I said with a shrug, searching his face for any trace of emotion. "I guess I just thought we were done."

His hands moved to my belly, still unlined and relatively smooth after my two pregnancies so long ago. "You feeling okay?"

"Yeah, just tired mostly." I ran my hands through his hair, loving the way he'd let it grow long enough to pull back into a short ponytail at the base of his neck. "You want a boy this time?"

"Already have a boy."

"I know, I just meant—"

"Already have a boy, Ladybug."

I sighed. "Yeah."

"You're more beautiful today than the day I met you," he told me seriously. "And I'm lucky as fuck that you put up with my shit."

"You really are," I answered with a nod, making him smile.

"We're almost forty years old, baby. This is the last one, all right? I'm happy as hell that you're giving me another. I love our kids—best thing we've ever done—but I don't want you putting that strain on your body anymore."

"Okay, handsome."

"I love you."

"Love you too." I leaned forward and kissed him, running my tongue over his lips before pulling back. "But if you don't fuck me in the next few minutes, we're not gonna have time before people start showing up."

"Fuck 'em," he growled, wrapping his hands into my hair.

He stood up, pushing me with him, and kissed me hard. His beard was rough against my skin and I reveled in the feeling, knowing that within a few days it would be long enough to feel soft again and the sensation would change.

Over the years, I'd felt his face against my skin a million different ways. Long beard, short beard, five o'clock shadow, or clean shaven, I'd never had a favorite. His aunt Lily had told me something before she died, and I'd never forgotten it. She'd said, "Handsome comes and goes, but if a man's face is dear to you no matter how wrinkled he gets? Well, that's worth keeping." And

Cody's face was dear to me.

"Elbows on the bed, Ladybug," Cody murmured into my mouth before spinning me away from him. I loved the way his hand pressed at the center of my back as I bent over the bed, and though we'd done this dance thousands of times before, it still surprised me when he dropped to his knees behind me.

"Love the way you taste when you're pregnant." He groaned into my skin, running his tongue from front to back. "You're always fucking ready for me."

I was moaning quietly into the bed when I heard a knock on the door and my head snapped up in panic.

"Shhh." Cody climbed to his feet behind me with one hand to my back so I couldn't move. My heart started racing as the door handle jiggled, and less than a second later Cody was slamming into me.

"Dad's takin' a shower, Lilybug, leave 'em alone," Cameron called down the hallway.

"Where's Mom? People are starting to show up!"

"She's probably helping him—"

"Gross!"

Their voices faded away as they left the hallway, and I dropped my head in a huff. "I almost had a heart attack."

"I locked the door, Ladybug," Cody said in exasperation. "I always lock the fucking door, 'cause you always forget to lock the fucking door."

He began to slide in and out slowly, and I turned my head to look at him. "One time!"

"Cameron's probably scarred for life."

"Shut up." My breath caught as he pulled out and slammed back in, the sound of our bodies moving together filling the room.

Casper

My house was filled with people, and I knew Farrah loved it, but fuck if I didn't want them all to leave.

She was tired as hell and trying to hide it, but the mask she'd worn all those years ago was pretty much nonexistent anymore. The confidence she'd faked for so long had somehow become real years ago, and I think our kids had a lot to do with it. When you were going to parent-teacher conferences at twenty-one years old and trying to keep your adopted son out of juvie, you tended to grow a thick skin.

I glanced over to where Cameron was following Dragon's daughter Trix into the house, and grinned. That was what the fucker got for trying to stop me from talking to *his* boy earlier about *my* daughter. Asshole.

"Trix, you don't stop walking away from me. I'm gonna paddle your ass!"

"Fuck off, Cam!"

Ah, to be young and fucking clueless again. I had a feeling those two were going to fuck things up pretty bad before they got their shit together. I probably needed to talk to Cam before Dragon killed him.

Brenna and Dragon had done a good job with that one. Trix had just graduated with a degree in business or some shit like that, and had already found some cushy job in Portland, which was probably why she and Cam were fighting. I didn't understand how we kept making these girls who were fucking princesses, all with a good head on their shoulders and a backbone of steel, yet all our boys seemed to be little assholes who couldn't keep it in their pants. It was probably a good thing Brenna and Dragon had stopped having kids after Leo; I couldn't deal with another one of their boys going after Lily in a few years.

"You need another beer, handsome?" Farrah asked with a tilt of her head.

Goddamn, the woman got more beautiful every time I looked at her. I shook my head as she sauntered toward me, and couldn't help the smile that pulled at my lips. She wasn't trying to walk that way, but I was pretty sure she was sore as hell after the way I'd pounded her earlier. I'd probably have to be a little more careful in the near future.

I pulled her onto my lap as she reached me, and laid my hand on her head as she pressed her face into my neck. Poor baby.

"You just sit here with me, Ladybug," I ordered her, kissing her face. "Dinner's over, people are relaxing, nothing more for you to do."

"I think it went good, don't you?" she asked sleepily, her body already relaxing into mine.

I looked around the yard filled with people.

Dragon and Grease were bullshitting by the horseshoe pits Cameron had begged me to build after we'd moved in. I hated them because all I could see every time I looked at them was one of my little girls impaling themselves on one of the posts.

My sister was yelling at the group of kids that had just come running around the corner of the house, their faces red with guilt.

Vera and Gram were sitting at the picnic table in the grass with Poet and Slider, our youngest, Lily, on Slider's knee. I wasn't surprised she was sitting with her grandpa instead of running around with the rest of the hellions. The girl was born a watcher; she preferred to stay on the sidelines instead of being in the thick of things, exactly the opposite of her sister.

Where the fuck was Cecilia?

I looked around the yard and finally found her standing with

Leo and Brenna under one of the trees that peppered the property.

"Three feet!" I bellowed, startling Farrah, who must have already fallen asleep on my lap.

The yard grew quiet as I stared at Cecilia until she finally turned to look at me in exasperation.

"We're standing here with his *mother*!" she yelled back.

I almost laughed when I saw how hard it was for her to keep her cool.

"I don't give a good goddamn if you're standing there with the pope! Back the fuck up!" I snarled. That little prick better move before I put my boot in his ass.

She threw her hands up and took an exaggerated step back before turning her face back toward Leo.

Fuck.

Farrah giggled into my throat, and my chest grew warm. "You embarrassed her."

"Don't care."

Everyone was still glancing our way in amusement, waiting to see what I'd do. *Shit.* Like they hadn't done the same exact thing when their daughters started dating. I knew for a fact that Poet had knocked the shit out of Dragon when he found out Dragon had knocked up Brenna.

Speaking of knocked up . . .

"Got an announcement!" I yelled, feeling Farrah's body tense against me. She still hated being the center of attention. "Farrah's pregnant!" I raised the beer bottle in my hand in a toast, and then finished it off in one go.

"Crazy fucker!"

"Congratulations!"

"Whoa."

"Seriously?"

"You just couldn't hold it in, could you?" Farrah whispered, kissing the side of my neck.

I leaned down to kiss her but stopped, my eyes growing wide as Cameron called out quietly from the back door, "Trix is too."

My head snapped toward where Dragon had been standing, but he was already stomping toward the house with Brenna close behind, trying to catch him.

Oh *shit*.

Acknowledgments

Mom and Dad: We did it again. Can you believe it? Thanks for the coffee ;) Love you.

My girlies: I love you. Thank you for always being so patient with me, and telling all your friends that your mom is an *author*. I know you think it's cool, and I can't even describe how that makes me feel. I think you're pretty freaking cool too.

My sisters: I love you.

Toni: You're the cheese to my macaroni. Thank you for loving Farrah, and just plain *getting* her. You're one of my biggest cheerleaders, and I never want to do this without you. I hope you know that I'm forever cheering you on too. Love you.

Ashley: Thanks for reading and pushing me . . . and talking me down off the ledge when I was freaking out. Stay awake tonight, because I'll probably feel the need to text you at two in the morning . . . again.

Madeline: You, my friend, are bad luck. Or maybe it's me that's bad luck. Or maybe together, we're a bad luck duo, and I wouldn't have it any other way. Let's toast to luck changing, synced cycles, and many more books that just can't stay in our heads but beg to be written down.

Donna: Here we are again. Can you believe it? I've said this before, but it bears repeating—I would never be where I am today without you. Thank you a million times.

Pam: Thanks for polishing my baby and teaching me in the process. Even though you have a ton of stuff going on in your life, you've still done a stellar job, and I can't thank you enough or describe how much I respect you for it.

Kara, Jasmine, and Sommer: Thank you for the beautiful cover!

My betas: Gina, Kenna, Kim, Ashley, and Tania: Thank you for all your help. You guys are worth your weight in gold.

Bloggers: Thank you for doing what you do, not only for writers, but for readers too—because I am both. You guys are so freaking cool and I'm watching you, and following you, and checking out your reviews and recommendations daily.

To the bearded man sleeping on the couch: Thank you for once again giving me the nice comfortable bed to write on, and for mopping the floors and making dinner.

And to you, who is reading this: I couldn't do what I do, if you weren't doing what you do. Thank you for falling in love with the Aces, for posting on my FB, for spreading the word, for reading and commenting and reviewing and making artwork. You'll never understand how humbling it is that you've taken the time to do all those things. Thank you.

About the Author

Nicole Jacquelyn is the mom of two busy little girls. She hasn't watched television in well over a year, she still does things that drive her mother crazy, and she loves to read. At eight years old, when asked what she wanted to be when she grew up, she told people she wanted to be a mom. When she was twelve, her answer changed to author. By the time she was eighteen, when people asked her what she wanted to do with her life, she told them she really wanted to be a writer, but the odds of that happening were so slim that she'd get her business degree "just to be safe." Her dreams stayed constant. First she became a mom, then she went to college, and during her senior year—with one daughter in first grade and the other in preschool—she sat down and wrote a story.

Nicole may be found on social media at:
Facebook: Author Nicole Jacquelyn
Twitter: @AuthorNicoleJ